Praise for *STRIPPED*

"Tantalizing . . . Their chemistry is intense."
—*The New York Times*

"A witty, wonderful romance that speaks to who we are, who we are meant to be, and who we are meant to be with."
—*The Washington Post*

"Vivid and naughty." —*Entertainment Weekly*

"Much like *Magic Mike, Stripped* is swoony, exciting and an all-around entertaining ride." —*Booklist*

"A sweet and sexy story that shows how life-changing—and gratifying—it can be to step outside of your comfort zone and question expectations." —Shondaland

"A perfect read for fans of *Magic Mike*."
—Smart Bitches, Trashy Books

"A sexy, funny contemporary romance . . . devilishly fun."
—NPR

"Castile delivers genuine chemistry . . . thoroughly entertaining."
—*Publishers Weekly*

"Take one sexy stripper hero, add one wild, witty school teacher heroine, and watch the fireworks. This book is my cherry pie!" —Ann Aguirre, *New York Times* bestselling author

"Castile's writing sparkles with wit. Readers will swoon for Robyn and Fallon's love story."
—Alexis Daria, author of *Take the Lead*

"In a perfect mix of sexy attraction that sizzles on the page and enchanting romance between characters you fall in love with, Castile's novel hits all the right notes!"
—Priscilla Oliveras, author of *Her Perfect Affair*

"Zoey Castile is a fresh and fun new voice, and the characters in *Stripped* will capture your heart (and possibly your dollar bills)." —Alisha Rai, author of *Hurts to Love You*

Books by Zoey Castile

Stripped

Hired

Published by Kensington Publishing Corporation

HIRED

A HAPPY ENDINGS NOVEL

ZOEY CASTILE

KENSINGTON BOOKS
www.kensingtonbooks.com

KENSINGTON BOOKS are published by

Kensington Publishing Corp.
119 West 40th Street
New York, NY 10018

All Kensington titles, imprints, and distributed lines are available at special quantity discounts for bulk purchases for sales promotion, premiums, fundraising, educational, or institutional use.

Special book excerpts or customized printings can also be created to fit specific needs. For details, write or phone the office of the Kensington Sales Manager: Kensington Publishing Corp., 119 West 40th Street, New York, NY 10018. Attn. Sales Department. Phone: 1-800-221-2647.

Kensington and the K logo Reg. U.S. Pat. & TM Off.

ISBN-13: 978-1-4967-1527-2 (ebook)
ISBN-10: 1-4967-1527-6 (ebook)
Kensington Electronic Edition: March 2019

ISBN-13: 978-1-4967-1526-5
ISBN-10: 1-4967-1526-8
First Kensington Trade Paperback Printing: March 2019

10 9 8 7 6 5 4 3 2 1

Printed in the United States of America

Natalie Horbachevsky,
for your friendship and love

1

Suavemente

AIDEN

I'm not the kind of guy who would end up in this kind of hotel bar at this time of night, but here I am, sipping my fifth hurricane of the evening, trying to figure out exactly what led me here. It's easy, really. The answer is a series of bad choices and a woman. And, well, myself.

The bar at the swank Hotel Sucré in the heart of New Orleans is quieter post happy hour, leaving me with a prized corner all to myself. I pick up my strangely voluptuous glass, fascinated by the fat condensation running down my hands. My mom always said I had fine hands, romantic hands. It sounded a lot prettier when she said it to me in Spanish, because what are romantic hands supposed to look like?

I set the empty glass down and try to flag my bartender. "One more, please."

Angelique, the bartender, struts toward me. She's a dancer, same as me, though her performances are a lot more family friendly. Her hair is shaved at the sides, and a thick braid runs down her back, laced with bits of gold, giving her a warrior-princess vibe. Brown skin shimmers under the twinkling bar lights, and her thick painted lips smirk while her eyes contain nothing but sass.

"I can't in good conscience let you have another hurricane."

"Mi reina," I say. *My queen.*

But she cuts me off, her glossy white teeth showing as she tries to suppress a smile.

"Don't start that *suavemente* shit on me," she says, leaning on the bar to make better eye contact. I notice how her black tank top is digging into her shoulders, leaving marks on the smooth plane of her skin. "You know it's not going to work."

"Come on. I've been behaving, haven't I?" I spin in my seat and instantly regret it when she laughs at my expense. Five hurricanes and balance do not blend.

There's a flurry of activity as security guards stomp through the bar and toward the lobby. There's some sort of big meeting or convention happening, lots of suits with black sunglasses and lanyards and press badges hanging around.

"Maybe," Angelique says in that sweet Southern accent of hers. "But you've spent the last two nights here in this bar. You should be out celebrating. With people. Especially today."

I suck the straw to get the sugary liquid at the bottom of my drink. "You're people. They're people." I point at the couple at the opposite end of the bar who are so wrapped up in an embrace that the rest of the world doesn't exist.

I want to roll my eyes at them, but I turn to Angelique instead. I breathe deep and sit back. I give her the *look* she says won't work on her. I may not know a lot of things, like what I want to do with the rest of my life or how to be in a relationship for more than a week, but I know how to make women feel good.

I love them. All of them.

So much, that I've never allowed myself to be in a relationship because it wouldn't be fair to hurt anyone. I am the way I am. For twenty-four years, I've known how women react to me.

Fine, fine—Latino culture gives me all these advantages. I get that. My cousins Ginelle and Adriana remind me of the fact every time I visit home and get all the attention. My mother, for instance. There has never been someone as perfect as me in the eyes of my mother and my grandmother and my aunts. Even if it isn't true, they made me believe it. I grew up adored, loved so deeply that I'm afraid I can't ever replicate that. Part of me doesn't want to. My mother said that when I was born, the nurses in the hospital were all in love with me. My elementary school teachers gave me good grades because they couldn't bear to make me look sad. My desk was overflowing with Valentine's Day cards. Girls fought for me in high school hallways. I mean, I also got beat up a lot, but that's another story.

Is it right that I get the kind of attention I do? No. Not always. But I've never claimed to be an angel, have I? Because of all of that, I've created a system to try my damnedest to stay out of trouble over the years. It's a work in progress. Rule #1 in the Aiden Rios playbook: Don't play games.

A little voice inside my head says, *And what have these twenty-four years of adoration and rules and women brought you?* Well, twenty-five, now.

"Don't look at me like that," Angelique tells me. And because she avoids my eyes and smiles once again, I know that I've already won.

"There is nowhere else I'd rather be tonight," I say, hand to God, because rule #2 is *Don't lie.* Lies are messy, even small ones. Even if I have to lose a client, it's all better than getting caught in a web of my own making.

Angelique picks up her shaker and fills it with ice. "Okay, but this is the last one."

"See?" I say, unbuttoning the top two buttons of my shirt and rolling up the sleeves of my royal blue blazer. It's a little tight on my shoulders, but it was meant for taking off right away. "I've got everything I need right here and now."

"You seem awfully dressed up for someone who wasn't planning a night out on the town," Angelique says, like she's trying to draw out more of the story from me.

"Listen, mi reina, if I wanted to go out into that rowdy mess and step into some frat boy's puke, I'd be out there. I have a good feeling about tonight."

She purses her lips. "That's generally the feeling rum gives you."

"I can handle it."

"You prepped your liver in Vegas?"

I chuckle, but look away. "I don't want to talk about Vegas."

She shrugs her shoulder but doesn't pry. As with most of the people who come and go from her bar, she only knows superficial details of my life.

These are the things she knows: My name is Aiden Rios and I'm a dancer from New York by way of Vegas, previously starring in an all-male revue. When I'm in my cups, my Colombianness becomes more pronounced, and she seems to smile every time I drop "mi reina" in a sentence. I'm staying in the hotel, and I'm in town for a celebration that was cancelled about an hour ago, when my lady friend got a call that took her away on some official business I'm not allowed to ask about. Rule #3: No full names. No real names is even better.

These are the things she doesn't know: I recently quit a really good thing in Vegas. A sure thing. I left my brothers in Mayhem City to pursue something else, a greatness I knew I was destined for. But that's the thing—I'm not exactly sure what that something is anymore. I got greedy. I made shit bets. To get away from it all, I followed my lady friend, who pays me handsomely for my time and company.

I'm a stripper. An escort. Fucked, but not in the way I like. Sometimes my job can get messy, but that is what my playbook is for now. I know if I keep to my rules, the mess might just get less messy. I hope.

These are the rules I've always kept: Business is business. No feelings. No last names. No pictures and no videos. No sex unless both parties are into it after the contracted period has come to an end. No personal addresses. Hotels only, which I learned the hard way when one of my clients' husbands came home early from some conference and I was massaging her feet.

I've always found it fairly easy to keep to these rules. But this time, something changed. I'm not in love or anything. I don't think I've ever been in love, that's the thing. I know, sad Aiden Rios. I've never had trouble finding a woman who will console me. And yet, when my client left an hour ago, I felt a hurt I haven't in a while.

When I met Ginny, I was still in Vegas. She was on some errand for her husband, who I didn't ask after. She's a fine woman, tall and blond. A housewife, but without the Real Housewife surgery and claws. Just a smart, classy lady who picked me up at a whiskey bar in the Mandarin Hotel when I was at my lowest point. I hate whiskey but rich people and hipsters love to pay twenty dollars for an ounce of "the good stuff." Anyway, Ginny told me she wanted to take me on a special trip. That New Orleans was incredible. That I should celebrate. That she needed to take her mind off her woes. But I've been here for two days, and I've only seen the river on the drive in and the inside of this hotel bar.

It is a very nice bar with a marble top and fancy lighting that makes everyone look a little bit better. So I've got that going for me.

To be honest with myself, I didn't really want to come to New Orleans, but Ginny knew I was in a bad place after the mess I left behind. Like I said, she couldn't bear to see me upset, and so she brought me here on vacation. Funny thing is, I'm not used to my clients trying to take care of me, and it started to feel nice. She's from Louisiana and went on and on about college teams and let it slip her daughter is at university. Things were looking solid.

But then something happened. I didn't ask why, couldn't ask why, but Ginny came into the suite (prepaid in cash for the week, of course) to pick up her weekend bag, stuffing in things from the safe and closet in a hurry. Just by the frown lines on her forehead, I could tell something was wrong.

"I'm so sorry, but I have to go. My husband—" She massaged the bridge of her nose and slumped onto the living room couch. I brushed her hair over her neck and rubbed the anxious knot there. She melted right away. Her tension slipped into my fingers as they dug gently into her shoulder muscles.

"You don't have to explain," I said. But part of me wanted an explanation. I had no right to ask for it. Rule #4: She can call things off at any time. I made the rules, after all. "I'll be here when you get back." But part of me wants to go somewhere. Anywhere. I've never felt as alone as I do right now.

"I'll be back in a week," Ginny said. "The room is paid for and I left my card for incidentals. I ordered up some champagne." She pressed the red stain of her lips on my cheek, and walked out that door.

I shouldn't be upset. Ginny is a client, and I'm what I've always been: a well-dressed escort at an upscale bar.

Alone, a little voice chides me in the back of my head. That voice sounds surprisingly like my boy Fallon. Just because Fallon got himself wifed up, he's been trying to get all of us to settle down.

Dust settles and I am not dust.

Here, in the Hotel Sucré's bar, Angelique is all the company I need. Plus, she makes killer drinks, and I love her stories about performing in Vegas. She's cool people, even if she seems to see right through me in a way others don't.

"If you'd rather spend the night in, then *why* in God's green earth have you been sulking all night?" Angelique asks.

I clear my throat and sit back. "I'm not sulking. I'm brooding. There's a difference."

"And an ass is just a horse with shorter legs," she says, and narrows her rich brown eyes at me. "A good-looking guy like you? Don't you have a girlfriend?"

I evade the question. "You think I'm good-looking?"

She sets her rag on the marble top. "You *know* you're good-looking. A boyfriend? A wife?"

"No on all accounts. You know how it is."

"I haven't found the right girl, either, Aiden," she says.

"Well, I haven't found her because I'm not looking," I say, and drink the watered-down remnants in my glass and crunch on some ice. When I was in junior high, my cousin Suzie said that she'd read in a magazine that chewing on ice was a sign of sexual frustration. I tilt the glass back too far, and ice comes tumbling around my face. Man, I'm in rare form.

Angelique hands me a stack of napkins. "Now you're cut off unless you start drinking some water."

So I do as my alcohol therapist tells me and drink some fancy bottled mineral water that advertises a mountain range in the Alps. I shoulder off my suit jacket and drape it over my chair to save my seat because I've had to go to the bathroom for hours. I just didn't want to get up and lose precious real estate.

Plus, I can't shake the feeling that I have to be here in this moment at this time. I'm superstitious but not *as* superstitious as my mom was or the way Tía Ceci and grandmother Socorro still are. They believed in the Almighty's divine intervention. My tía Ceci knows what I do for a living, but no one else does. They believe you catch people's bad energies, and I know they'd say that what I do puts me around a lot of that. I know if my grandma Socorro felt this same feeling I have right now—that I shouldn't move or go out or even back to my room, though my bladder is about to burst—she'd tell me that something is happening and to wait for it.

But I can't wait for it, and maybe that's my biggest problem.

As I make my way through the bustling lobby, I try to tuck those thoughts away. I concentrate on the party of bachelorettes that are having pre-night-out drinks in the lounge. The bride looks decadent in a white minidress that's painted on. Her bridesmaids are in color-coordinated black and gold dresses that complement the different shades of brown and black of their smooth skin.

I flash a smile and a wink as I walk past them, full swagger. One of them whistles at me, and maybe it's the krewe of cocktails that have paraded down my throat, but I can't seem to think of a good enough line to say back.

I freeze up. We stare at each other for twenty awkward seconds before they turn around and ignore me.

I keep walking, past the reception desk, the flowers with their cloying scent that threatens memories of things I'd rather forget, the signs that read *VOTE CHARLES FOR CHANGE*, and a woman dolled up in a red pencil-skirt suit that makes her look like a rose waiting to bloom.

"Watch where you're going," she snaps as I nearly walk into

her. But I smile and she seems to unfurl, her anger dissipating into thin air. "Here for the fund-raiser?"

I shake my head, rake my fingers through my hair. Maybe Angelique is right. I shouldn't be alone and sulking. Er, brooding. The night isn't wasted. Won't be wasted. Maybe this is the reason I've clung to this bar all night. This lady in red. I know I should say something clever, something that will make her laugh at my joke, something that will bring a smile to her face. Her lipstick is drawn on in precise lines, and her eyebrows etched in perfect arcs. She wants to look a certain way, and I, more than most, can identify with that.

But for the second time in so many minutes, I freeze. For the life of me, I can't even go through the dozens of pickup lines stored in my mind for a rainy day.

"Uhm, I have to pee," I tell her.

No, no, no, no, I scream internally. That's *not* the line. We know better. *I'm not here for the fund-raiser, I'm here for your pleasure.* Hell, I could have said I was here for turndown service. To wash the fucking windows. Whatever. Anything but talking about my bladder.

"Good luck with that, kid," she says, and pats my cheek with her scarlet-manicured hand.

Feeling thoroughly shut down, I go to the bathroom to do my businesses. I wash my hands and splash a bit of cold water on my cheeks.

When I look in the mirror, I see the resemblance to someone I'd rather not think about: light-brown eyes, not green enough to be hazel, and a square jawline that took me eighteen years to grow into. So I grab a hand towel and dry my face. Shake off whatever has me clenched and sloppy.

When I stroll past the lobby again, the woman in red is gone and so is the bachelorette party. More than anything, I feel like I'm walking alone through a moment, not part of it. An outsider looking in, though I've felt that way for most of my life. Out in the streets there's a sea of people shouting, music pouring through the air like champagne out of a just-shaken bottle, neon lights flashing every kind of sin and desire you didn't even know you had. It's all there, just at my fingertips.

Here I am, alone at a bar, and for the first time in the evening, I know why I'm supposed to be here.

And she is sitting in my seat.

2

Daughter

FAITH

My mother always taught me that if I was going to embarrass her, I might as well stay in my room.

That was when she'd have her fancy fund-raisers at our house and I'd be forced into frilly dresses that itched and made me look like a five-tier cake with meringue frosting. At various points in the night I'd get reprimanded for being too quiet or too loud. For not being enough like the other city council members' daughters. No matter what I did, I couldn't seem to make her happy.

Not much has changed since I was thirteen, it seems.

Well, that's not quite true. I no longer wear the meringue dresses.

Over in a quiet corner of the room, my father is patiently and dutifully smiling at the cameras and reporters asking him all kinds of invasive questions.

How did it feel being a stay-at-home dad?

How does it feel to be married to such an ambitious woman?

Are you prepared to be the First Husband of New Orleans?

Are you proud of your wife's work? Of your daughter?

And the answers are always the same. My father, Lorenzo Charles the third, comes from one of the oldest families of New Orleans and is used to talking to reporters because of his law firm's efforts to preserve the wildlife in Louisiana. I should be walking in his footsteps. It's been two years since I graduated Yale Law and did a year's clerkship at my dad's firm, plus grunt work for a nonprofit environmental agency. I know as a Charles I have a job waiting for me. But I want to be able to *earn* it. I know what people think when they look at me. Daddy's girl. Rich girl. But I've had to work for everything I've accomplished, just like my parents did. The next step is taking the bar. I failed once, and while I was studying, I decided to help my mother achieve her greatest dream. Being mayor of New Orleans.

I've been studying for two years now.

I hold the clipboard with the guest list. All of that schooling and here I am, checking people's names off as they enter an overly air-conditioned event space. Every person here has come for a fund-raiser, but there's an underlying current. The recent speculation has been that my mother was going to drop out of the race after the opponent, Reginald Louis Moreaux, suggested that my father's decision to stay at home to take care of me was because of some sort of infidelity. God forbid the man wanted to give up his career all those years ago to be a dedicated father and good husband.

My family might be dysfunctional in different ways, but I'd suggest my father was a serial killer before I'd believe he was unfaithful. People in glass houses, but I won't go down that petty path.

Still, the Moreaux side has played dirty for the duration of the campaign, and there are three weeks left to go. Everything from lies to trying to pry into my mom's past as a waitress. They even put *waitress* in air quotes, as if my mother's beauty suggested something else. As if no one can believe a Black woman from her station in life could achieve the things she has honestly. I don't know how my parents don't lose their shit. *Always be the better person,* my dad used to tell me. *Especially when they don't want you to be.*

"Name?" I ask the woman who walks in next. She's dressed in all red with heels that give her five inches on me, and I'm five nine.

"Betty LePaige," she says. I match her credentials to the list.

The N'*awlins Gazette* is nothing but gossip, probably trying to dig up something else on my mother. They haven't come to any of the press conferences or run any coverage on the race, so this new presence sends up a red flag in my head. Perhaps the Moreaux camp tipped them off to be here. . . . Perhaps people really think there's something to confess. . . . Whatever it might be, I should tell my mother.

"You're all set," I say and return Betty's tight smile, then hand over the clipboard to an intern.

Weaving through the crowd of reporters and donors, plus a few friends and family, I feel watched. It's like having a spotlight on me.

I find my mother giving some sort of rousing talk to three businessmen. Dressed in a fine forest-green suit, my mother cuts a lovely figure. People who don't know her wouldn't notice the way she always keeps her hands moving. It's not because she likes to talk animatedly, but because she's embarrassed by them. The hands of a woman who had to lift boxes and clean floors and burn herself on plates coming in fresh from the oven in run-down diners. Working hands. But her face hasn't changed since she was, well, my age. I have an insight into what I might look like in thirty years.

Though I hope not half as wound up, but maybe I'm well on my way. I wave at her a few feet from where she's in conversation.

My mom notices me, I know she does, but she waits before catching my eye. She excuses herself, leaning in close. "I hope this is important. Those could be very valuable donors."

Everyone is a very valuable donor, I want to say, but I'll never be old enough to avoid being smacked on the back of my head. Though now, she'd only ever do it in private.

"There's someone here from the *Gazette,* I thought you should know," I say. "I was thinking the Moreaux campaign might have sent them to keep an eye on us."

My mother shakes her head. Years of council meetings have taught her how to hide her ire, but she's my mother, and even if she doesn't think so, I know her better than anyone else. It's the slightest purse of her lips, giving way to the same dimples I share. Though she's yet to get a wrinkle on her smooth light-brown skin, her right eyebrow, carefully drawn in, ticks up like a check mark. She is nothing if not observant. Especially when it comes to me.

"Faith, my darling, I didn't know I hired you on to write fanciful stories."

I take a deep breath because I can't make a scene. Not today. "It's a likely possibility. The Moreaux article is the reason we're having this event in the first place. One of your last donors pulled out."

"That might be so, but you should know better than to pull me away when I'm having an important conversation." My mother smiles her "people are looking at us" smile, and so I turn mine on. A mirror I can't escape.

I take a deep breath. Everything is important. She's made that clear since I could walk. "Fine. I've told you. Here's your speech."

"Watch your tongue, young lady," she says in a whisper, then takes the folder from me. "Maribelle already gave me a copy. You should spend more time with her, Faith. She's learned the ropes faster than any intern I've ever had."

Maribelle's name makes something inside of me snap. She's fresh out of college with her eye on local government. She's qualified to do exactly nothing, but my mom seems to think everything she does, from the way she pours coffee to the way she irons her blouses, is perfect. Every day or so, my mom tells me to "spend more time" with Maribelle, but says nothing of what I contribute.

"Then why did you ask me to do it if Maribelle already did it?" I know my voice is too loud, because my mom slings her arm over my shoulder. In her sensible heels, she's my height—because the one thing I got from my father is his height, if not his patience.

"Lower your voice, please," she says brightly, but I hear the undercurrent there. I'm in trouble.

Hell, I'm always in trouble. Why should today be different?

"I don't understand why you're like this. Nothing I do seems to please you." I can feel the anxiety in my chest unravel. It's a snake waiting in the grass. Ready to lift its head and snap. This has been coming for months, years really, and now I know that it's going to get ugly and I can't seem to stop it.

"Faith . . ." Her smile is wider.

"Please, don't patronize me. I've busted my ass for the last two years for you."

"For *us*. And don't you give me that back talk. I gave you something to work for while you were doing I-don't-know-what—Look, I don't want to fight—"

"No, you can't afford to fight. There's a *difference*."

Heads swivel in our direction. From the corner of my eye I can see Maribelle, her perfect curls bouncing against her back as she zigzags to rescue my mother from her own kid embarrassing her.

"Faith!" Maribelle says in that perky voice of hers. "Can you help me out with something?"

That's code for "you're making a scene."

"You know what?" I say. "You clearly have all of this under control. I'll see you at headquarters tomorrow."

"Why don't you take the day off?" my mother says.

I know I should take a breath. I know that maybe she's a little bit right. Maybe I'm the one who's wrong. But I say, "You know what? I'll take the week instead."

And with that, I turn tail and leave. My daddy is trying to catch my eye, but I can't bear to look at him. I have to focus on making my face into a carefully carved statue. It works for my mother, why doesn't it work for me?

I take the elevator, squeezing in with partygoers and people ready for a night out in the Quarter. I can't even remember the last time I went out for something that wasn't a political function or a party full of stuffy old lawyers.

Something in my chest is wound up so tight, I feel like if it snaps completely, I might explode. I have to cool off.

Thankfully, I know the bartender of this hotel.

I exit the elevator and pass a group of bachelorettes conga-lining out the door, then I turn the corner and sigh with relief at the sight of Angelique Jacobs. Angie and I have been friends since high school, and we both went to undergrad at Loyola. Neither of us really wanted to stray too far from home. But after that first year, she transferred out and switched her major from political science to dance. Her last gig was in Vegas, swinging from trapezes and all kinds of things I can't even fathom with Cirque du Soleil. I can barely do the warrior two pose in yoga, and she can fold herself like origami. But she fell and hurt her shoulder real bad. So she came home.

It's been a year, and I think she's got a bit of stage fright after the incident. Bartending is holding her over, but I can tell she wants more. Or I'm possibly projecting on her because here we are, eleven years after we started college, and we're right back where we started. New Orleans.

"I take it by the look on your face the party is all peaches?" She slides a coaster in front of me.

There's a half-drunk hurricane already there, but she moves it aside a bit. Even the look of that drink gives me a toothache.

"Is someone sitting here?" I ask, not ready to talk about my tiny temper tantrum.

"Yeah, but he's in the bathroom." Angie has a *look* in her eye. It's mischievous and downright conspiratorial.

"What?"

She smiles, her red lip gloss like a candied apple. "Nothing. You want the usual?"

"You're an angel."

"Fallen angel, maybe," and when she says that, I can practically feel her wince. She turns around and grabs a bottle of Woodford Reserve, one fat square ice cube, and pours me a double.

I hold the drink like it's a potion with the solution to all my problems.

"What did Daria do this time?" Angie mutters.

She and my mother never really got along after Angie decided to change her career for one in the arts. Daria Charles was probably more worried that I'd get the art bug and move to Rome to paint naked folks or some such.

"Nothing this can't fix for the moment." I take another sip and try to relax.

"The answer to your problems isn't at the bottom of that glass," Angie says.

"That's not a very good business motto for your line of work," I sass but swallow my drink easily. It goes down smooth. I think of all the times I watched my daddy come home from work after a long day, before he quit to raise me while Mom started her political career. He'd go into his office and pour himself a glass of what he called *medicine*. Part of me wonders if I'm too young to be feeling this way. But I think I know the weight that tugged on his shoulders just a little bit.

"I'm just saying. I think your stress comes from multiple places. One of them being that thing you've got under lock and key between your legs."

I nearly spit my drink out. The couple canoodling at the other end of the bar comes up for air to watch me choke on the burn of bourbon in my windpipe.

"Please never refer to my vagina as a treasure chest." I reach for the water she sets in front of me, her head tilting back in a great big laugh at my expense.

"Look, you know I love you, hon. I can't stand to see you upset. I know you're not going to listen to my first suggestion, so I'm giving you another one. In my honest opinion as your best friend, you need to get some. Like yesterday. What's it been, like, two years since Stuart?"

I hold my hand up. "What's the first suggestion I'm not going to listen to because you know me so well?"

"Quit your job working for your momma."

A troubling feeling tugs at my stomach. My mother and I have never had the best relationship. But I keep trying because I know that when I wake up tomorrow, I'm going to want my mother to look at me the way she looks at Maribelle or whatever new assistant is popping up like a weed.

I look into my glass like my reflection will have an answer. It doesn't.

"You know I can't do that. How would it look?" I sigh. "Especially now. We're supposed to be *the* family you want to be. Maribelle's probably coming up with a lie about why I stormed out and said I'd take the week off."

That's the funny thing about my impulsive decision making. I usually regret it fifteen minutes later.

"Is that really the image you want to give out?"

"It's the image my mother believes we have. And anyway, once we win this thing, because we will, I'll find a different job."

"Hm," she says.

"Do you have a third suggestion?"

"I like the second one the best. He's six four, Colombian, too fucking beautiful for his own good. He was a dancer in Vegas, so you know he *knows* how to swivel them hips."

"Angie!" I look around. Then it dawns on me. "What kind of dancer?"

She slaps her hands on the gray bar top. "The take-off-all-your-clothes kind. And don't make that face. He's been at the hotel for two days and I've only ever seen him by himself. He hasn't taken anyone up with him. I don't know his deal, but he's not in town for long. You need to blow off some steam and I think he does, too."

"Is that your professional opinion?" I say, laughing because her idea is absurd. "The only steam I need to let off I'll do at a Bikram tomorrow."

Angie makes a face that is equal parts disappointed and hopeless. "Just remember who you talk to about your frustrations with your mom. It's time to take action."

I suppose she's tired of the same old song. I threatened to quit my *nonpaying* job on my mother's staff last year. And a few months before when my mom won city council, and the year before that when my mother had her second successful run at a local office.

I start to stare at myself in the mirror of my whiskey, when Angie's eyes widen at something behind me.

Someone.

By the sparkle in Angie's eye, I know it has to be one of two things: Tessa Thompson in a bikini or the Vegas stripper she's trying to set me up with. Angie is convinced she's going to find me a man that'll quench my dry spell. Sometimes you just go for so long without something that you lose the taste for it. Like dairy. I brace myself for what's in store.

His voice comes first. Slow as gin, and I know, I just know that when I turn around to look at him, the sight of him won't disappoint.

"Excuse me, miss. I believe you're in my seat."

Angie is smirking like a little kid with a birthday cake all to herself from orchestrating this little encounter. She let me sit down on a chair that was already taken. She never does that. She knows I like to drink in a corner of my own. My seat happens to be occupied by a couple obnoxiously making out. For the first time I notice I'm sitting on the sleeve of a rich blue blazer. Angie must've known his jacket was there.

I turn around in my chair and steady myself. The snake coiled in my chest morphs into something different. Something tangled and unsure and a feeling I can't quite place.

This guy is deliciously rumpled. Like he just rolled out of bed with his dark hair mussed up despite the product I can smell in it. A rebellious chunk flops over his eyes, and he brushes it back with strong, fine hands. His angular jawline and cheekbones were made to chisel gemstones into perfection. His eyes are the clear light brown of my whiskey, and when he blinks, I feel like I could just sit here and count every single one of his thick black lashes.

I recognize the feeling I couldn't place. Has it really been so long that I couldn't put a name to it? Two years, to be exact. The word flashes across my eyes like neon strobe lights. *WANT.* Like candy on days I have a sweet tooth or water during a long hot day.

This is a guy who knows what he's doing. Knows the way my body reacts to him, turning just so forward. I'm not even meaning to do that, but I'm leaning like a flower thirsty for the sun.

I instantly don't like this feeling, and I'm going to have to give Angie hell for trying to orchestrate this.

"Sorry," I say, and start to get up.

"No, no, I can move." His voice has a treble that thrums across my spine. "Though I will need my jacket back."

I find myself stuttering. I haven't stuttered since junior prom, when I was unsure if Jerry Carlson was going to kiss me or not. (He didn't.) "Th-this jacket?"

I have it in my hand. A soft, expensive fabric. I peek at the brand before I hand it over. I'm doing the thing that Angie tells me I do too quickly. I overanalyze. His suit is easily three grand from head to toe. Shoes that are classic, polished leather. No one wears cufflinks anymore, but he has two simple gold buttons on both sides. Designer watch with a minimalist face around his right wrist, fingernails manicured meticulously and kept short.

If Angie hadn't told me his profession, I'd play that guessing game she and I have when I let her take me out to "troll for dick" as she puts it, though we always end up getting her a hookup instead. It's fine with me, and so I developed the guessing game I have going on now.

I would have gone with a hedge fund guy. He's too happy to be a lawyer, and too well dressed for a tech start-up, and too classic for a musician, or at least one who would be in this hotel when Jazz Fest isn't clogging up the city's arteries.

I hand him his jacket blazer, and he extends a hand for me to shake.

"Aiden," he says.

"Faith," I say.

"Faith," he repeats, and the sound of my name on his lips is a ridiculously beautiful thing. "I could use a little bit of that."

I cringe a little inwardly. I hate pickup lines. I've heard most of them. *I've said all my prayers tonight.* Every version of that one about falling from heaven. The men of New Orleans keep thinking I'm angelic, and this one can be added to that pile of cheesy one-liners.

Then when I notice the sad tug at the corner of his lips, I wonder if he's sincere. Or a very good actor.

He points to the just-vacated seat beside me. "Do you mind?"

I shake my head and try to breathe through the sudden rush of excitement I feel, despite my better judgment. His muscles flex against the stark-white material of his shirt, and just before he sits I can't help but admire the way his tailored slacks hug perfectly tight buns. Because I can sense Angie smirking, I force myself to look away from the lines of his body. Is it possible for someone to be soft and hard at the same time? I can feel a flush creep up my neck because I picture him stepping out of a fire-man uniform or whatever it is he wears onstage. He certainly moves like he's aware of his body. A sensuality, a gracefulness as he turns to me with his whole self, like I'm the only thing worth looking at. For a flash of a moment, he looks unsure, but it's only a second. Then he licks a set of full lips, and that image tugs a smile at the corners of my own mouth.

"Can I buy you another drink?" he asks. That irreverent flop of hair falls over his eyes, and I wrestle with my own desire to reach for it if only to stare into those whiskey eyes. My heart flutters, but then I cross my legs, because so does another part of me.

I bite my bottom lip. I should go home. I should apologize to my mother. But I'm drawn to this handsome stranger in a way I can't explain.

I have a feeling I might regret this.

So I say yes.

3

Crush

AIDEN

When I saw her, my entire body reacted.

I've always loved looking at women. They're all beautiful in more ways than I can count. My mother taught me that I had to show respect, especially if I was going to try to talk to her, and no matter what the outcome.

This woman, sitting in my seat, was a sight I was not prepared for. My eyes widened at the sleek curve of her profile. An hourglass figure that I'd like to turn in my hands. Her black dress was sensible, elegant, with a playful red sash to accentuate her waist. *Delicate.* The word danced around my mind as I took in the hair gathered at the base of her neck. With every step I took to get to that bar, I imagined her hair falling down her back if I pulled the pins holding it together.

I was holding my breath right up until I reached her, my heart hammering as I anticipated looking into her eyes. I could see a fraction of her in the mirror, a sliver of a promise I wasn't sure I was ready to make.

Then I saw Angelique's mischievous grin as she watched me approach. A Cupid with horns instead of wings.

I start talking to her, and she tells me her name is Faith. Honestly, I've been throwing cheesy-ass lines all night. Off my game and all that. But when I hear her name is Faith, it feels like God and the Universe might be trying to tell me something.

"Whatever the lady is drinking," I tell Angelique.

Faith traces the mouth of her glass, empty, with the drippy remnants of an ice cube sliding back and forth.

"And I'll take another hurricane," I say and knock on the marble.

Faith smacks her hands down. "You *cannot* order that."

"Why do you guys keep judging my drink of choice?" I say, flashing a smile.

Faith and Angelique share a long stare. It's the way I might look at a friend. "Do you two know each other?"

Neither of them answer, but my devilishly beautiful bartender says, "I told you. I can't in good conscience give you the immense sugar crash you've had with hurricanes. It's your—"

"It's my sixth one of the night," I say quickly. "But you've taken such good care of me. Besides. It's basically juice I'm drinking."

"I can't sit here and watch this happen. Will you let me order you a grown-up drink?"

"Technically, any drink I order is a grown-up drink because I am over twenty-one."

She smiles again, wide and playful. "Listen, I understand the need for cocktails. They're pretty. They're sweet. But when you wake up tomorrow, you're going to regret it."

The way she speaks makes me want to lean in toward her. Everything about her fascinates me. The way she holds her drink with a confident ease. But when she catches me checking out her thick brown legs, she fingers a lock of her hair. Maybe that trip to the bathroom did me good because my head is clear, focused. My dick twitches with instant desire for her, while the rest of me is steady, comfortable. Like her stare is anchoring me here to this moment. I can practically taste the cloud of worry around her, like she just fought with someone. A boyfriend. A friend. Someone important. Whatever it is, it has to be the thing behind her words.

"Are we still talking about a drink?" I ask.

She lifts her chin, watching me defiantly. I can count the

smatter of freckles across her cheeks and nose the way I count stars.

"Yes," she says, in a calm alto voice. "Drinks. Now. I'll let you buy me a drink if you let me buy you one."

"Doesn't that cancel them out?"

She tilts her head. "Isn't it the gesture that matters?"

"Okay, but I hate the taste of licorice." I notice the way she crosses her legs tighter. "I'll eat just about anything else."

"Drink," she corrects me, a little ruffled.

But I smile and shrug, leaving her to conjure up whatever image she wants.

I watch as Faith rests her chin on her closed fist. Her eyes are trained on the array of bottles in front of us, and my eyes are trained on her. There's a tiny freckle on her right jaw, and I find myself overwhelmed with the urge to brush my thumb across it.

Whoa, hey, no. I clear my throat.

This woman is stunning and has me shook in a way I haven't felt in years. Perhaps ever. But I can't let myself get carried away.

"Let's go with a classic," Faith says. "We are in New Orleans, after all."

She hasn't actually said the drink, but Angelique seems to read her mind. While the bartender has her back turned, mixing spirits, Faith and I have a moment to ourselves.

"So, you do know each other." I leave the statement plainly there.

Faith looks at me with the slightest hint of coyness. There's a solid gold ring with a garnet stone on her middle finger. It's the only jewelry she's wearing other than elegant but simple pearl stud earrings, so I'd wager it's a family heirloom. She's not the usual kind of woman I've met sitting alone at a bar. She wasn't searching for someone. Probably got off work and swung by to grab a drink where she knows the bartender. I want to ask her. I want to know why she seems so tense. But that breaks some sort of playbook rule. It must.

"We went to school together, actually," she says. It took her so long to come up with an answer that I can sense how guarded she is. "Have you been in town long?"

"Not long. I've barely left the hotel, actually." I instantly regret saying that because it leads to more questions I can't exactly answer.

I tell myself that I'm not working. That I was left here all by myself by a client. I tell myself that I'm not doing anything wrong, because getting to know this woman can't possibly be wrong.

"You're in the greatest city in the world," Faith says. "How have you not left the hotel?"

I make a sound like a record scratching. I tug on my tie until it comes completely undone and turn in my seat to face her. "Excuse me. I'm from the greatest city in the world, and that's New York. You might have heard of it. There are a bunch of songs about it."

"Greatest?" She purses her lips and holds up a finger. "So you like paying $4,000 for a closet and $20 for cocktails? No wonder you're getting your fill of hurricanes here."

I laugh at her burn. From her lips, it's not a burn at all. "Actually, I grew up in Queens, so I paid $1,500 for a two bedroom, and where I'm from I don't drink hurricanes so I can't tell you if they're $20."

It's her turn to laugh. "Angie said you came from Vegas. You're not going to defend that place, too?"

Chances are that since they're such good friends, my favorite bartender must have already told Faith that I dance. It's a good sign that she's still talking to me, but I'm going to dive right in and see if I can swim.

"God, no," I say, edging just a tiny bit closer to her. "I couldn't cut it, anyway. I danced for a while with Mayhem City. I don't know if you've heard of us, since you don't know New York is the greatest city in the world, either."

Her eyes widen, like she's shocked at my directness. But her smile is so full, so brilliantly real as she laughs that my insides feel a strange tingle.

"I don't know why but it sounds familiar," she says, unable to look at me when she continues. "But I've never been to a, uh, show."

When her dark eyes flash back to mine, I hold her gaze and say, "I could always give you a private one."

She presses her hand on my chest and gives me a little push. "You are too much for your own well-being."

The pressure of her fingers on my chest is enough to light me up, the pleasure of it settling right in my crotch.

"How long have you danced?" she asks.

"Since I was eighteen." I never talk to women like this. Yeah, one of my rules is honesty, but for the most part they never ask. They just want to go straight to the goods, and I'm usually okay with that. "I never had it in me to be something terrible like a lawyer or a—wait, are *you* a lawyer? Did I just totally fuck this up?"

She looks down, and her insanely pretty lashes rest on her cheeks when she smiles. "No, I'm not. I'm between jobs."

"Well, I'm glad we have that in common."

Do you ever get several voices in your head all at once? Sometimes when I'm doing something I know I shouldn't be doing, that voice sounds like my tía Cecilia. She basically taught me everything about girls that I couldn't talk to my mother about, and my father, well . . . Tía Ceci was there to rise up to the challenge. She's always telling me how to treat a girl. Like a queen. Una reina. She has to mean everything to me in that moment. If I'm not feeling it, don't fake it. The problem is, when I was younger, I wanted everyone to be my queen. Here, right now, I'm more aroused by Faith's freckles, her eyelashes, than any other woman in this bar. *Slow down*, the voice says.

Faith's lashes are a perfect curl, framing narrow eyes as dark as midnight. She takes a breath, a little sigh I want to capture with my mouth. "You're staring."

"So are you," I shoot right back.

Her eyes flick down to her lap. Her body language speaks volumes. She's not moving from her seat but has swiveled, turning her knees toward me, smooth and polished in the bar's light.

She's tapping her heeled foot, which tells me she's just a little bit nervous. A girl like this doesn't seem to lack confidence, but here she is, avoiding my eyes and smiling all the same.

Angelique brings our drinks around, and I wink at her. I owe her a huge thank-you for introducing me to Faith. I know she's looking for another dancing gig, and I'll have to remember to ask my buddy Fallon to look into it.

Faith cocks her head to the side. "What should we toast to?"

I hold my drink level to hers. When I look at Faith, everything feels sharper. Like clouds have parted to reveal her eyes and nose and lips and cheekbones.

"To grown-up drinks," I say.

"I know what else you should toast to," Angelique mutters, cleaning a glass with a rag.

The girls look at each other, but Angelique doesn't share the reason I'm so dressed up even though I'm staying in.

Faith clicks her glass to mine.

My drink is like bitter medicine with muddled fruit and a sugar cube. I don't love it but I don't hate it and I wonder if it's only because she ordered it for me.

"What is this?"

"A Sazerac!" Faith says with gusto. "You should have had one as soon as you got off the plane."

When I watch her take another swig of her plain old whiskey, I shiver. I'll drink tequila and rum on their own all day. But there's something about straight whiskey that is incompatible with me.

"How can you drink that stuff?" I ask, watching her down the amber liquid.

She looks into her glass, I can tell there's a depth I haven't even begun to see. "When I was little my dad used to come home from work, walk into his office, and pour himself a glass. Sometimes when he was tired, I'd do it for him. Measure two fingers, he'd say. Well, three for me because I was little. Then I'd fetch one ice cube. No more, no less. I guess I take after him. What about you?"

"My mom didn't drink. I mean, except for Communion

wine. My dad, on the other hand. When he was around, he'd finish a bottle of this stuff, aguardiente. It literally means 'burning water' and it tastes like shit. But he'd drink that with orange juice. My mom kicked him out a bunch of times but she just— and *wow*, sorry. Too personal." I stare into the abyss of my cocktail to avoid the sympathy I'm sure is swimming in her stare. Why did I tell her that?

"Hey, Angelique," I say, knocking on the bar. "Is there some sort of truth potion in here?"

Angelique is busy shaking a drink at the other end of the bar. "Yeah, it's called alcohol."

Faith's observing me. Maybe even trying to decide what my game is. A girl as fine as this? She wouldn't give me the time of day if she knew what I did in addition to dancing . . . the reason I'm stranded in this city for at least a week. I know that I should be more straight up with her. But for a sec, just for a sec, I tell myself that I'm off the clock. Ginny is off with her husband. So I'm just a guy buying a drink for a gorgeous woman I don't want to pry myself away from.

It's scary as fuck.

She tucks a strand of her hair back. My heart gives a little thump when I imagine whispering sweet nothings in her ear. I clear my throat and sit back.

"That's okay. You can tell me your darkest secrets right now and it'll stay between us," she says.

"What makes you say that?"

"Because we're strangers."

"Do you want to change that?" I ask, and once again, our bodies are like magnets, drawing closer inch by inch. What the hell am I doing?

She shakes her head. "I'm not sure. But I'm not ready to go home just yet."

When she sets her drink down, the back of her hand is touching mine. I can't ignore the tightening sensation in the pit of my gut. The nerves slamming against my chest. The way my dick twitches every time I stare too long at her sensual lips.

"Good. Neither am I."

The place is filling with late-dinner goers. They squeeze in around us, and a second bartender joins Angelique to help with the rush of orders.

Someone screams from the other end of the bar. We turn around to find the source of the yelp, and it's a group of young women.

And they're headed right toward me. Now, I never get recognized from my shows with Mayhem City, so this is particularly weird.

"Excuse me," one of them says, holding a pen. "Are you Maluma?"

I grin at her, and Faith is trying not to laugh behind her hand.

"I'm not—"

But they shove their napkins and pens in my face and jump behind me for selfies. I scribble the singer's name on scraps of paper and one rib cage.

"So you're a singer," Faith says as the girls run off, blowing kisses my way and telling me that they love everything about me.

"You definitely don't want to hear me sing, mi reina," I say. "But I can sign dozens of autographs like a pro."

She narrows her eyes, and I love when her nose scrunches up every time she does that because it feels like she's trying to see through me, through any lies I might be telling.

"Vegas must have been the best place for that."

I shake my head. "I don't really miss it."

"Everybody misses something from everywhere they've lived. Even if it's one thing. Like, Connecticut is not my thing. But there was this patch of green on campus. There was this tree that had the perfect place to sit. Like the roots grew to make a chair just for the students. It was perfect."

I try to picture this incredibly smart girl reading in the shade, a breeze blowing leaves across her lap. Even that thought of her—sweet, simple—sends alarms of pleasure to my cock. I grab my jacket and drape it over my lap.

"I mostly miss people, not places," I say. "My sort-of mentor, Rick Rocket, wanted me to replace him one day."

"What happened?"

I got caught up in the things they warn you about. Women. Rich women. Promises that lead to nowhere. But it hurts to admit that to myself.

"Made a bad investment. Lots of regret. That's why I'm here alone, drinking."

"You seem awfully young to have so much regret."

"Age means different things to different people," I tell her. "Ever since I was little I've had people telling me that I can't do something. I've been trying to prove them wrong for so long—I don't know. It's hard to keep motivated when the people you care about don't believe in you."

Faith squeezes my hand. "This is going to sound insane. But I know exactly how that feels."

"Is that why you're here with me on a Friday night instead of breaking hearts on Bourbon Street?"

Faith looks away, trying to suppress a smile. Her smirk is equally as satisfying. "First of all, you're from New York, right? How often do you go out to Times Square?"

"Point made. Still. No hot date?"

She picks up her drink, purses her lips together. Her eyes flick over my shoulder. Is she expecting to see someone? Maybe I'm being used to make someone else jealous. But if that's the case, she can use me any way she wants. I would gladly lend her my body for all kinds of things.

"I was at a work event," she says, finally. "My boss and I disagreed on something and I walked out."

"Damn. That's ballsy."

"Gutsy," she corrects me. "And not as gutsy as I wish. I didn't exactly quit. I know I should."

"What's stopping you?" I ask, leaning in closer. It's like the bar is getting louder and louder so we have to lean in closer and closer to hear each other better. Right now I'm so near that I can smell the sweet perfume lingering on her neck, floral and citrus and that primal essence that fills my dick with an urgent need. Any closer and my mouth would be on the silky skin of her neck, which she bares to me by brushing her hair away.

"You can't walk away from family," she says, punctuating

her sentence with a sip of her whiskey. "Besides, if all goes well, I'll be able to go my own way next year."

"Cheers to that," I say, clinking my glass to hers. My drink has been gone for a long time, but I have never felt so aware. So grounded to one person that the place could catch on fire and I wouldn't want to move, not without her moving first. That's a dangerous thought, and it's the only thing that makes me draw back a bit.

"What do you have going on tomorrow?" I blurt out.

"Tomorrow?" Her eyes flick from my stare to the unbuttoned space at my collar. Then, she glances over my shoulder. I force myself to not follow her stare. What is she looking at? What makes her wide-eyed? She turns her body a bit. Is she hiding? A boyfriend? An ex-husband? Then she says the words that make every cell in my body come alight with possibility. "Why not tonight?"

I stand, to shield her with my body. If she's hiding from someone, the least I can do is provide cover. Maybe this is wrong. Maybe I don't know the full story of what's going on with Faith. But I know that I don't want to tear myself from her presence.

Angelique walks over with a knowing smirk on her face. "You guys done?"

I reach into my pocket for my clip. "Check, please."

"You can charge it to your room if you want."

That sends a shot of panic through my blood. That's not a good idea. Ginny left me her card, but that feels all kinds of wrong, even for me.

"Nah, it's all right."

I leave a few bills, and when I turn, Faith has something in her hands. Her thumb brushes across the surface of my expired New York State ID.

"Aiden Peñaflor," she reads, then there's a tiny gasp in the back of her throat, a throat I desperately want to feel. "Today's your birthday?"

Dressed up with nowhere to go.

"Twenty-five isn't really a big deal." I smile, but I don't feel it reach my heart. I run a hand through my hair. I don't know what else to say. I mean, all of my birthdays have been pretty crappy. Why should this one be any different? But I don't want to bring her down. I want to hold on to this sensation she instills in me with her voice, her stare, her body. Around us the music grows louder and the people have multiplied once again.

Her finger reaches for the strand of hair that flops over my eyes. It doesn't stay put, but her fingers find their way, tracing my ear, my cheekbone.

"I know a way we can celebrate."

4

Pour Some Sugar on Me

FAITH

I know, I know—everyone says that they've never done anything like this before. Especially when it comes to impulsive decisions to run off with a stranger. The most attractive stranger I've ever met.

This goes against everything that I've ever learned as a girl growing up. Don't trust people you've just met. Don't be alone with a man you've just met. What would my mother think if she saw me right now, clutching my purse as I leave with this Aiden Peñaflor? What would my dad say?

When I left the bar, Angelique gave me a wink. If she thought there was something wrong with Aiden, she wouldn't have encouraged me. I trust that.

Ultimately, the decision is mine and mine alone.

Walking behind him, I find my hands are not my own. They want to reach for him. To see what he feels like beneath the layers of tapered cloth. He has the kind of face that surely leaves a trail of broken hearts in his wake. Heartbreaker.

I follow him to the elevator.

The easy solution is not to involve my heart. Aiden is just a man. I am just a woman. We're consenting adults who don't have to answer to anyone.

I just have to step into that elevator.

What if we stop on the conference-room floor? What if someone gets in who knows my face?

There's a ding to my right. Familiar voices chatting back and forth. Maribelle. She's stepping out of the other elevator, and before she can turn to see me, I hop in.

"Why does it feel like you're running away from someone?" he asks. He takes out a room key and presses it against a sensor, then presses a button. Penthouse.

How is an unemployed male stripper able to afford that?

"Would it matter if I were?" I ask.

We're on opposite ends of the elevator. There's a feeling at the base of my stomach that tightens just by watching him lean against the wall. He exudes an effortless confidence without being overbearing.

"It doesn't matter to me," he says. He starts to move a step closer, but the doors open and in walk a couple of men. They glance at Aiden, but decide he's of no interest to them, and barely look at me.

They were at the fund-raiser. Harry Coleston and Kyle Bellachamp. Two of the people my mother's team has been courting for sponsorship.

My heart thunders in my chest. Neither of them look at me, but when they eye Aiden up and down, they acknowledge him as a fellow businessman. I inwardly roll my eyes.

This is a bad idea. What if they remember me?

Harry and Kyle are speaking in such hushed tones that I can't actually make out anything they say, but I catch a loose "could be very good for business."

Then they exit the elevator, and Aiden and I are alone once again, and I let go of an anxious breath.

His clever eyes slink from them to me, relieved. To him, they were just men intruding in our moment. Had they noticed me, it would have been a costly mistake. I am being reckless.

But then he pushes himself from the metal wall and asks, "Where were we?" I close the distance between us with two sure steps. It's like wading into water the first day of summer to figure out the temperature. When I press my hand over Aiden's chest, I can feel the way his heart pounds, speeds up when I rub my fingers in the dip between his pecs. It's a strange thing to react like this to someone you've never met before today.

But maybe that is why I like this so much.

I'm not supposed to be the kind of girl who does this.

I'm not supposed to want him this way.

I'm not supposed to do so many things.

Aiden presses his hand over mine. His thumb strokes back and forth across my skin. Heat spreads up my arms and down my spine. It's like my body isn't mine. I'm pushing myself up on my toes, reaching for his mouth.

And then the elevator bounces. Aiden's arm wraps around my waist and pushes me into a corner to cover me from whoever might be coming next. There's no time to pull apart without looking suspicious.

A group of girls ready to go out on the town hoot and holler at the sight of us.

"Ohhh girlll, get it!" one of them shouts.

I feel hot with all of this attention. I'm not supposed to have this kind of attention. *Supposed. Supposed. Supposed.*

That's all replaced by one word. *Want. Want. Want.*

Aiden laughs his sweet, cool breath against my neck, and I cling to him like a shield.

The group gets off on the next floor, which has a rooftop pool and bar. He gives me breathing room, but I want to feel the pressure of him against me once again.

"I can mark public exhibition off my list," I say when the doors close.

Aiden points at the way out. "I mean, we could always go back to give them a real show."

That magnetic feeling overcomes me again, but we've arrived. This time, he moves backward. One, two, three steps, and we're down the hall from his suite.

Nervousness flutters in my chest as he opens the door. He searches for lights.

"Make yourself at home," he says.

He sweeps inside. The suite is huge, with beautiful carved fixtures and gold trim that makes everything feel like I'm in a French painting.

I set my purse down on a little table by the front door.

"Do you want something to drink?" he calls out from the sitting room.

I peek into the bedroom. The linens are pulled so tightly that there isn't a single wrinkle on the comforter. There's a glass of water and a bottle of aspirin on the bedside table. A black duffel bag and an open suitcase. Sneakers and dress shoes near the bed.

"I've always wanted to have something from a minibar," I say, walking into the living room.

"You can have whatever you wish."

I grab a bag of fruit candy for something sweet to nibble on. When I turn around, Aiden has taken off his jacket and unbuttoned his shirt one more notch to reveal a thin gold chain with a tiny gold stamp.

"What's this?" I ask, and maybe it's to have a reason to be close to him again. To get my hand near the warmth and beat of his heart. The gold stamp is light to the touch.

Aiden smiles, and his whiskey-brown eyes bore into mine. "My mother gave this to me when I was born. I carry it with me wherever I go."

"My father gave me something like this once." It was a pair of diamond earrings that I got during my cotillion. They were his mother's and intended to be worn on my wedding day.

"My mother said that this would protect me."

"Do you need a lot of protection?"

He takes a minute to consider this but finally admits, "Yes. But so far it's worked. Come, let me show you my favorite part of this room."

He stops by the minibar first and grabs two champagne splits. Then, instead of taking me to his bed the way I expect, he leads me to a small balcony.

My belly flip-flops at the sight of the city sprawled out, a blanket of twinkling lights in every color, a chorus of music and revelry. We're in the middle of it and yet in a corner of our own.

"See?" I tell him. "This is the greatest city in the world."

"It certainly has the best view."

When I look at Aiden, he's not staring at the city. He's staring at me.

"Happy birthday, Aiden," I tell him.

He twists off the caps to the champagne bottles and hands one to me. "Ah, it's no big deal."

"I think it's a bigger deal than you want to make it out to be."

He starts to raise the bottle to his lips. "You're a shrink?"

I laugh and shove him a little with my hand. "Cold. Not even close. What do we toast to this time?"

"To being spontaneous."

"*Spontaneous* isn't my middle name," I say.

He comes closer. We're leaning on the railing of the balcony, and even though it's sturdy and I know it won't give, I have the strangest sensation that I could fall at any moment.

I drink my champagne quickly, which is a mistake because the fizz spills over. "Sorry, I'm a mess."

He chuckles. Takes our drinks and sets them on a table. His fingers close around my wrist. I raise my eyes to his and my breath catches. His smile is just as disarming as his touch.

And the strangest thing happens.

Aiden kisses the spot along my jaw where the champagne spilled. His tongue licks against my skin in the softest brush. My free hand instinctively reaches for his neck to cling to like a life-line. It is the thing I've been wanting to do since I laid eyes on him. Why do we stop ourselves from wanting things?

I knew I wanted this man at first sight. It doesn't make sense. Shouldn't make sense.

This is wrong.

Is it? Why is doing what you want wrong? Why is that the lesson I've had instilled in my head all my life?

Because being kissed by Aiden doesn't feel wrong. Not one bit. His next kiss lands just below my lower lip. I dig my fingers into his neck. He pulls me closer. I'm a magnet. A force meant to collide with him. I let out a small moan, and then he's kissing my lips. His mouth closes over mine. My eyes flutter shut, and I can taste the lingering orange sweetness on his tongue. My fingers dig into the base of his hair, tugging lightly on the short crop there. He grips hold of my waist, squeezing so tightly I have to gasp and slide my hands across the solid plane of his torso. I find his mouth again, because he's a beautiful kisser. Firm and gentle and attentive. Like my mouth was made for his to revere.

I reach for the buttons of his shirt and undo them until I reach the waistband of his trousers.

He breaks the kiss first to take off his shirt. Tosses it to the side somewhere in the dark of the suite.

My hands don't feel my own when I reach for him. He's too far, even though he's one foot away. I have to kiss him again. I have to touch the rapid pulse of his heart beneath his skin. We come together again, lips searching for lips with the neon lights of the French Quarter as our backdrop.

I reach for the button of his pants, but he grabs my hands and says, "Your turn."

He graces me with another kiss, and it's like my legs have turned into liquid melting at his feet. Those slick fingers of his find the clip at the back of my dress, and with one hand flat on my back, he uses the other to tug down the zipper. The cool night air touches my bare skin, warring with the fire igniting in my veins with every kiss he lands on my mouth.

I feel greedy, wanting to explore the scape of his body without taking my mouth off his.

He stands back, giving me space. Space to enjoy myself.

I feel his eyes on me as I let the sleeves of my dress fall down to my waist and then into a pile at my ankles.

"Fuck," Aiden hisses. But he doesn't make a move. He stands half a dozen feet away with one hand on the balcony as if for support.

I did that. I made him feel that way. It sparks a tingle between my legs. I don't even have time to be self-conscious that I'm not wearing matching underwear and bra because when I woke up this morning I didn't think I was going to be on a balcony, getting undressed with a guy I met at a bar.

And yet here we are, two strangers in their underwear before midnight.

"Your turn," I say.

He undoes his pants and pushes them down. He's in black boxer briefs that stretch across the muscular mounds of his thighs. The hard strain of his dick against the fabric.

There's that smile of his again, and that magnetism returns. He grips my arms tightly, holds me at arm's length and waits.

"Why are you keeping me so far away?" I ask.

"I just want to remember you," he whispers.

Then he pulls me to him, my mouth hungry for his in a way that scares me. I wrap my arms around his. His hand explores my back, slides around my derrière and along my thigh. I lift it up in response to his touch, and in that movement, our parts line up perfectly.

I break the kiss to let go of a sigh.

Aiden cups his hands firmly around my bottom and picks me up. I cling to him as I let go of a tiny, sharp gasp.

"I got you," he whispers into my neck. "I got you."

I lean down to kiss him once more as we cross the threshold leading back into the suite, continuing past the living room, and toward the bed.

He throws me onto it.

I start to take my heels off.

"Leave them on," he says, and parts my knees. Presses a kiss on the inside of my thighs, moving quickly and surely to the heart between my legs.

My chest is wild with new feelings, my mind worse with thoughts. This is so, so very not like me, and yet, it feels so, so very good.

When Aiden pulls my underwear down, I wriggle with anticipation. It ends in the pit of my stomach as he closes his mouth over my clit, expertly licking circles and figure eights and all kinds of twists that I've never experienced before. I don't want to think too deeply about how much he's practiced to get this particularly wonderful skill. But I squeeze my thighs around his head, searching for that rush, the overwhelming crash of pleasure that I've only been able to find with the fun vibrating toy in my nightstand. Aiden is a living version of that toy. Better even, because the next thing I know, I've got my fist in his hair as everything within me comes crashing down and there is nothing but us and this room and his tongue licking up the wetness between my legs like it's his birthday ice cream cake.

When my breath settles, and I let go of his hair, he eases himself to stand over me. When he wipes his mouth with the back of his hand, I want to lick the corners of his devilish smile.

"I should've been drinking you instead of those hurricanes," he says softly.

No one has ever stared at me with the intensity he has right now. It thrills me down to my bones. So much that I want to do something I don't do. Not for the last three guys I dated. Not since the first time I really didn't enjoy it.

I tug the side waistband of his underwear and free his heavy erection. My hand looks small around the shaft, not quite able to close around the width. A tiny moan escapes my throat.

"Faith," he says, shutting his eyes as I move my hand up, and up, my thumb caressing the outline of his frenulum. It's inches from my mouth. I touch it to my lips for a breath of a kiss. I can feel him shudder, stiffen in my hold even more.

Then, just as he says, "This is the best birthday I've ever had," I close my mouth around the tip.

"Oh, no," Aiden groans.

When I open my eyes, he's startled, and I'm afraid I've hurt him or done something wrong. Because he's jerking away from me, and Aiden, the most beautiful man I've ever met, has finished his birthday celebration before I could get started.

5

Blow Me (One Last Kiss)

AIDEN

So I'm going to put myself on the line and say that something like last night hasn't happened since I was thirteen and I touched myself for the first time.

As I lie on the pullout couch in the living room of my suite, just as alone as I was when I started off my birthday, I replay that moment over and over. Things were going as well as I could have asked for, and yet, the sight of Faith on her knees, taking my dick into her hands, unraveled me faster than yarn in a kitten's paws. I was fine, and the second she took me into her mouth, all I could think of was getting away from her because blowing a load on her face would be downright rude and disrespectful.

Thankfully, she didn't completely laugh at me. It was just a giggle, a deep purr as she crawled into my bed on all fours. Just the sight of her on her side, facing me, daring me, waiting for me, made me hard all over again.

"I'll go clean up," I said.

And I did. Ran right into my bathroom in search of condoms I keep in my toiletry kit. That's how little sex I was after. I didn't bring condoms out with me because I didn't expect any sort of fucking to happen tonight.

It was like finding the golden ticket. There, shining in my hand as I returned to her. Faith.

Faith, the sexiest woman alive, asleep on my bed.

So, here's the thing about my line of work. I always set these rules. Rules are the key to being professional, but they're also the key to not going to jail or getting beat up by an angry husband or boyfriend. But most importantly, to keeping the women in my life safe.

Rule #5: Don't cop feelings.

Rule #6: No sex.

There's a stipulation there, though. Technically—technically—I don't have sex with my clients. That's not part of the agreement. Now, if at the end of everything both parties consent, then why not?

And so on and on go the rules. I've had to adjust for when things don't work, like when I had to add Rule #17—no costumes—after a client destroyed my image of Little Red Riding Hood when she put on a little dress and a red cape and bought me a wolf mask. I mean, exceptions are made. Addendums slipped into deals to keep everyone happy and safe.

For instance, I should be adding Rule #45: Don't bring a girl over to a hotel room being paid for by one of your clients.

For the record, I've never done that before. When I consider myself on the clock, I'm on the clock. But Faith.

Faith was unexpected.

The shy smile when she uttered those words at the bar. Her body reacting to mine. The way she arched her back when I buried my face between her legs. I'm pretty sure she ripped out some of my hair, but I don't care. I'd gladly take a bald patch just to be able to taste her once again.

That brings me to Rule #7. If she falls asleep and I can't get her safely back home, I sleep somewhere else.

Now, don't get me wrong. I'm not offended at all that she fell asleep on me. I'm flattered really. I felt her. The walls inside her squeezed around my fingers like a vise as she came all over my mouth. She purred like a kitten, stretched, and then that was it. It was fucking sexy.

Sweet dreams, Faith. I pulled the sheets over her and told myself to ignore the strange twinge in my chest. Fucking hurricanes.

I grabbed a blanket from the closet, closed the door to the bedroom, and made up the pullout couch.

I checked my text messages. One from Ginny texting a selfie of herself in the bathroom of wherever she is.

I bought this with your eyes in mind. It's a red nighty with hearts over the nipples.

I don't want to lie to her. Some of my friends argue that it's what I'm being paid for. But I'm not an asshole. At least, I hope I'm not. I don't want to be. The response she wants from me is not the one I could give her, because my mind is consumed by the other woman in my bed.

Beautiful, I text back because she is a beautiful woman.

What are you doing?

Just in bed.

It's N'awlins darlin'.

Believe me, I can hear it from here. Just jet-lagged, I guess. He's back. Xoxo.

<3

I take a quick, cold shower, then jump into the sofa bed. And drift off to the sound of Bourbon Street and my thoughts of Faith.

When I wake up, I replay last night. Ginny leaving. The bar. Faith. My premature birthday surprise. But, really, Faith. She appeared like a sign, a gift wrapped present from the Universe. Or maybe I'm trying to make more of this one-night stand because I'm embarrassed by how my body reacted to her. Frantic and needy and all the things I've tried so hard to not be.

And there she is, still asleep. I wonder if she's one of those workaholics who live on coffee and four hours of sleep a day. The tension in her yesterday was unbelievable.

I've never had a second date that wasn't a client. And I don't think I can start now. To make her the most comfortable, I'll go out and get breakfast and let her leave on her own. I don't want there to be any awkwardness, and maybe it'll be better if I'm not here.

I write down a quick note: *Thanks for last night, Aiden.*

That's fine, right?

Before I can second-guess myself, I put on gym shorts and a T-shirt and head out.

The streets are deserted. None of last night's debauchery is anywhere to be found. Even the streets are clean. Mostly. There's still the lingering scent of stale booze and staler vomit as I cross the streets in search of breakfast.

My phone buzzes. It's too early for anyone normal to be calling me, so it has to be one of my boys. Fallon's ugly mug is on my screen, and I swipe.

"Jim's Taco Shop, how may we service you this morning?" I ask.

"Always with the jokes."

I laugh and scare an old woman walking opposite from me.

"What's up?"

"I spoke to Ricky this weekend," he says.

I let a silence run for a bit before asking, "Is he still pissed at me?"

There's grunting in the background, but before I can let my mind wander to somewhere perverted, he says, "Sorry, I'm at the gym. And he's not pissed anymore. It's been three weeks so now he's just disappointed."

I get quiet again. Start, then stop. How do I explain myself? "I wish I could take it back."

"What the hell happened, Aiden?"

"I played the wrong cards, man. I thought I had a sure thing with that heiress. She offered me my own club, my own show. And then she bailed. I couldn't face him. Not after I walked out on him like that."

Fallon sighs my name. He sounds more like a dad than the one I had. Even in that one sigh. "She was an heiress of almond milk, bro."

"I already feel like shit, I don't need—"

"I know, but you have to talk to Ricky. Patch things up. You're still a brother to him. No matter what."

"Then why hasn't he reached out?"

I can practically see Fallon's face on the other side of the phone. "Why haven't you?"

"Always the peacemaker, right? How's Robyn?"

"She's good. At school right now. I'm at the gym and then I have to go handle the liquor license stuff for my brother."

"I'm glad you guys are partnering in that, man."

"Whatever moves I have to make to provide. Where in the world is Aiden Rios for his big twenty-fifth birthday?"

I laugh, but I feel myself choke. "New Orleans."

"Damn, I love that place. Eat a hundred beignets from Cafe du Monde for me."

"That's where I'm headed. You know me, breakfast of champions."

"I do know you. What lady do you have falling in love with you these days?"

"You remember that woman I met in New York a while back? Ginny Thomas?" I clear my throat. "I bumped into her on the Strip and we came here. She left yesterday morning. Some emergency business of whatever."

"Yeah, alone birthdays suck. I'm sorry, bro."

"Whoa, whoa, who said I was alone?"

Fallon laughs. For a little bit, it's like nothing has changed. He never left Mayhem City and I never betrayed my mentor and we're just chilling in the dressing room. "So that's who you're getting beignets for."

"First of all, I'm pretty sure Faith's going to want to be gone in the morning. She's a very uptight business type. I feel used," I joke and tell him about what happened last night. Minus the premature excitement part.

After he's done laughing at me for a bit, he settles down. "Faith, huh? Look at you using first names. I don't think I've ever heard you refer to a woman by her first name. Touch your forehead. Do you have a fever?"

"I just said Ginny's name."

"A woman who isn't related to you or your client. A woman you're sleeping with."

"That's not true," I say, scratching my head as if that would unlock a memory.

"Think on it, Aiden."

"Don't start. Just because you're attached at the hip to your girl doesn't mean everyone is about that life."

"Hold up, hold up. I didn't even say anything. You're projecting." There's the sound of weights dropping and cheesy Europop in the background. "Who's the mystery girl? What's she like?"

I jaywalk across the street, and a couple of drivers slam down on their horns. "I don't know. Hot?"

But who am I kidding? She's more than hot. She is incredible.

"Very descriptive," Fallon says.

"She's—gorgeous, bro. I don't know. I guess I was off my game yesterday. There was something about her that made me just spill shit I don't even tell you."

"Hm."

"What do you mean 'hm'? What's 'hm'?"

"Do you want to braid her hair, too?"

"I'm hanging up now." From here I can smell the muddy Mississippi River. It looks murkier than the Hudson, but it's probably cleaner.

"Wait wait wait! I'm just fucking with you. Though, since you're so sensitive about it, I think that there's something else going on here."

"There's nothing going on. I had a nice time. That's it. Plus, I'll be on the clock again when Ginny comes back."

"Aiden, listen to me. I'm not trying to be a grumpy old dad or anything."

"You're right about the dad part, but you're still grumpy and old as fuck."

"Mature. Twenty-five looks good on you. Tell me, what are you going to do if you get back and she's still there?"

"She's not still there," I say. Faith looked like she was trying to escape something last night and I feel blessed to have been her escape. "I can't explain it. There's no way she's sticking around."

"Don't sell yourself short," he tells me.

I stand in front of the restaurant. A couple of college-aged girls strut past me, and I flash them a smile. "Buenos días."

They giggle and whisper to each other, turning around every now and then to keep staring.

"You're a stereotype of yourself, dude."

"Whatever, man. You're just jealous because you're never going to have sex with another person ever again."

Fallon laughs. "Yeah, totally jealous. Answer my fucking question."

"If she's still there then I'll—" What do I do when someone who isn't a client sleeps over? I can't remember the last time that happened. With clients, I know exactly what to say. I know what they expect from me. When I'm having my own fun, there are no sleepovers. Ever.

Fallon is still laughing. "Did you finally realize you broke one of your own dumbass rules? Number a hundred: No slumber parties or something."

"There is no rule number one hundred."

"Get her a coffee at least, though."

"Okay, I'm really hanging up this time."

I pocket my phone and head into Cafe du Monde, where the scent of fried dough and powdered sugar is arresting. My stomach growls. An older waitress takes note of me. I guess it's still pretty early, because the crowd is thin.

"In or out?"

I know she means whether I want to sit inside or outside, but what Fallon just said about me comes to mind. Dickbag.

"To go, please."

She smiles, takes out the pencil behind her ear. "What're you having, sweetheart?"

What if Fallon is right? What if Faith is still in my room when I come back? Or worse. What if Ginny gets there before I do? No, that won't happen. She said she'd be back in a week. Is that guilt that's making me think like this?

"I'll have a dozen beignets and two coffees, please."

"Milk and sugar?"

I don't know how she drinks her coffee. "I'll take two black coffees, one with milk, and a fourth with milk and sugar."

"So four coffees instead?"

"Yes, please." And I realize, that's a lot of coffee for someone who may or may not be there when I return.

And it's a strange feeling hoping Fallon is right.

FAITH

The first thing that I realize when I wake up is that I'm not wearing any underwear.

"Oh fuck," I groan. "What time is it?"

I sit up and peer around the room. The bedroom door is closed, and the curtains are drawn. I'm in my blue polka-dotted bra, and the pink, incredibly unsexy panties I was wearing last night are on the bed. Half of it is still unmade, which begs the question, where is Aiden?

I crack the bedroom door open. "Aiden?"

Silence.

I consider wearing one of his shirts, but that's a strange territory. Clearly he didn't want to be here—to avoid the awkward morning-after chat. Still, I don't want to walk around someone's hotel room without any underwear on.

In the closet I find a bathrobe and slip into that. I go out onto the balcony to find my clothes. Last night comes to me in flashes. The press conference. Seeing him at the bar. Kissing him. The champagne here. If I close my eyes, I can remember the way his mouth tasted. His mouth on my—

"Oh God," I say, placing my hand over my racing heart and the other on the railing beside me. I fell asleep! I don't know if it was the combination of the bourbon, the comfortable bed, and the first orgasm I've had in two years (by a man). But I was out like a light. I remember fluttering my eyes open and Aiden placing covers over me.

That's when I notice the messy bed in the living room. He slept on the sofa and gave me his bed.

I don't want to give him too much credit for being decent.

But in my experience, another guy would have crawled in bed with me and tried to wake me up with a boner breakfast.

"What's wrong with you, Faith?" I say aloud and head for the bathroom.

I pass by a note.

"Thanks for last night, Aiden," I read out loud. Ugh, what was I expecting? His phone number and a promise ring?

We both knew what this was. I think about texting Angelique but I know what she'd say. "At least you got yours, honey."

And she's not wrong.

Today might be the first time that my first thought upon waking up wasn't poll numbers. Though now that I'm going down that spiral, I wonder what the poll numbers are. We'll have to wait until tomorrow for the Sunday papers.

I don't know how long it's been since Aiden left. Part of me wishes that I could see him again. But I know better than this. That was a one-time thing. I wouldn't call it a mistake, because it wasn't. Just before I started college, my mother told me, "Young ladies do not pick up men."

Is that why I did it?

I look at my watch. It's eight in the morning. I have to go to headquarters in two hours for my mother's briefing. My stomach rolls at the thought of walking in there, my heart twists in a not-so-good way before I realize that no, I don't have to. I see myself telling my mother that I was taking the week, my petty, bratty reaction to her asking me to cool off. I run my hands over my face, try to calm my breathing.

A few months ago I saw a therapist. I was getting panic attacks and such bad anxiety that I couldn't even leave my house. I stopped after two sessions, but the most useful thing she told me was to break up my tasks into the smallest possible sections. I get overwhelmed with the big picture, so if I see things as a bunch of little pictures, then, just maybe, I can get through the day. Then another day. Then a week. A month. And so on.

I need to get out of here. I've only done the walk of shame a couple of times in college. To be honest, the only person who makes it feel shameful is me. I haven't done anything that I wouldn't do again. Well, except fall asleep.

I mean, I feel this way right now, but we'll see about later.

My mouth tastes like old whiskey, and my hair is all out of sorts. I grab my purse and take myself to the bathroom. I plug my phone in the wall outlet to charge. I scroll through a few messages from Maribelle asking where I am. One from Dad telling me he loves me. One from my mom asking me to stop being dramatic. A last one from Angie sending me water and eggplant emojis. She has no idea what really happened here last night. It's a good thing I didn't get Aiden's number, because that way this is a clean break. He made that clear by not being here in the morning.

Though, it would have been more convenient if he left a time with the note. It could say something like, *"You're welcome for the cunnilingus. Be back in 15 minutes."*

I run the shower, and there's one of those bathroom kits. Thank God this is a fancy hotel. I find the shower cap and tuck my hair inside. There's a bottle of men's body wash in here. It's one of those three-in-one things. How do men use the same product for their bodies, hair, and face? Meanwhile, all women products are like, "here's a special lotion for your elbows." There's marketing for you.

I get out of there as quickly as I can. I'm the kind of person who can take a bath for hours. It's the only place that gives me true peace and quiet. But for now, I have somewhere to be. Anywhere but here.

I hop out and use a towel. If he wants more, he can call room service. I slip back into the same clothes I wore yesterday. I can't bring myself to wear the same underwear, so I stuff it in my purse.

My bag is always complete with a first aid kit. Though it wouldn't help in any kind of survival setting, I have everything my mother would need throughout the day. Lotion, face wipes, Q-tips, coconut oil, and lipstick.

When I was a little girl, I used to watch my mother apply her lipstick in the mirror. She'd always get it precise on the first try. I don't have the same skills.

I press the home button on my phone. Eight fifteen a.m. No Aiden.

I realize that I'm stalling. That despite all of my talk of this being the perfect escape, a part of me wants to see his face again. Even if it's just for a little bit. Even if it's awkward as hell. There's something about him that's possibly too pretty, too sly. Heartbreaker. I said it myself, didn't I?

Get out of here while you still have the chance, the voice in my thoughts says.

I take a look at myself. I should add dry shampoo to my first aid kit. That's going to be my takeaway of this whole ordeal.

I grab my purse and exit the bathroom, making sure to do one last sweep for my clothes.

The balcony. The bedroom. The bed in the living room. Here the sheets are rumpled and smell like his cologne and something else—oranges.

That's weird, Faith. Step back away from that pillow.

I stuff my feet into my heels again and run the hell out of the room.

Thankfully, Saturday mornings in the Quarter are quiet because of the amount of people nursing hangovers. I look at my reflection in the elevator's mirrored walls. I don't look terrible for someone who spent last night being eaten out. I close my eyes, and the thought of Aiden's mouth between my legs brings a tiny pulse there.

Heartbreaker.

Is that truly what I think or what I want him to be so that it's easier to walk away like this? There's nothing to walk away from. We were two ships passing in the night, that's all.

Stepping outside of the hotel feels like I'm wading through mud. Every step comes with aching muscles. I suppose that's what it's like being close to twenty-nine. One night of hard drinking, and my body revolts. Though I slept eight hours for the first time in months! I should be well rested. Thankfully, I have nothing else to do today except to catch up on sleep and try to avoid my mother. I step into the taxi waiting at the curb.

"Where to, darlin'?" he asks.

"1230 Harmony Street," I say, reaching into my purse for my phone.

My phone.

My heart spikes, sending a hot flash across my body.

Not in the taxi. Not in my purse. I don't even have any pockets in this dress.

My mind goes back to the place I was trying to leave without a trace, where I left my phone plugged into the bathroom wall outlet.

"Stop! I forgot something," I shout at the cabbie. I get out and ignore his shouting at me. I feel terrible, but he only drove half a street.

The doorman smiles at me and lets me inside. I get to the elevators before I realize I can't get to the penthouse without a key. I palm my forehead and think of what I can say to the reception desk that might get me upstairs.

A tall man stands in front of the elevators beside me. The sweet smell of powdered sugar reminds me I'm hungry. I didn't have dinner.

"Rough morning?" a familiar, playful voice asks.

It *was* a rough morning, but that smile Aiden flashes tells me it's about to get a whole lot better.

6

No Me Ames

AIDEN

We ride the elevator back to the suite. Fallon was right. She's still here. But she's only here because she forgot her phone.

Still, seeing her, being around her, fills me with a strange satisfaction. Comfort. I might have been tipsy last night, but right now, I'm stone-cold sober.

Faith is stunning. Her hair is rumpled and her mouth is plump and pink from all of the kissing we did.

I so badly want to kiss her again, but I don't know how she feels after last night. Does she regret it? Does she want to keep running? Does she want to laugh in my face?

My life's work is being able to know how to talk to women. How to say the right things to make them happy, make their days better, make them feel like I'm worth the price tag.

Then why is it so hard to find a way to talk to Faith?

I know if Fallon were here, he'd tell me some woo-woo shit about being honest with my feelings.

Feelings get you hurt. It ends in breaking the people around you.

"I'm sorry I left this morning," I blurt out anyway. "I didn't want to wake you."

"Plus you thought it would be easier to make a clean break," she tells me. She doesn't look at me, but at the numbers lighting up as we climb to the top.

This elevator ride is less fun than last night's. But there's something about being in the same space with her that makes me want to stay right where I am.

Of course, that's when the doors open and we walk back to my suite. *Ginny's suite.*

"Are you having a party so early?" she chuckles.

"Hm? Oh, this?" I let us in and lead the way to the living room. "I wasn't sure what kind of coffee you liked. Just in case you were still here."

I set the greasy bag of beignets and tray of coffee on the table. She sits down on the armchair, and I busy myself with putting the sofa bed away.

"Milk and sugar," she says.

I sit across from her. Why am I so fucking awkward right now? I grab the black coffee and add a packet of sugar to it. I make a face when I drink it.

"You don't like chicory coffee?"

I chuckle. The stuff is slightly sweet with a burnt aftertaste. "I'm more used to the Colombian coffee my mom always bought."

"Is that where she's from?" She helps herself to the bag of basically donuts. Her hands are graceful. Long fingers. I can picture her now wrapping those same fingers around my dick. As she brings the beignet to her lips, I am fully erect.

Then, I frown. She shouldn't be here. She should go about her day so I can go about mine. I haven't been to the gym in two days. Ginny could come back. Housekeeping could barge in.

But when I picture her leaving, I feel irrationally angry.

"She was from Medellín," I say. I look into my coffee. What is it with this city that it has me spilling all the things I never share? No, not people. Just Faith. "My mom left for New York when she was twenty and met my father there. He was Colombian too but from Barranquilla."

She licks her lips. I wonder what she's thinking. "You were born in Colombia?"

"It's actually a crazy situation."

"Tell me."

And I do. My mouth opens, and this *thing* I have locked in my chest climbs out. "This was right before I was born. My parents were together for about six months and he'd just put a ring on her finger. But, he had to go back to Barranquilla to visit his ailing mother. Then he went missing."

Faith watches me, her rapt attention giving me the feeling that I'm telling someone else's story instead of the series of events that led to my mother's heartache.

I clear my throat and continue. "So my mom went to Barranquilla with her brothers, and my grandfather drove all the way from Medellín to see what was up. Like showed up with machetes in case he'd been taken or whatever. My dad always seemed to owe someone money. But when they got there, they found that he was totally fine. My grandmother was the picture of health. He just wasn't planning on coming back because my mom was pregnant."

Faith's mouth is a perfect O with surprise. It's not the right time, but the image of her wriggling against my mouth last night pops into my mind. I'm the most fucked up, if that's what I'm thinking of while reliving my family history.

"What happened?" she asks.

"Well, my grandfather wouldn't have it."

"Shotgun wedding?"

"Machete wedding more like it."

She shakes her head but smiles at my twisted humor. "And I thought my family had stories. Is that why you were born there?"

"Yup," I say. "We were supposed to go back to New York but my mom went into labor a month early. Then we just stayed for about nine years." I clear my throat and then drink more of the bittersweet coffee. "That's my origin story in a nutshell."

When Faith smiles it feels like sunshine after a long bout of rain. "I bet there's a lot more to your origin story."

"What about you?"

"My parents didn't have a machete wedding. They almost didn't have a wedding at all because my mom is so stubborn."

I hold the coffee in my hands because I have the impulse to pick her up and gather her in my arms. Relive the kiss we shared on the balcony. She looks down at my mouth, and I know, I know, she's thinking the same thing.

"So what happened?" I ask.

"My dad was in environmental law. He comes from a long line of lawyers."

I chuckle. "I knew it."

"*I'm* not a lawyer," she says defensively. "Anyway, my mom's side comes from farmers in North Carolina, but they lost everything when my uncle sold his plot to land developers. My mom was the only daughter and they left her nothing. So she moved here at sixteen. Started waitressing, cleaning, doing it all. She met my dad when he was lost trying to take the *bus*. Can you believe a twenty-one-year-old man hadn't been on the bus before? Love at first sight, but I never believed that."

"Yeah, I say. Me neither." But when I look at her, really look at her, I feel a strange sensation beneath my ribs. If it's not love at first sight, it's definitely a deep want. Or heartburn.

I should ask her to leave.

But when she drains her coffee, I say, "Help yourself to another one."

Her laugh is as sweet as the sugar packets she takes and pours into the second coffee with milk. "I'm actually going to need something with sustenance."

"Do you have any plans today?" I ask. I shove two beignets in my mouth because maybe food will shut me up.

She seems to consider this. She's thinking about how to get out of here. This is it. She's going to leave, and I'm going to take another cold shower because breathing the same air around her makes me hard, and I'm going to crawl into bed and think about how amazing and beautiful this woman is as I jerk myself off.

"I do," she says.

I swallow the lump of sugary dough. "Yeah, me too."

"Oh yeah, what?" The tilt of her head and the smile on her lips tell me she doesn't believe me.

"Let's see, get breakfast. That's it. That's my whole plan for today. I suppose I should walk around and see what the big deal is about, but I doubt I'd be impressed."

She knows I'm fucking with her. That's why her eyes beam like lasers and she makes a tiny grumbling sound. I want to kiss the pout of her mouth and lick the remnants of powdered sugar that cling to the left corner.

She looks out the window, like she's considering her options. Then, at her purse open on the floor. I realize the pink bunch at the center is her underwear. Then that means she's sitting there wearing nothing. My heart spikes to my throat, and my traitorous dick threatens to rip through the fabric of my sweats.

"Aiden?"

"Yes, Faith?" I'm startled by her voice because I am so hard I can't see straight.

"I asked, would you like to have breakfast with me?"

Cafe Fleur De Lis is on the relatively quiet Chartres Street. Packs of brunchgoers gather outside different restaurants. Some of them still wear purple, green, and gold beads. Some of them look like they never sobered up from last night.

Bars are wide open, and small strip clubs are rocking the day shift. It makes me think of my boys of Mayhem City. I wonder if they're touring yet. I take out my phone with the thought that I should text Ricky. But that's not what today is about. Today is about having a nice brunch with Faith. After I accepted her breakfast invitation, she went home to change. But I saw those panties in her purse, and I know she needed to go and clean up and so did I, though I'm not sure if she had quite as much fun as I did. I covered myself in so many suds I had to stand under the rain shower for five minutes before I was soap-free. A series of images flashed before my eyes. Faith on the balcony biting her lip. Her dress slipping off her shoulder and onto the floor. My tongue parting her lips. Her mouth on the swollen head of my cock.

I grabbed my dick. Each stroke dedicated to a memory of Faith.

Her mouth, her nails raking my neck, her sexy fucking laughter, those eyes looking only at me, that precious little freckle on her jaw. I rode those memories as I came into the shower drain.

I thought I was done.

Here, in the middle of the street, I see her turn the corner, and my body lights up like New Year's at midnight, and I know I've only just gotten started.

Faith is in a bright yellow dress that gives her light-brown skin a golden sheen. Her heels are a deep-red leather. Even on the uneven paved streets, her powerful legs strut toward me with the confidence of a reigning queen.

Her shoulders are bare, a simple gold necklace catches the light at the center of her chest. Her hair is half up and half down, pinned in an old-fashioned look. Her hands are covered in white lace gloves.

"Wow, you—" How do I even finish this sentence? You look like a dream I didn't even know I had? You look like ice cream on a hot summer day? You look like the thing that might break me if I let it?

"You too," she says, brushing a strand of hair out of her eyes. "I have to go to church after this."

"Aren't you and your mom fighting?"

"Still have to show." She keeps her hands to herself and so do I. It's like we both know that when we're too close, we won't stop until we're pushed together. But maybe the streets of New Orleans are used to people devouring each other in public.

I go in for a kiss on her cheek, but she turns her face, and I catch the corner of her mouth.

She backs away quickly. "Did you get a table?"

"No, just got here."

She's unusually skittish. Though I've known her for about a day, so I'm not sure what her usual is. It was the same at the bar last night, like she was afraid of being caught. Before we walk into the restaurant, she gives the street a good once-over. I can't think why she's that suspicious. Maybe she's just paranoid. Or she's truly married and I have a type.

"Good morning!" a pretty hostess with several nose piercings greets us. She grins at me, her dark-brown skin like polished stone. "Two?"

"Yes, please."

When the hostess's eyes fall to Faith standing behind me, they widen. Faith smiles but gives the girl a small shake of her head.

"Do you two know each other?" I ask.

The girl's eyes ping-pong between Faith and me. But whatever girl-code is going on, the girl only smiles a wide white smile and leads us to a small corner table in the back.

The crowd here is mostly tourists with lobster-burnt skin. Though, I feel like I wouldn't be able to recognize what a local from New Orleans would look like.

"Are you some sort of celebrity?" I ask Faith. "You seem to know everyone."

She laughs. "Please."

"That's not an answer."

"It's part of an answer."

A waitress rolls around and sets down two giant mimosas with the fattest strawberries I've ever seen. "On the house."

"Thank you," Faith says, and gives the girl a small squeeze on her arm.

I pretend to gasp. "Are you local mafia? Am I on a date with a mafia princess?"

Faith rolls her eyes and playfully bats my shoulder with her gloved hand. It stays here. Why does one touch from her ignite something in me I didn't think I was capable of? It's like I can feel her, through the fabric of my shirt and that of her gloves. She looks at her hand and removes it.

"It's nothing like that."

I rest my chin on my knuckles and watch her. "Are you going to tell me?"

"Not yet. We just met."

I grab hold of my drink and smirk. I lean into her, my nose and lips inches from her ear. "I know you well enough to remember the way you taste."

She swallows hard and lifts her drink to mine. "What should we toast to?"

"To mafia royalty," I say. "And generous waitresses."

Speaking of, the young waitress swings back around. "Miss Charles. What're you having?"

Faith Charles.

I could google her. I could go behind her back and go into a deep dive of an Internet wormhole and never come out because I want to know everything about her.

But I won't. Because I can't see her after today. Shouldn't see her . . .

"I'll have the Seafood Benedict." Faith looks at me. "How do you feel about pancakes for the table?"

"I feel like it's everything I've been missing all my life." I hand the waitress the menu back. "I'll have the Big Easy Breakfast."

She jots it down with a wink. "What flavor pancakes?"

"Banana chocolate chip," we say at the exact same time. The waitress grins because we're probably ridiculous.

"Faith Charles," I say. It's like learning a new language. The language of her.

"Aiden Peñaflor," she says.

It's cute the way she pronounces it. Pen-ya-floor. But after a moment, the name sends a red flag up in my head because I haven't gone by that name since I was eighteen.

"I'm sorry, I saw your ID. Remember?"

"It's nice to meet you, Miss Charles." I lean back and admire the way she smiles when I say her name. "Now, will you please tell me why everyone seems to know you?"

She folds her hands in front of her. She could be a local model. But her beauty is not small town. "Angie and I have this game where we guess who people are and what they do whenever we go out. She spoiled you for me, though."

I envy the straw that gets to rest in her clever mouth. "I'll play. But I'll have you know that I'm coming up with all sorts of ideas."

"Let's hear one."

Telling her I think she's a model sounds cheesy as fuck. She's so witty that I do think she's some sort of law professional. Her teeth are perfectly straight. "Dentist."

She shivers. "You mean mouth torturer? Wrong. You get two more guesses."

"We didn't agree to that." I cross my arms over my chest.

"I make the rules."

God, I want her to say that to me while we're both naked. "Hotel owner."

She sighs, and I almost feel like she's disappointed. "Not even close."

What's the opposite of hotels? Or cities? I remember she said her dad was in environmental law. And then it hits me, I'm trying to figure out why everyone knows her, but what I should be doing is guessing who she is—deep inside. I go with the wildest, most random thing a classy, sexy woman like her might be. "Park ranger?"

She laughs, the stiffness from before melting away. I love making her laugh. I shouldn't love this the way I do. "Close, but no."

"You have to give me another shot."

Her chin juts out in the most adorable way, a playful turn to her lips. "I think this already is your second shot."

I palm my chest to my heart, like she landed an arrow there. "Solid burn. I was hoping you didn't remember that part."

She lowers her eyes and edges close to me. Her voice drops an octave as she whispers, "I liked knowing I made you feel that way."

I lick my lips and my eyes flick to the bulge straining against my thigh. "You still do."

Maybe that was too much, because she clears her throat, signaling a subject change. "Your weekend in NOLA is coming to an end. Where are you off to next? Ibiza? Santa Monica?"

I adjust my seat to give my hands something to do. "Actually, I'm here until Friday. Then I'm out. Not sure where yet."

My contract with Ginny will be up. She made it clear that it was the last time she could ever see me. It was a little strange, actually, but lots of my clients are.

As long as I get paid, it shouldn't matter.

"Where do you *want* to go?"

"I don't know," I tell her. Is every drink in this city just strong? Because I can't seem to stop the words flowing out of my mouth. "A part of me wants to go back to Vegas. Beg my friends to take me back. But I messed up so badly and then instead of being an adult, I just split."

Faith's eyes are so full of patience as I speak. Something inside of me feels like it's been cracked, like a fissure in glass. I think it's going to keep spreading the more I'm with her.

Tell her you can't see her again.

"Faith, I—"

"Pancakes for the table!" the waitress says, dropping the massive stack in front of us.

"Yes?" Faith asks once we're alone. Or as alone as two people in a restaurant can ever be.

"I—I'm glad you brought me here. I haven't had pancakes in forever."

"Don't tell me you're one of those no-carb people," she teases, cutting a triangle out of the stack.

"I guess now that I'm not in the show anymore I can eat whatever I want."

I stuff pancake into my mouth. I don't like this oversharing I do with Faith. It's too vulnerable. Too much like letting someone inside your house and *begging* them to look into your closet. Not like regular closets, either. The closets where you keep your sex toys and dirty magazines.

"Well, I'm glad you feel like you can finally have pancakes. My daddy used to say that life isn't worth living without good food. Of course, he grew up comfortable, so he could say that."

"If you could eat one thing for the rest of your life, what would you eat?"

She thinks on this for a little while. "Mangos."

I joke-smash the table. "Mangos? You could go with pizza or

triple-bacon cheeseburgers and you go with fruit? I don't think you get the point of this game."

"Mangos are delicious. Plus you can eat them sweet or salty. When I was in college I went to Mexico for the first time."

"Spring break?"

She gives me a little shove, and I have to resist the urge to take that hand and hold it.

"Studying the effects of marine pollution in the Yucatán."

"So, no wet T-shirt contests and margaritas."

"I mean, you've never been around a bunch of science nerds. Things get pretty wild." She takes a drink of her mimosa. "Anyway. This might sound ridiculous but up until that point I couldn't remember ever having, like, a whole mango. It's always in concentrate or mango flavored or in juice. And across the street from where we were staying this lady had a tiny cart where she peeled them and put them in a bag with salt and hot sauce. I ate that every day. Pretty sure that's why I can't have spicy foods anymore. But it was worth it."

"In Colombia we had a mango tree." I don't talk about Colombia this much. Not to my friends, not even when my tía Ceci wants to go to dinner and catch up. But I'm talking about it with Faith and I know that I should stop but I can't. "My mom used to cut it up for me and squeeze a whole lemon over it and a little bit of salt. But when she wasn't looking, I'd add so much salt my mouth would be like prunes when I was done."

Faith laughs and sets her hand down. "You can't choose mangos for yours, too."

I brush my finger across hers. My heart is racing because she doesn't pull away. She hooks her index finger around mine.

"Banana chocolate chip pancakes," I say.

FAITH

Do you ever feel happy watching someone eat? Not in a sexual way. It's more of a "wow, you love my city" kind of way. Aiden enjoys life's pleasures. Does he enjoy them too much? Does it matter?

"I've never had a shot for breakfast," he comments on the bourbon that comes with the breakfast special. "It's not as bad as the stuff my friend Fallon likes. Want to taste?"

It's early, but it's Saturday and we're in the best city in the world. So I take a sip, pressing my lips right where his just were. The bourbon burns smoky and sweet.

"What are you thinking about?" he asks me.

"I'm thinking that I've never met someone who enjoys things the way you do."

Aiden arches a thick black brow, a sensual smirk on that heavenly face of his. "There's so much to love in this life. Food. Sunshine. Drinks. Sex. I've always done what I wanted. Now I realize things can backfire, though."

When he says *sex*, his eyes are intense on me. "That's a very long way of saying *YOLO*."

He leans close to me. "No one says that anymore. But basically. My mom didn't have a lot to give me, but she always made sure that what we did have—food, books, whatever—that I appreciated it. I wish she were here now so I could give her everything we didn't have."

I suck in a tiny breath. Pieces of Aiden start to come together. The way he always speaks about his mother in the past tense. The sadness in his eyes when he was sitting at the bar alone on his birthday. It wasn't just the birthday. It couldn't have been.

"I'm sorry," I tell him.

"I don't know why I said that." His jaw clenches like he's trying to not cry, so he frowns instead.

I rest my hand on top of his and I feel him ease. "Thanks for letting me be the one."

He shakes his head and tries to smile, tries to be the guy that loves life and does whatever he wants. I glance at the time on my watch and realize I have about fifteen minutes to get to church.

"Shit," I mutter. "I have to go."

He nods, understandingly, a smile tugging on his lips. Then, he finishes his morning whiskey and grimaces.

"Thanks for having breakfast with me, Faith," he says.

I watch him for a moment—this fascinating, lovely, sexy man. Even the thought of walking out of this restaurant without him pulls at my heartstrings in a painful way. "Have you ever been to a swamp?"

He chuckles, then realizes I'm serious. "I can't say I have."

"I'm visiting a friend tomorrow. Would you like to come with me?"

"To the swamp?"

"It's a national wildlife refuge, but yes, the swamp."

Without hesitation he says, "Yes."

Before I throw myself on top of him in front of a restaurant full of brunchgoers, I ask for the check. He tries to pay, like really tries to take the bill from me, but I don't let him.

"I'll pick you up at nine in the morning," I say as we step out of the restaurant.

"See you—" I watch him reach for me, then a body mass comes out of nowhere. He collides into someone. She yelps, losing her balance, but Aiden is fast and grabs hold of her.

My body runs cold when I realize who it is. Dread pools into the pit of my stomach, and I know I can't run in these heels.

"Faith!" Maribelle says, brushing her curls out of her face.

"Maribelle," I say with a guilty smile.

Aiden looks back and forth between us, trying to sense the tone. He tries to hang back but Maribelle's wide brown eyes look him up and down. I wonder what kind of stories she's making up in the painfully long seconds we stand staring at each other.

"We missed you this morning," Maribelle says, always one to fill in awkward silences with chitchat. She's holding a stack of pamphlets about my mother's campaign, which she's probably papering the town with. "Your mother's worried because you weren't answering our messages."

"I'm sure I'll hear about it in a few minutes."

Aiden is just standing there. I know I should introduce him, but I don't want to because he's been *mine* since yesterday and I don't want to expose him to the circus of the campaign. I know he's not mine-mine, but he's the only space that I have that isn't part of politics. I don't want to let that go just yet.

"Hi, I'm Maribelle Suarez," she says, holding her hand out to Aiden.

"Aiden Peñaflor," he says.

"Peñaflor?" Maribelle smiles wide. She even pronounces his name better than I can. "My roommate at LSU was a Peñaflor."

Aiden's so good at meeting new people. How does he do it? Maribelle's usual hyper energy seems tapered down. "No relation. I'm the first generation to live in the States."

"Oh cool," Maribelle says. "Me too. My parents moved to Florida from Puerto Rico, but I've *always* wanted to live in New Orleans. It's been my dream for forever."

I didn't know that about her. A voice that sounds strangely like my dad's says, *You never asked.*

"Faith has been trying to sell me on New Orleans hard," he chuckles. "But New York has Colombian food."

A tiny bolt of jealousy strikes my thoughts. It's not that I think that Aiden is trying to get with Maribelle. It's that he's sharing things about himself that I want for me. Ridiculous, I know. Selfish. Bratty.

"Yeah, when I'm older I want to open a Latin restaurant somewhere here. Right now I'm concentrating on politics. Of course, you know all about it."

And there it is. The thing that I've been trying to keep out of this thing—whatever it is—that Aiden and I have. It's gone.

Aiden looks to me to fill in the blanks.

"I have to go," I tell Maribelle. "And I'm sure Aiden is busy, so—"

"It was nice to meet you," Aiden says, and because he's himself, he hugs her and kisses her on the cheek.

"Maybe I'll see you around?" she asks, with a shy, significant look at me.

I can practically feel the machinations in Maribelle's mind working. She's going to tell my mother that she saw me with a guy on the street before church. A man she has never heard about or seen.

Self-preservation. That's what I'm going with. That's what's making me wrap my arm around Aiden's. Because for some reason this is safer, easier than trying to lie to my mother about who this man is.

"You will," I say. "He's my date to the masquerade ball."

"I am?" he asks for a moment. Then he repeats, but confidently, "I am."

Maribelle's shock lasts until she waves good-bye and continues down the shops.

"Masquerade ball?" Aiden says, but he doesn't seem upset.

"It's in two weeks. I know you're leaving so you can't come. Maribelle's just going to run off and tell my mom she saw me with you and I panicked."

"Could be fun," he says, shoving his hands in his pockets. "What's it for?"

I take a deep breath. "It's an election fund-raiser. Both candidates host and raise money for the city."

"Mafia princess." Aiden smiles and cocks his head to the side. "You know the candidates?"

I hand him the pamphlet. *Vote Charles for Change.*

"My mother *is* a mayoral candidate."

7

Up Around the Bend

AIDEN

"Holy fuck," Fallon says.

Back in my hotel, I pace on the balcony of the suite.

"Holy fuck," Fallon repeats.

"I know. Say something else. Because right now I don't know what I should do. I mean, I don't think she would have said anything if we didn't bump into that girl Maribelle after brunch."

Fallon, my supposed best friend, laughs. He's fucking laughing at me. "You went to *brunch*?"

"I had a bourbon."

"Really? Fine, but first you tell me that you let her take you to *brunch,* which in your words is yuppie bullshit, and now she's taking you to a swamp."

"I'm hanging up now."

He's almost done laughing, but he's practically wheezing. "Okay, I can be serious. But you have to answer something honestly."

"What?"

"After all you said this morning, why are you going to keep spending time with Faith?"

I sit down on the deck chair. From here I can see people swimming in the rooftop pool, and below that, the foot traffic coming and going. Somewhere out there is Faith Charles, daughter of a mayoral candidate. Before today she was Faith, a girl who makes me spill my secrets within ten seconds of being around her. Before that she was the most gorgeous woman I'd ever seen.

"I like her."

"You like her?" Fallon repeats. "Sweet summer child. The last long-term relationship you had was in elementary school."

"Best two weeks of my life." Ali Matsuma drew me cute little cards. She dumped a milk carton over my head when she found out I was also getting Valentine's cards from half of the class. "Your point?"

"My point is that you don't know what you want, but you want her."

"But I'm not moving to New Orleans."

"Robyn never thought she'd move to Boston."

I groan. "That's different. She's going to school there. You're engaged. I'm not getting engaged. Marriage doesn't work."

"Nice."

"You know what I mean." Fallon knows how I feel about my father. Everything he did to my mom. Stole her light. I don't want to think about that anymore.

"What do you want to hear?"

"I want to hear that I should enjoy the time I have with her."

"Even if it means staying an extra week?"

"Ginny's coming back on Friday. We check out the next day. I'll get another room. It'll be a clean break."

Fallon makes a thinking sound. "Here's an idea. Cancel your contract with Ginny."

"I can't."

"Why not?"

"Rent money? Do you know what I do for a living?"

"If you say you like this girl and you're actually going to stay a stretch, then man up and do the right thing. Get a tux. Go to this ball. Move out of that penthouse and get your own place. Be honest with her. I know what it means to lie to people, bro. You're just going to hurt her."

"I don't want to hurt her."

"Not to drop another bomb on you, but I spoke to Ricky again. They're hitting the road today."

I cut him off. "I can't deal with that right now."

"If you say so." Fallon's quiet for a little bit. "How's that hotel? The Sucré."

"Touristy but swank. Why?"

"No reason."

He does that sometimes. Changes the subject by making a hard left. "Okay, I have to go."

"To go to your swamp tour."

I squeeze the bridge of my nose. "It's important to her."

"You're catching feelings, little bro."

"You're going to catch my fist if you keep with that."

"Pfft. I'd like to see you try. And remember what I said. Seriously."

I sigh, but he can't see me shake my head. "Give my love to Robyn."

That call was supposed to help me figure out what to do. I know Fallon is right. I have to be honest with Faith. I will be. That's the only way I should keep seeing her.

I don't want to hurt her, and now that I know who she is, everything about me could do that.

"After the swamp," I tell myself. I repeat it over and over until I make myself believe it.

FAITH

Aiden in the daylight is a startling sight.

His pale gray T-shirt hugs his torso like a second skin, and the gym shorts he chose are better suited for a stroll down a South Beach street than the Quarter.

Underneath all of that muscle dripping of sex is someone nervous. Sweet. Insecure.

I don't know if that's why I invited him to the swamp.

There is nothing sexy about a swamp. But after yesterday's full-on passive-aggressive wars, my skin feels so tight I might shed it. Mom and I have played the silent-treatment game for years. I'm always the one who relents because I don't want her to be mad at me. It's a good thing my week off from the campaign will give me *some* reprieve.

When Aiden gets in my car, my mood already feels lighter. He leans in and kisses my cheek, and warmth spreads down my neck.

"Ready to go?"

And he says, "I'm yours for the day."

We drive for about an hour outside the city with the windows down and music playing from the radio.

"I'm not knocking your choice of activity," Aiden says. He leans his face to the warm air. "But you don't exactly look like the outdoorsy type. Not when I first met you."

I pretend to be affronted with a wink. "I'm glad I exude city slicker. When I was about thirteen my mom caught me kissing the neighbor in the treehouse behind our backyard."

"Scandalous."

"For real. To this day I'm not even sure if she told my dad. I think she was afraid I was going to be one of those girls—"

"Independent?"

My laugh is dry. "A pregnant teen whose boyfriend leaves her and then her parents are stuck taking care of her."

"Not all teen pregnancies go like that," he says, and I feel bad for my snap judgment. "Not all families feel stuck, either. But I think I get your mom's reaction. My mom couldn't even *talk* about sex. She made my tía Ceci do it. Gave me my first condoms even though I wasn't having sex yet."

"Late bloomer?" I glance at him.

"Yeah, but I was a fast learner." His light-brown eyes flick down to my lips. I shake myself out of the trance that starts when we look at each other. Especially because I'm the one driving. Am I the only one feeling this? I can't be.

"Anyway," I say. "My mom sent me to this summer camp in the swamp."

"I do not do sleeping on the ground."

"Neither do we!" I laugh. "There were only three Black girls there and the only reason was because they had to do it or take Earth Science at summer school for twice as long. But I don't know. There's something calming and strange about the swamp. My nana used to tell me stories of witches and mermaids that lived in there along with the gators and fish."

"What did you have to do at this camp?"

I put on my turn signal as the signs for Bayou Sauvage National Wildlife Refuge come into view. "The camp was part of the conservation center, so we helped the park rangers mostly. Collected water samples to test for pollution. Nursed baby ducks who lost their mothers. Tried to protect alligator eggs from being snatched by people."

"People do that?"

"Yup. The first three days were terrible. I wanted to leave. My arms were swollen with mosquito bites. I was certain I had yellow fever."

"What changed?"

I pull into the parking lot. "It's silly. I was tricked. This camp counselor gave me the job of taking care of these ducklings that had gotten sick because of the dumping of waste. They were so cute, I couldn't resist. That was when I felt, I don't know, responsibility."

"For the ducks?"

"For the ducks and this land."

"I guess it was a good thing that you got caught." He looks at me. We sit in the car for a minute that stretches like molasses. "That kiss was fate."

I know, in this moment, that he's thinking about kissing me. I want to. More than I can admit to myself. But that's the thing about the days after *the* morning after—it makes us second-guess. Overthink.

I clear my throat. "Come. I know a guy."

AIDEN

"I know a guy," she says.

It's the thing that pulls me out of the daze. All this talk of kissing and swamps and endangered ducks isn't exactly the setup to the most romantic date I've ever had. But I wouldn't rather be anywhere else. It sure beats wandering around the puke-scented streets of the Quarter by myself.

Faith walks ahead of me. My heart does a hard pitter-patter with the way she walks. Her black and blue workout pants shape her sexy-ass curves.

I can't touch her. We're not there yet. But damn, I can dream about wrapping my arms around her waist. Feeling the softness of her belly, the smooth skin of her thighs. That little sigh she made just before she came.

The sharp call of an animal snaps me from my reverie. Faith looks over her shoulder. "That's just a heron."

I laugh nervously. "Sorry, I've never been to a swamp. I don't think I've ever even been to a national park. The only outdoors I ever did was soccer in Flushing Meadows with my uncles."

She extends her hand for me to take. "Don't worry. I'll protect you."

I take her hand in mine, and even though it's smaller and softer, it feels secure. "We're not petting alligators, are we?"

She laughs, a real belly laugh. "What in the world makes you think that? Do you want to lose a hand?"

"Faith!" an older blond woman calls from a log cabin. It says *PARK ENTRANCE*. "Isn't this a surprise! We haven't seen you in so long. Blue Bill's really missed you."

"Blue Bill?" I ask.

Faith leans into me and says, "You'll meet him in a bit. Gladys, this is my friend Aiden. He's from New York City."

"New York City!" The woman's sunburnt cheeks brighten with a smile. She holds her hand out to shake mine, but I pull her into a hug.

"Sorry, I'm Colombian. We hug."

"Hoo boy. That's the most action I've seen in ages. Whatever brings you to these parts, Aiden?" She pats my arms, eyes wide at my muscles.

Faith is trying to hold back her laugh.

I glance at Faith. "Just exploring a bit. Faith kindly offered to show me a bit of the less touristy places."

"No one loves this place the way Faith does. It's a right shame she left us to—"

Faith cuts the woman off quickly. "Enough of that, lady. He didn't come to get my life story."

Gladys looks me up and down and makes a face. "Sure looks like it to me."

"Maybe Gladys should be my tour guide," I say, slinging my arm around the old woman.

Faith throws her hands up. "Fine. But she'll make you clean out the gator cages."

I must have a stricken look on my face, because the pair of them fall into laughter.

"Ha ha, laugh at the tourist."

For the first time I realize that there is a group of teenagers inside the log cabin. Some of them are watching us, and others are busy on the computer or going through papers.

"Mind the registry, Annie," Gladys says. "I'm taking out the Jaguar for our city guest here."

Faith takes my hand again and starts leading me deeper into the swamp.

"Wait, like a car?"

FAITH

This boy really just asked me if we're going in a car. I start cracking up despite myself. His tan skin has a sweet red blush on his neck. I think about kissing it and leaving marks. The thought startles me because it feels so raw and aggressive.

He squeezes my hand and tugs me to him. "I love it when you laugh like that."

"Keep throwing those lines at me," I tell him. But I love those lines.

We hop into an airboat, and Aiden's wide-eyed response to the metal contraption is priceless.

"Scared?" I ask him.

"Are you kidding? When I spent summers in Colombia, my grandfather used to take me on the river. It was a literal raft. Almost lost a foot to piranhas."

"I thought you said you weren't outdoorsy," I say.

"That's what happens when you almost get eaten by a school of tiny fish."

"Don't worry," Gladys says. "Jaguar here's safe as houses. I've taken her out for the last ten years."

But Aiden's stricken face tells me he's not reassured at all. "Even houses fall down in the right circumstances."

"You're in the best hands. Gladys took me out my first time here." I hand him a life jacket and then we're off. Aiden sits beside me and Gladys steers. She knows every part of this swamp. She grew up only one county over and tells Aiden just as much.

"You were a bratty thing, Faith," she says. "Wouldn't wear a hat because she didn't like the way it looked on her. Learned right quick that a neck and scalp sunburn's nothing to joke about."

With the hypnotic sound of the fan behind us, we glide across the water at an easy pace. Aiden seems to relax, though when our knees touch, he tenses once again. I can't deny I feel the same knot in my belly.

Still, I have to defend my honor with Gladys. "I didn't want to be here. All of my friends were vacationing in Disney World and I had to be getting water samples and spending hours doing nothing but watching a bunch of birds and keeping track of them. My parents' friends never really understood why my dad cared so much about preserving national parks and lands."

Aiden furrows his brow. "Why would they be surprised?"

"Because Black people weren't allowed in parks for a long time in this country," I explain.

"The feds made it official in 1945," Gladys says. "Still, you can feel the impact even now."

"But my dad's favorite place is in the middle of nowhere," I say. "If not for my mother, he'd move to the woods and chop his wood and have his bourbon and peace. She always tells me I'm just like him."

Aiden nudges his knee against mine, the breeze playing with his hair.

"We all become our parents," Gladys says as she steers.

Aiden scoffs lightly. "I sure hope not."

"My daddy was a mean old fisherman. Lost his leg to a gator one year. They fought for their dominance of their little patch of water. My momma was a witch. She could hear the swamp speak to her. They passed on when I was young, but they gave me their love of the land. I've always preferred the wild to people."

"Except me, right?" I grin at Gladys.

When she smiles, her slightly too-big teeth are on full display. "Of course. The summer program did you right. Showed you that there's more to life than chasing a dream in a cubicle. Wish we could give the same opportunity to other kids, but with the budget cuts, the summer programs will go first."

"Don't you worry about that," I tell her. "The fund-raiser will help."

A white heron swoops down low, snatches a bird with its long beak.

"Holy shit," Aiden says. "And I thought subway rats were savage." Then he jumps back. "Holy shit. Is that an alligator?"

A massive gator breaks the water. "That's Blue Bill."

Aiden's laugh is a little panicked, a little shocked, as the creature makes its way toward us. The snout snaps open and closes like a bear trap as it glides half-submerged in water.

Gladys does little to contain how much she loves to see people freak out. "Bill here hasn't had a human yet. Don't you worry your pretty head off."

I see Aiden practically trying to convince himself that he needs to put on a brave face in front of me. This isn't for everyone. Even Angie hasn't let me bring her out here. She prefers her nature behind a thick wall of glass, where it won't touch her skin or hair.

Gladys winks at me. She loves telling stories so much that I'm not even sure if she's sure which ones truly happened and which are of her invention. I rest my hand on his back.

I've never seen someone fall into the water, except for Gladys, and I'm convinced she can actually talk to these creatures.

"My cousin Adriana had a pet snake," he says.

"Yep, a snake and an alligator aren't much different," she says.

She knows that they are, but she's using her teaching voice. The one that gets all patient and slow. When I was younger I used to think that it was patronizing. Now, I wouldn't mind a little of that patience.

Aiden leans over quite a bit as Bill shimmies next to us. For a moment, he seems pretty pleased with himself, like he's at a small farm petting zoo. Until the water breaks with a splash, and Gladys grips him by the sleeve and yanks him back away from Blue Bill's reach. My scream is delayed, watching the creature nearly take off his whole arm.

"This almost never happens," Gladys says by way of apology. Then she shouts, "Bill! We do not behave like that with company!"

"Holy shit," he says, and when I hold his hands, a laugh shakes his body.

Gladys slaps Aiden's back. "Keep all arms and legs inside of the ride at all times, darling. Now, let's get you back before you lose that pretty head of yours."

We tease him the whole way back, Aiden fully convinced that Gladys has the gators trained to jump on command. Gladys is only mildly affronted at being compared to "those SeaWorld ringmasters."

Back at the ranger station, we try to wash off the stink of the muck, but no matter what, it lingers.

"Thanks for letting me take you on a weird date," I say.

"It was the smelliest and most dangerous date I've ever been on," he says, staring down at me like he wants to kiss me in the air-conditioned room lined with swamp facts and taxidermy. "There's so much more to you than bourbon and fancy dresses. But I draw the line at camping."

"Cross my heart," I say. When Aiden looks at me the way he

does now, it feels like my heart has grown feet and is tripping over itself.

We say good-bye to Gladys and promise to return.

As we drive with the windows down, he tells me about the time his grandfather took him out on a canoe in Colombia and one of his cousins almost drowned. He has a scar on his knee from a reed that cut him there.

Out here, with Aiden, my mind is unburdened. I don't remember the last time my abs hurt from laughing out loud. I wonder if that's why I'm clinging to him. Using him to forget my own problems. I wonder if that's fair to him.

He did say he was only passing through, searching for his next step in life. It would be foolish to think that this can ever be more than a flirtation. And yet, when I park around the corner of his hotel, neither of us make a move to get out of the car. His eyes are bright. His lips are full.

That kiss was fate, he said earlier.

I don't think I believe in fate.

I believe we make choices. We work for the things we want. Maybe it's the same thing, only being called by a different name.

But we lean into each other. Lips brushing lips like the touch of feathers. My heart swells in my chest, and a hunger sparks in my belly. *Want.* Our kiss deepens, tongues searching for secrets and teeth nipping for more. I want so much more than his kiss.

Aiden pulls away first. "Can I see you tomorrow?"

I want to. I know I shouldn't. "I can't, there's a banquet thing. I might not be working this week, but I have to show up as the daughter."

He flashes that smile at me. But there's something sad in his eyes. Like a memory that never seems to leave him. Or maybe I'm imagining it, because I can't possibly know that. "Thank you for today, Faith. For the other night and this. It makes me want to see more of your city."

I squeeze my legs against the memory of him. "What about the day after? A night tour?"

"What kind of tour?"

"I'll surprise you."

He leans in, but I'm already closing the distance to his lips. He tastes like pleasure and secrets, the things I'm not supposed to want. Not now.

This time, I force myself to pull away, because a car is beeping behind me. My bottom lip is swollen, but he presses a sweet kiss on it and says, "It's a date."

8

Tango del Pecado

AIDEN

The doorman at the hotel gives me a fist bump as I walk past him and into the elevator.

My mouth is numb from kissing Faith in her car. My entire body is filled with different sensations. Can your stomach hurt from laughing? I don't want it to sound like I don't have any fun. I have lots of fun. But it's been a strange couple of weeks, and the biggest gap is my family. Not my tía Ceci. I talk to her all the time. But the family that chose me.

Today was one of the best days I've had in a long time. Alligator and all.

I whistle all the way to my door. I don't even know the song, but it was playing on the radio both times we were driving.

The suite phone is ringing when I arrive.

"Hello?" I say.

"Mr. Buenos Aires?"

My heart sinks. That's the fake name the room is registered under. It was Ginny's idea because she seems to think every country in Latin America is the same.

"Yes?"

"You have an urgent message from Ginger Thomas to call her back as soon as possible."

Fuck. I dig out my phone. Of course it's dead. Rule #10:

When you take a job, text back right away. "Thank you. Can I ask you—are there any rooms available for tomorrow?"

"Is there something wrong with the suite, sir?"

I feel stupid because she can't see me shake my head. "No, I have some friends who might swing into town for a visit."

I hate putting on that voice. It's one I've picked up at parties and functions I get taken to as a date. A voice I use to blend in, to make everyone around me forget that perhaps I don't belong there.

"One second, sir," she says, and I hear clicking on her end. "We're booked solid until the end of the week."

"Thanks for checking," I say.

"Of course, sir. Is there anything else we can do for you?"

"That's all for now," I say.

"Don't forget to take advantage of our spa services. We can send someone up for a couples massage, if you wish."

"I'm okay, thank you." I hang up and charge my phone while I shower. The swamp smells like, well, swamp, and I can feel it in my pores.

I step out of the shower with a stupid grin on my face. Maybe I *should* go downstairs and get a massage. My bubble is burst within seconds when my phone lights up with a FaceTime call.

Ginger Thomas lights up the screen, and I swipe to answer the call.

"Aiden? Are you there? I can't see you?"

I stand in the middle of the room and hold the phone up. My insides feel like they're tripping over each other, twisting into gnarly branches. I don't like feeling this way, have never felt this way.

"Hey, doll. Where you at?" I lie down on the bed and hold the phone so she can see me.

Her eyes are a bit red. She was crying. A dark part of me wishes I could stand face-to-face with her husband and read him the riot act. It triggers images of my mother sitting at the kitchen table ripping a napkin in her hand. Crying and waiting for my father to come home from one of the neighbors' houses.

"What's wrong?" I ask.

"Oh, nothing. Just my husband never considers my feelings. But that's not important." She's sitting by an empty pool.

I have no idea what Ginny's life is like, to be honest. I met her in New York at a party on the Upper East Side. She needed a date to the opera after her husband cancelled on her, and she hired me. That was a year ago. After everything went down in Vegas, it was a stroke of luck that I bumped into her at the Mandarin bar. We were both at our worst. I know that her family is wealthy. She supported her husband all throughout college, but we don't get into specifics. In my experience, women like Ginny just want someone to treat them well. Everyone wants that.

I sit back on my bed and hold the phone up. "What would make you feel better?"

She looks around. She's got her headphones plugged in. I wonder if her husband is close by. At first I wonder if they're home, but then a waitress slinks by and hands her a dirty martini with extra olives. "Sing to me?"

So I sing. My voice is not going to win me any awards, but I can carry a tune in a specific key for a specific song. My mother loved this song "Nuestro Juramento." It means "our oath" and it was her favorite song. When she was sick she asked me to sing for her and I would do it even if my voice cracked the entire time. This song isn't right for my alto, but I get through it now, and the entire time I think I shouldn't be singing this for Ginny. But it's the first thing that comes to mind in a strange panic, and it's like reliving the worst day of my life again. I clear my throat, finishing in a rush.

She sits there and sips her martini with her eyes closed, listening to the sound of my voice.

"Thank you, sweetheart," she tells me when I'm done. "I'll see you at the end of the week."

My throat wants to close up because the reality of who I am and what I do is unavoidable. Ginny will get here in a few days. And I know that as much as I want to, I can't see Faith again.

FAITH

There's someone at my house when I get home. I can smell my father's cigar the moment I step inside. He's sitting outside in my yard, but the window is open. Some people think it's gross, but I love the smell of cigars. It reminds me of cool summer nights when my daddy and my uncles would sit around our large front porch and look at the stars, telling stories of their parents and grandparents. *Old men and their stories,* my mom would say and go inside the house. But I loved sitting out there, just listening.

Because one of my mother's campaign promises is to reduce the effects of smoking, she won't let my dad smoke in the house. Though I suspect there's another reason he's here.

It's early in the evening, but the sun is already starting to sink. I pour us two glasses of Four Roses bourbon, one ice cube in each, and take them outside.

His only acknowledgment is a tiny nod when I sit down. He rests the cigar on the ashtray and taps his drink to mine. Takes a sip.

"You missed the meeting this morning."

"You know why I wasn't there." I let the bourbon coat my throat. I can't lie to my father, so I don't.

"Do you want to tell me what you were doing with your time instead? Your mother and I were worried when you stopped answering messages."

I look into the whiskey, and my belly flip-flops because I don't see my own reflection. I see Aiden's eyes.

"Worried about me or about how it would look that I wasn't there after Friday night?"

He chuckles. "Do you know what your mother said today?"

"What?"

"That you're exactly like me. But what you just said this moment is exactly like your momma."

I smile and lean against his arm. "I went to visit Gladys."

"How's that old swamp witch doing?"

"Daddy!"

"What? You told me yourself she runs through that marsh naked in the moonlight. Sounds like a witch to me."

I roll my eyes. "She's a little *eccentric*. And she's good. Losing her budget, as usual."

He switches his drink for his cigar. I'm not like my mother. I'm like him. He hands the cigar to me. The first time he did this, I was sixteen and was caught smoking. He made me smoke an entire cigar in front of him. I didn't touch another one for six years.

Why is this family full of tough love? Why do we pass that on?

I take the cigar between my lips and let the smoke burn my throat.

"When you were little you always knew exactly what you wanted to do. Always. I knew I couldn't fight you. Just let you go at your own pace."

"Why do I feel like there's a 'but' coming?"

"But, you know what this election means to us all. What it means to your mother. Mayor of New Orleans? That is a dream she never thought she could have. Every day I watch her stand in front of the mirror and remind herself that she's good enough. She's worked harder than anyone I know."

"My entire life she's always reminded me of the fact that she's worked harder than I ever have or ever will."

My dad rarely gets angry. But I know he's close when his forehead frowns like this. "Is that really what you think?"

"That's how she makes me feel."

He finishes his drink. "I love you, baby. You know I love you."

"But?"

"That love is unconditional. I hope you feel the same about us with the way you're behaving." He stands, and I follow like a good little soldier. "You should pay a visit to your mom's old diner. Remember where she started."

"Daddy—"

"I've said what I came here to say. The election is in three weeks, Faith. Remember what's on the line. Whatever is going on, fix it. I'll see you at the banquet."

"Yes, Daddy."

* * *

Angie comes over to pick up a dress she wants to borrow from me. It's Tuesday and I've been pacing my house waiting for Aiden.

"You would not believe the shift I had yesterday."

I chuckle and embrace her. "Did another guy try to jump from one of the suite balconies into the rooftop pool?"

She rolls her eyes. "You know, even a giant sign that says NO DIVING doesn't dissuade drunk fucking tourists? I'd still take that over girls who mix drinks and puke everywhere. Everywhere, Faith."

I grimace and lead her to my closet. "At least it didn't get on you. It didn't get on you, did it?"

"Look at you being glass half full."

She makes a beeline for my closet and helps herself. She pulls out a sleek red number I got for the day my mom announced her campaign.

"When have you worn this? This is sexy."

I ignore the jab and ask, "What do you need a dress for?"

Angie throws the red dress on my bed. Her "maybe" pile. She grabs a powder-pink one. "When have you ever dressed as a fairy fucking princess?"

"That was from prom, remember?"

Angie cracks up and puts the dress back. "I'm sorry I touched that. Didn't Gordon Derringer blow his load in his pants while you were kissing? Why have you kept this?"

"First of all, ew—I haven't thought of that in years. And secondly, it's dry-cleaned. I lent it to one of mom's coworkers' daughters for her prom."

Angie widens her eyes. "I hope *she* also got it dry-cleaned."

I hop on my bed and watch her. "You haven't answered my question."

"I have a meeting," she says.

"Use your words. What kind of meeting?"

"There's this show swinging into town for the weekend. I have an interview with the owner for a possible job."

"That's amazing!" I jump on her and hug her until she shoos

me away, never one for showing sentiment. "I'm so happy for you. Why didn't you tell me?"

"It sort of came about last minute," she says, but there's something she's not telling me. I know I can't push her, so I sift through the dresses and pick out an electric-blue wrap dress that will show off her powerful dancer legs.

She holds it to the mirror and then decides to try it on. "You haven't asked me what it's about."

"Because I know you'll tell me when you're ready."

She looks over her bare shoulder. I've always envied her toned, muscular back. But athletics and I have never gotten along. When we were thirteen, she was as thin as a beanpole, while my hips and derrière betrayed me. I looked too grown even though I didn't feel that way. I hid under shirts too big for me and wore the uniform trousers instead of the skirts.

"Promise you won't judge?"

"I'm no one to judge you, darlin'." I brush one of her curls away from her eye.

"This show from Vegas is looking for a choreographer. It's a male revue. The owner wants to meet ASAP."

I tilt my head to the side. "Male revue as in—strippers?" I think of Aiden and smirk. Angie would rock that gig.

"Don't make fun!"

"I'm not! Besides, why would I ever judge you for that? It's an amazing opportunity."

I wonder if it's the same group Aiden was in. It has to be.

She adjusts the top of the dress. Because the material is flowy around the hips, it looks too big on her. She takes it off and adds it to the "no" pile. She tries on the red one.

"It's different for them, you know," she says. "I stripped for two months at Sapphire before I got the job at Cirque du Soleil. I wasn't cut out for stripping. But the money is amazing. When men strip, it's about the sensationalism of it. Men can love stripping. When women do it, they have to be in need. They have to feel like there's no other way out."

She's absolutely right, and I feel ashamed that she'd think I'd judge her. "How'd you meet the owner?"

Her eyes flick to me. "Your *fling* from the bar. Aiden. He mentioned they were touring and I got in touch with a recruiter to get me an interview. I would have gone to Vegas but they're coming here."

Having her call Aiden my *fling* reminds me I haven't told her about our subsequent meetings. I get up to help her zip the dress up. It's sleeveless and doesn't cover the surgery scar on her shoulder, but when she looks in the mirror, I know it's the right one.

"Now," she says, looking at me through our reflections. "Why did you have a dreamy look in your eye when I walked in?"

"Angie . . ."

"I told you my thing. Your turn."

I clear my throat. Looking at Angie is like looking at a reflection of myself that I can't lie to. "Do you remember my *fling*?"

"The one so pretty, even I'd consider having sex with him, and I'm a lesbian? Yes, go on."

I have to glance at my feet, but the words won't come out. She turns and squeezes my arms. "It's been, like, how many days since? It couldn't have been that good. Tell me everything. It's been so long, your hymen probably grew back."

"Angie! That's not even scientifically accurate." She follows me to my bed. So many of our secrets have been told this way. Sitting on each other's beds, trading the things we don't want anyone else to know. I tell her about going to his room. Him going down on me. Me falling asleep. We have to pause for about five minutes because she can't stop laughing. "Anyway, we've seen each other almost every day since."

Angie bites her bottom lip.

"What?"

She hesitates. "Are you sure you want to be dating before the election? It's bad enough you're best friends with a bartending college dropout and former stripper."

"And I love you. Whatever you do I love you. Ride or die, remember? I'm not the one running for office."

"I don't think your momma sees it that way."

"You're the one who encouraged me to go after him."

"For a one-night stand, not to date. Wait. I know that guilty face. You didn't. You invited him to the ball, didn't you?"

I let go of an exasperated breath. "Yes, but I told him he doesn't have to come."

"The way he was looking at you? I doubt he'd say no to anything you suggested." She gets up, and in the set of her mouth and forehead, I know she's done talking until she has something vital to say.

It makes keeping details of Aiden all to myself easier.

AIDEN

When I turn the corner on Chartres and Saint Peter Street by Jackson Square, my feet stop working. My body has a physical reaction. Nerves swirl in the pit of my stomach with every step I take to get closer to her. My mind spins, trying to make sense of the lies that will catch up to me. I don't want to lie to her. I don't want to hurt her. I don't want to stop seeing her.

That's the thing. I can't do all of those things at once.

Faith stands apart from the crowd, even though she's right beside a cluster of tourists with sunburnt shoulders and baseball caps detailing their favorite local teams. Faith is in a pair of jeans that taper to the finest ass I've ever seen. I could take a bite out of that like a fucking peach. Her white shirt hits home in a way I didn't even know it could. It's a flowing white lace top that hangs off her shoulders. She reminds me so much of the festivals in Colombia. I know it's not the same, but the way her hair falls in black waves over those bare shoulders—all I want is to trace kisses across her warm brown skin.

I need to calm down with those thoughts in public because the front of my jeans are starting to feel tight. I take my jacket and drape it over my arm. The night is breezy, and it smells like it might rain later.

When she sees me, I don't imagine the spark in her eyes. If she looked at me like this every day, I'd die a happy man.

But she can't. Because when I tell her the truth about me, about why I'm here, that spark is going to fade.

"Hey," I say. Clear my throat because I feel my voice crack the same way it did when I was thirteen. "Hi."

Her smile is radiant. She stands on her toes to kiss my cheek. "I got our tickets."

I smack my forehead. "I should've thought of that."

"Don't be silly. Aiden, this is my friend, Violet Beauchamp."

Violet has a head of wild dark-red hair that falls down her back. I'd say that she's wearing a vampire costume, but on her it looks like it's her everyday clothes. A black corset and black patent leather pants. Dozens of metal necklaces around her neck and wrists. Her eyebrows are pencil thin, and her lips are pitch black. She holds her hand out to me.

"Nice to meet you," she says in a husky voice. "Glad Faith has an excuse to join one of my vampire tours."

"*Vampire* tours?" I ask, taking Faith's hand in mine. "I can't say I've ever been to one. Have you been doing this long, Violet?"

She lifts a shoulder as if it's no big deal. "Went to school for history, but after I graduated I came here for a summer and I never left. The only thing I'm good at is memorizing things."

"She's modest," Faith says. "Vi has a catalog of little-known history from all over the world. But now she specializes in New Orleans stories."

Violet takes a pocket watch out and flips it open. She counts the crowd gathered around her and returns the watch to her pocket. The streetlamps cast yellow light around us. I tug Faith a little closer to me, and she grabs hold of my forearms with both hands. I've seen Robyn do this to Fallon when they stand in line to go to a game, or waiting for the subway. Like *I'm* her anchor this time.

"Ready?" she asks, and all I can do is nod because I don't trust myself to use my words just yet. I'm basking in the glow of her cheekbones, the earth brown of her eyes.

I press my thumb to the base of her jaw, touching that cute freckle, and then we're off. Her hands slide down my arms and because neither of us let go, we link our fingers together. As Violet leads us down a dark street, she talks about the history of New Orleans, the legends of vampires that might have and might still roam this city. The cobblestone streets and alleys leave so much to the imagination. I've never been into things like this, but I remember thinking Aaliyah was the hottest woman on earth when I watched *Queen of the Damned*.

This is the strangest date I've been on, not because of the subject matter, but because Faith and I aren't talking. Whenever I do date, the goal is to see if we like each other enough to spend the night fucking. Sometimes we skip the date part to the end.

Violet talks about a group of women called the Casket Girls, who were sent over to New Orleans to become wives, and are now the basis of vampire legends in this creepy-ass convent. Faith watches her friend and the reactions of the other people. Some might be too tipsy to actually pay attention, but there's something in Violet's voice that makes the hair on my arms stand up. Faith seems to notice and rubs my arm.

Her touch sends all kinds of signals throughout my body. It's like I'm a pinball machine and every time she puts her hands on me, I'm all frantic light and sound.

"Scared?" Faith asks.

I lower my mouth to her ear. "Only if it means you'll protect me."

She smiles widely, and we walk a little faster, getting left behind each and every time because we stand too long, stare too long at each other.

I want to kiss her in the middle of this haunted, dark street, and I want to press her up against a wall. See if her heart is beating as quickly as mine.

Violet gets to a building on a corner with metal posts and a balcony that wraps around the corner. One of the lampposts is burnt out here, leaving us more in shadow as she tells the story of Jacque St. Germain, who was a ladies' man, wealthy as fuck, and threw tons of parties. Only at his parties he wouldn't eat anything, only drink out of a goblet. To be honest, this is what Fallon was like before he met Robyn. Only instead of a goblet, it would have been a Solo cup. Anyway, St. Germain brought a prostitute up to his house one night, and the lady then jumped off the balcony and onto the same street where we're gathered. She said he bit her neck enough to break skin. The next day, St. Germain was gone, and when the police raided his apartment, they found bottles of wine that were mixed with blood.

This city is so fucking weird.

But when I look at Faith, I know that it's also beautiful. Unexpected. Just like she is.

Toward the end of the tour, we stop in a small dive bar. A woman in her late fifties, with the voice of someone who has a shot of whiskey and a pack of cigarettes a day, greets us. Faith and I trade in our vouchers for the shots of tequila.

She makes the cutest face when she bites down on her lemon. There's a bit of salt on her lip, and I don't know if it's New Orleans, or the adrenaline beating my heart senseless, but I bend down and kiss it from her.

She chases my mouth with hers, and then we're full-on kissing. A flash of lightning hits outside. The rumble of thunder. She jumps, like she's only just realizing that we're in a public place, that people are watching us. She lowers her face and tucks her hair behind her ear.

"We should go. Everyone is outside."

Vi smirks at us as we exit the bar. "All right, it's about to pour, but the next stop is our final one." She launches into the story of a pirate left caged above the church during a storm. The next day, the cage was empty and still locked.

Faith's hand finds mine, and we walk the rest of the way like this. I cling to her like a drowning man to a raft. And when the tour is over, I know that I should pull her aside and do the thing I promised to do. Tell the truth. Come clean. Be a good man.

But when she says, "Do you like jazz?"

All I say is "Lead the way."

Faith and I hop into a cab and take it to Frenchmen Street. It's the middle of the week, but the bars are bursting with all kinds of people. Music spills past every door we pass. Jazz, reggae, all sorts of horns and drums that have my feet wanting to split into a dance.

Man, I've missed *music*.

The way the sounds make me feel like a marionette, every single one of my muscles reacting to the rhythm and beat of a song.

That's when I hear it. The sway of the music I grew up with. Faith tugs on my hand because I've stopped in front of a tiny bar. I can see the band against the wall. A bunch of old men with white pants and Panama hats. Saxophones and congas and guiros. One of them has a beaded Puerto Rican flag around his neck. A small crowd is dancing to the salsa, but most of the people there are sitting around the bar and watching.

"Do you want to go in?" Faith asks.

I flash a smile and then we're inside the bar.

We weave through the small crowd. I can't stop my shoulders from bouncing to the song. It strikes a chord instantly because I remember it. One of my mother's favorites, a cover from a Colombian band. The feeling is overwhelming, and I have to push it down.

The bartender slides two napkins in front of us, a lanky young guy with a short blond Afro and a septum piercing.

And I don't know if it's the tequila I had on an empty stomach or the nostalgia of the music, but I say, "Dos margaritas, parse. Sorry—"

He looks at me with wide eyes and cuts me off. "Parse? Qué hubo, paisa?"

We make the same strangled cry because we recognize each other as Colombian. He takes my hand and shakes. "Just passing through or new in town?"

The music gets louder, so I don't have to answer this question. "Aiden."

"Javi." He throws a bar towel over his shoulder and takes up a set of shakers.

"Do you know each other?" Faith asks.

I shake my head. "No, but he's Colombian."

"Did you recognize that from a word?" She looks amused.

I smile into her hair and nod. This is perfect. I have the perfect girl. The perfect bar. If I could capture this moment and this feeling forever, I'd have no reason to leave.

"Even when I was a kid, I didn't grow up around a lot of Colombian kids. When we moved to New York, my tía Ceci was always working and my mom was sick. I mostly stayed in the apartment building."

"There weren't kids your age?" She swivels on her barstool. Whoever invented these has my praise forever. Her knees are between my legs, her fingernails tracing circles on my thighs.

"There were. I grew up around kids from everywhere. It was mostly a Caribbean neighborhood. But I always had to explain my accent. So every time I meet someone from Colombia I get a little overexcited."

"No, I get that. I did a summer program in Boston once. Every time I saw a Black girl in the room we'd make eye contact. Like, *you good? We good.*"

"Why were you in Boston?"

She lifts her hand to brush her hair out of her eye. "It was a land conservation summer program."

"I think the only reason I'd ever be back out in nature would be because of a beautiful girl."

She smirks, like she's trying to reject my flirtation with the cute wrinkle of her nose.

We watch each other for a moment that stretches into infinity. I can feel it wind around us like a cord. So tight that I can hardly breathe. I don't like this feeling. I don't want this feeling. It's like being hit in the gut over and over again. The salsa band's song hits all the high notes, my heart thumping along with the rhythm, her fingers tapping out the same beat against my thighs.

"Toma, hermano," Javi says, pushing the drinks toward us. "On the house."

"Thank you for being Colombian," Faith chuckles.

"It's a blessing," I say. "What should we cheers to?"

She thinks on it. "To Colombia. For giving me Aiden Peñaflor."

Peñaflor. A name I never use, but the one I've given her. My lies are snowballing into each other, and the only one who can stop them is me.

"Thank you," I say instead and squeeze her thigh with my free hand.

A horn blares, and the light dims a little bit more. Faith's stunning features are highlighted by neon lights. Her brown skin is incandescent in this light, a vision in the night. This is my world. Night clubs and sex and money. Hers is in the sun, among trees, with brunches and banquets.

But both of our worlds also have music.

"I love this song," I say, standing with her hand clasped in mine. "Dance with me."

"I don't know how." She tries to be demure, but I've felt the way she kisses and the way she tastes. I've seen the spark in her eye.

"I'll teach you," I whisper in her ear, and I feel her shiver against me.

I place both hands on her waist and guide her. We move to the push and pull of the trumpets, her feet are fast and mimic each of my steps. I give her a little push. Hold my arm out and she reels back into me, against my chest. We sway together from side to side, until I turn her in place. Press my hand on her lower back. Her heat radiates against me. Her mouth is slightly open and inches from mine.

I want to kiss her.

I want to bury myself inside of her.

I want to worship the ground she walks on.

But instead, we just dance.

The song comes to a head, sweat trickles down my spine. My heart runs laps around my chest, as I hold her, tilt her toward the ground. Her hair spills back, her eyes searching mine as the lights go out.

And in the dark, she finds my mouth with hers.

9

When You Put Your Hands On Me

FAITH

Kissing Aiden in the dark sets my entire body alight. I could power this entire club with the heat of his body against mine. The sway of his hips grinding against mine to a song I don't know the language of, but I understand every word nonetheless.

There's a flutter between my legs as he slides his hands from my waist, around my hips, and he cups my ass. I dig my nails along the fabric of his shirt as if I could press him any tighter. If that were possible, then we'd be fused together in the pitch black of this club.

The music cuts, replaced by the chatter of the crowd, the metallic clinks of instruments. Apologies for the blackout. The rain. Something about the electricity coming back. Something that isn't about Aiden's lips on mine.

He comes up for air first, breaking the kiss to tease his teeth in the crook of my neck. I hiss against him.

"Did I hurt you?" he whispers in my ear, his face buried in my hair.

I kiss his ear, tug on his earlobe. "Do it again."

It's so dark I can't see him. Someone is talking about staying calm. But I'm not calm. I'm pushing him against a wall. Someone brushes past us, trying to exit. There's a flashlight guiding people out the door.

But I don't want to leave. I want to stay in this hidden place, my fingers exploring his hot skin under the sweat-stained shirt. I reach lower still. I find his erection.

"Faith," he sighs against my mouth.

I love the way he says my name. The way he reacts when I touch him. When I look at him. It's a strange sort of power to have. I keep one hand on his abdomen and lower myself to my knees. I rake my nails against his thighs.

I kiss him through his jeans. His fingers grab hold of my bare shoulders. Maybe it's the dark. Maybe it's the cacophony around us. Maybe it's the thrill he gives me. But I unbutton the top of his jeans. Tug the zipper all the way down. I hear the intake of his breath. His dick strains for release as I press another kiss there.

"Come here," he says, everything about him hurried, from his hands pulling me up to his mouth parting mine. His tongue searching. His fingers running a line between my legs, wetness soaking through my jeans.

"I want you," I tell him.

Then, a flashlight beams near us and we shake apart.

It's the bouncer. He keeps the flashlight pointed at the ceiling. Which I'm thankful for because my lipstick is probably smeared all over my face. "Everyone out! The storm's cut the power."

I head in the direction of the light outside. The entire street is dark. Some sort of power outage. I'll have to call my mom in the morning.

"Wow, it's the whole block," Aiden says.

The bottom of his shirt barely covers his still-open jeans. He keeps an arm around me, and I do my best to put myself together, fix the shoulders of my blouse.

Police sirens ring from the distance.

"You can't be here," he says. "Come."

We weave through the people in the dark. There's a fight somewhere. People pushing each other. This can get ugly real quick. Aiden keeps his hand firmly around mine, pushing his way past other silhouettes.

But I tug on him. "I have to make sure everyone is okay. If my mother were here, she'd do the same thing."

He sighs, brushing the side of my face with his fingers. "No offense, but you've got lipstick all over your face and mine."

I dig through my purse to find a face wipe and use the flashlight on my phone as a mirror.

"Do you also have a Swiss Army knife and an inflatable tent?" he asks, chuckling.

All of my lipstick comes off. There's a rumble up above, and that's when the sky breaks open and it begins to rain.

"I'm not leaving you here by yourself."

I look up at him. My eyes adjust to the dark only just, but I can make out the slope of his cheekbones, the curve of his nose. My heart makes a strange squeezing sensation. "Let's go."

AIDEN

I get back to the hotel by myself in a daze. Faith is unbelievable.

When the police chief arrived, they set up a barricade with high-powered lights. In the middle of the street with nothing but rain, somehow, they managed to get an evacuation route for everyone.

The police chief recognized Faith and shook her hand. She spoke to him briefly. It didn't feel right intruding, so I hung back under the mist.

Soon enough a couple of news vans arrived, but the street was blocked off, so they all clustered in a corner and tried to interview the police chief, people standing and waiting for the rain to pass.

An officer offered us a ride back to Faith's house, but neither of us wanted to explain why we were leaving together, so I lied and said I had a car on the next street. That I hadn't gotten a chance to drink, so I was stone-cold sober.

That's when things got awkward. A reporter in a long brown trench and a wrap around her head ran up to Faith, shouting, "Miss Charles! How did you happen to be at the scene of the blackout?"

Faith looked over her shoulder. "I decline to comment."

The woman looked familiar. I don't remember where I saw her before. "Did your mother send you here? Who's your friend?"

That's when Faith turned around. "Perhaps instead of trying to talk to me, you should ask Mayor Moreaux why this is the third power outage of the month."

The reporter looked at me, tilted her head as if she, too, recognized me.

Satisfied with whatever she got, the woman went away. It took an hour and a half, but Faith and I walked all the way to her house.

We could have called a cab, but the rain had stopped and the breeze was warm. We didn't talk much. To be honest, I don't know what I would have said. But even in her silence, I could feel her anxiety over what she'd snapped at that reporter.

It's not my world. Not my place to tell her what she should say. She handled it a lot better than I would have. When we could hear the teeming sounds of the Quarter I put her in a taxi.

Just before she closed the door she said, "Tomorrow night?"

And I said yes. Of course I said yes. If it hadn't been for that blackout, what would have happened? I replayed the intensity of the way I wanted her.

When I walk through the doors of the Hotel Sucré, I'm arrested by the cold air pumping through the lobby, which is probably a good thing.

"Mr. Buenos Aires," a small voice calls from the front desk. The young receptionist is alone and filing through papers.

"Yes?"

"You have a message from Ginger Thomas."

I try not to deflate at her name. Ginny. I keep forgetting about Ginny. Fuck.

"What is it?"

The girl slides a piece of paper across the counter and doesn't seem to be able to look in my eye.

I shove the paper in my pocket and head for the elevators. But what I see when I get there stops me cold. A poster of an upcoming show. Was it always there and did I miss it? No, it had to have gone up today.

Dated for the middle of next month.

MAYHEM CITY LIVE

And my face is still on it.

"When were you going to tell me the boys were coming here?" I yell over the phone.

Fallon mutters obscenities. He's probably asleep and waking up Robyn.

"I tried."

My body feels hot from top to bottom. I've only ever gotten this feeling every time I'm in trouble. Is this a hot flash? "You tried? When? During the dozen conversations we've had since I got here?"

I hear a door open on his end. "Look, you didn't want to listen. I know better than to try to make you listen before you're ready. But Aiden, this is why Ricky wants to talk to you."

"Uhm, also, my fucking face is still on that poster. I mean, I look good as fuck after doing nothing but live at the gym and work."

Fallon chuckles. There's a beeping noise, and I can't tell if it's coming from me or him. I let myself out onto the balcony.

Below on the pool floor, there are a handful of people still at the bar.

"You know what, hold on. I need to get out of this room."

"Wait, where are you going?"

"The pool. I've been here for a fucking week and the only water I've seen here has been a swamp."

"Okay," Fallon says. The fact that he's so calm about this makes me want to rage even more.

"Why are you so calm?"

"The poster was a mistake."

"How do you know?"

"Because I talked to Ricky, that's why."

I get off two floors down and use my key card to enter the pool area. I make a beeline for the terrace wall, where you can overlook the entire city. Out in the distance is a patch of black. It's the longest day I've ever had lately. Well, except for the day my business partner left me high and dry after I quit on my friends.

"Aiden?" Fallon asks. His voice cuts out for a moment, but then he's as clear as a bell. "Are you thinking 'what if people Faith knows see it'?"

"Or her dad." I lean forward on the cement of the terrace wall. "I should've told Faith everything. I had every chance. We're going out tomorrow. I should just let her, right?"

Fallon clears his throat. "I already told you what I think."

"Please, Fal. Please. What should I do?"

"You know what you have to do. I'm here for you."

That's a weird thing for him to say. Someone taps my shoulder. "Hang on."

But when I turn around, there he is. Zachary Fallon in his fucking Red Sox pajama pants and a black gym tank.

"I mean, I'm really here for you," he says, all stupid smirks.

I take the hand he offers and pull him into a tight hug. "I've missed you, man."

He pats me on the back and for a moment some of that loneliness I've felt over the last couple of weeks is gone.

"Now," he says, "what are we going to do about your problem?"

10

Wild Love

FAITH

My mother slams the newspaper on my desk. Though calling the *N'awlins Gazette* a "newspaper" is a courtesy. The headline reads: MAYORAL CANDIDATE'S DAUGHTER BLAMES CURRENT MAYOR FOR FRENCHMEN STREET BLACKOUT.

I inhale deeply and try to do the backward-from-ten count-down. I get to about *six* before my mom slams her hands again.

"Explain yourself, Abigail Charles."

You know she's really mad when she doesn't even say my first name.

In the foyer of my house, Maribelle hangs back, staring at the art on my walls. I only buy things from my friends, but she's staring at them like I've bought an original Klimt. Though if I were her, I'd hide from my mom's warpath, too.

"You know that's not what I said," I tell my mom. "I told her that instead of interrogating me, she should go talk to the mayor. That's all."

My mom is in a black power suit with a tiny American flag pinned on her lapel, a gold fleur-de-lis just below it.

"I was on Frenchmen Street last night," I say. "I had to help. I couldn't leave just because someone might recognize me as your daughter."

She tries to breathe. Moves past me to the pot of coffee nearly done percolating. "Thank you for doing that. Those things can get ugly."

It's not over. I wonder if she's trying the same countdown thing my shrink suggested. Though, my mother? At a psychologist? I bet I'd see mermaids come out of the bayou before that day.

I grab two mugs from the cupboard. She massages her hands, does that thing where she's trying to cover up the burn marks across her right knuckles from a grease fire accident when she was a waitress. The scars on her left hand from working at a canning factory before it shut down and left a whole town without work.

She takes her coffee black. She says she likes the flavor, but I don't think that's possible. I think she's too busy to stop for sugar and milk and all the other crap I put in mine.

"Who's he?" she asks after she takes her seat.

Even though I was bracing for that question, it still sends an alarm through my body.

Who is he? In the blurry picture that made the front page, I'm wearing a police-issue windbreaker. I don't look terrible, all things considered. I look like I'm giving out orders . . . kind of like my mom. To the right is Aiden. He doesn't really look like he's beside me because he's giving a statement with two others. His shirt is drenched and thankfully his pants are buttoned all the way up.

What was I thinking? How could I have acted like that? What if that reporter had been in the salsa club and seen me? That's a headline my mother wouldn't have forgiven me for. I can already hear her words: *reckless, stupid, selfish.*

"Faith . . ."

"His name is Aiden Peñaflor. Maribelle met him. I'm surprised she didn't tell you."

Mom arches her eyebrow. "Maribelle is not my spy. If you introduced him, she'd have no reason to think he was anything other than your friend."

I set my coffee down on the newspaper and cover my face. But Aiden is still there. How can my mom even tell that he's with me? Unless she didn't know. Unless she was bluffing and was going off a hunch.

"He's just your friend, isn't he?"

"Ma."

"What? Even in that photo I can see the appeal. But who is he? Where is he from?"

"If you want to interrogate him, you can do so at the masquerade ball."

"You can't bring a date to the ball."

"Why not?"

"Because, that's not part of the plan. Faith, you're part of this family. We can't present ourselves to the people of New Orleans with some guy you just started dating."

I pinch the bridge of my nose. "Since when did you start caring about what other people think of us?"

"Don't be naive, Faith. You know that for us it matters more. Reginald Moreaux could have an affair in broad daylight and it wouldn't get back to him the way it would to me."

"I'm sorry." I nod. "I'm sorry. I know. Look, he's just a friend."

"But bringing him to the ball . . ."

"I'll give him a press pass. He's a performer. The arts need fund-raising, too."

She makes a face, and even I can't believe I said that. "Faith . . ."

"Don't start. Please. Let's just get your speech ready."

She drops the subject for now, but I know we're not finished talking.

Maribelle runs in, her round cheeks pink. "We have a problem."

She holds up her phone. My mom looks at it for a second, and I see the way her face becomes steel, armor. I've seen that look so many times in my life. When she faced every teacher who told me I had an attitude problem, when she'd get hate mail from constituents that talked about her body, her skin.

"Slum it with Charles," Maribelle reads it out loud. The red posters are plastered all over downtown. Her face has gone from pink to a vicious red. "We've made it all this way without playing dirty. We can show them. Don't worry, Mrs. Charles."

"Those fucking bastards. I'm going to march over there right now and tear every sign down. I'll—"

My mom holds her hand up, like a queen silencing her subjects. "We will do no such thing."

"But—" Maribelle and I say at the same time.

"Oh, we will respond. I don't think the people of New Orleans are going to like these signs very much. Reginald will give his speech after mine."

"But, Mom. It doesn't always work like that. Having a better speech is part of the plan but we need something else."

Mom refills her coffee, and I think I was wrong. It's not that she's too busy to put things in her coffee. It's that straight black coffee is no nonsense. "I don't know why I'm surprised. Remember the last election cycle? They're just more and more of the same."

"More like *Moreaux* of the same," Maribelle snorts, then covers her mouth. "I'm sorry, that just came out."

But my mom's eyes are alight with something wonderful.

"Maribelle, you're brilliant," I say.

"Call the printer," my mom says.

AIDEN

"Look at you going on a proper date. On a weekday no less," Fallon tells me.

He's perched on my bed, flipping through the premium channels. "How come you get all of these?"

"Penthouse suite, baby. And not that I don't want you eating the food and beer from my minifridge, but shouldn't you be with your girl?"

"Woman, Aiden," Fallon says. "Woman. Robyn's getting her nails done and she signed up for some voodoo thing."

I pick out one of Fallon's ties from when he was on the road with the show. I go for a subtle blue one. Faith seemed to like the blue I had on before. My first attempt to tie it fails.

"You know, where I come from, con los santos no se juegan."

Fallon thinks on it for a moment. "You don't play with eggs?"

"*You don't mess with the saints*." I pull the tie off and throw it at him. "Seriously? Almost a year with Robyn and that's what you learn?"

"Spanish is hard. I'm old, I'm set in my ways." He gets up and tugs the tie between his hands. "Here, let me."

"Sorry, it's one of those stupid things that I never learned."

He nods, but doesn't bring up the obvious. My dad never taught me. When I was in high school, for some school dance my tía Ceci bought me a clip-on from the dollar store.

Fallon turns the tie this way and that. "My mom taught me, actually. When my dad would be too hungover to do his own tie she'd dress him. Then she taught me and made me promise to never be like him."

"You're not."

Fallon smirks, but I can tell he still doubts it because I still doubt it when it comes to me and my old man.

The tie is in place. He slaps my shoulder. "You ready, brother?"

I look at myself in the mirror. Charcoal-gray suit and blue tie. I run my hands over my brows, my freshly shaved face. A lock of hair keeps flopping over my forehead. On the outside I look fine as hell.

If my insides matched my reflection, then I'd be a wreck. My legs keep wanting to run away from me, running in whatever direction Faith is. But also far away from her because I don't want to do this. I don't want to watch the reaction on her face when I tell her that I'm not who I've said I am. Not completely.

"When are the guys getting here?" I ask Fallon, who's back to channel surfing and lands on the new Thor movie.

He doesn't even look up at me. "Tonight, I think."

"Wish me luck," I say and pocket my wallet and key card.

"Good luck," he says as I open the door, or I think he does. I can't hear him over the sound of my heartbeat bursting through my eardrums when Ginny walks out of the elevator.

FAITH

I find the dress that Angie didn't want to wear. The blue one that cinches at my waist and falls around my hips. It's a little formal for New Orleans, but there's something about today that makes me want to feel pretty.

I dodged a bullet with my mother, but tomorrow might be another story. She's not the kind of person who can take a lot of feedback.

I find matching underwear—a pale pink lace bra that pushes up my girls, and matching panties. I tell myself that this isn't a sex date. It's a friends date. I told my mother we were friends.

But friends don't dance the way Aiden danced with me.

Friends don't lick the way I did him.

Friends don't make your skin feel like fire every time they touch you.

Even thinking of Aiden makes my heart feel like it's disintegrating into bubbles. I can't catch feelings for a guy who's leaving at the end of the week. Part of me knows that my mother is right. I shouldn't bring him to the ball, because that's what you do for people who are serious. People who have a plan.

If that were so, I shouldn't go to the ball either because I don't have a plan. My future is as cloudy as the Mississippi, and yeah, maybe that's why I feel like Aiden and I connect so well.

I slip into a pair of black leather pumps and give myself a tiny spritz of perfume, then I'm out the door.

When I get in the car, I breeze down the streets and sing along to whatever pop star is new these days. I know the lyrics even though I don't know who's singing, but I need something to take my mind off the things I'm avoiding.

Aiden's mouth.

Aiden's body.

Aiden's d—

My phone buzzes for the third time in a row, so I check it at a stoplight.

Aiden: *Running*

Aiden: *Late*
Aiden: *Sorry.*

I throw my phone into my purse. Then I notice the neon purple lights of a shop on the corner. I pull into the parking lot. I realize I've forgotten something in my rush to leave the house.

I walk into The Big Easy Adult Sex Shop.

AIDEN

Ginny's eyes widen when she sees me. Her bright green eyes take stock of me. My hair, my tie, my shoes. "Don't you look dapper."

"*Dapper* is my middle name," I say and flash her a smile more sure than I feel right now.

She sticks her head out of the doors. "We have to talk."

"Pool?" I say calmly, but inside I'm a wreck. Ginny is here and Fallon is in my room and Faith is going to be here any minute.

I hop into the elevator with her, and when the doors close, she says, "Hold me."

There's something soft and sad about her. Even in her designer dress and large sunglasses, her hair coiffed into perfect blond waves, she looks *sad*. I wrap my arms around her and feel her tremble.

"What's wrong?"

She shakes her head. "I don't mean to dump this on you."

There are so many things wrong with this. She's paid me for a week of my time, but part of me, a sick, twisted part, cares that she's upset. It hits too close to home the way she cries. In my mind I flash to waking up in the middle of the night to my father shouting. He was always shouting about something. A leak in the bathroom, a doorknob that broke clean off, the way my mother arranged the meat on his plate. Whatever it was, it left her a wreck like this. And I'd hug her even though I was small, but I knew that it was the only thing I could do because I wasn't strong enough or brave enough to take on my father.

"What's wrong?" I'd say, and here, in this elevator, I repeat the same thing.

Ginny breaks apart from me and drags a finger under her black sunglasses. "My husband's work is draining. I shouldn't be here."

"Why are you here?"

The doors open and Ginny walks out first. She's a stunning woman when she's in public. It's dark now, but she wears those sunglasses anyway. Some of the younger girls around the pool watch her walk to the couched area in the corner.

I lag. It gives me time to text Faith that I'm running late, but my fingers have a mind of their own, so I end up sending three messages.

I don't look around the pool but stop at the glass doors. The air is cool, and the sound of emergency sirens and music horns and street crowd yelling melds into something that isn't quite music, but what I've come to understand is completely New Orleans.

I walk up to Ginny and point to the seat, as if we've just met. "Is this seat taken?"

A waitress rolls around and Ginny says, "A Hendrick's martini, dry with extra olives—and whatever he's having."

"Bourbon, neat."

Ginny takes off her sunglasses. I want to rage at the sight of the bags under her eyes, swollen from crying. "Since when do you drink something that isn't full of sugar?"

I smile, and her features soften. "This might be surprising, but while you were gone I drank so many hurricanes I made myself sick."

She throws her head back and laughs. "Oh sweetheart, that's a rookie mistake."

"Tell me," I say. "What's really wrong?"

"Without breaking the rules," she says. "My husband is involved in something that will come back on us."

"Legally?"

She shakes her head. "No, but it's ugly. I always thought I

knew the kind of person he was. But I don't. I don't know if I ever did."

"Is he hurting you?"

"Oh no," she says hurriedly. "Don't think that."

"I don't mean physically," I say softly.

Ginny places her hand on my face. "You're too good to be true, you know that?"

"I'm really not." I sigh.

"Reg has always been who he wants to be. We got married right out of college. Thought it would look good for his—Anyway, I didn't think I had many options, so I did it."

"What would make you happy?"

She looks at me for a long time, then her eyes flit past me to the city. "I don't know. I don't think about my own happiness a lot. Well, unless I'm outsourcing the company."

My stomach tightens. "That's a really nice way of saying *escort.*"

"You know you're my favorite. There's something about you that's genuine. Even if it's not."

The waitress comes over and sets the drinks between us. I take the bourbon and drink half. How does Faith drink this stuff?

"Why are you back in town early?" I ask her.

She takes a sip of her drink. Maybe she's not happy with her husband, but I can't see this woman who holds her pinky out to drink a martini living another life. "Business."

"Right."

"We're staying at the Monteleone. But I sneaked away. He thinks I'm out with my friends." She laughs.

"I'll be your friend," I say. I want to mean that.

"I thought we weren't going to lie, Aiden." She looks into the clear liquor and stabs an olive. "What are you doing with a woman like me? What am I *doing*? You're half my age."

I look at my phone. No messages from Faith. What if she comes up? What if she finds Fallon in my room? I look up, and sure enough, there he is. I can read the "what the fuck" on his mouth.

"You haven't done anything that you should be ashamed of," I tell Ginny.

"Just because we haven't had sex doesn't mean that my husband wouldn't have grounds to divorce me." She drinks more. "I don't want to talk about that. I'm sorry, he just makes me so—"

"Maybe it's time you think more about the things that make *you* happy. You're more than just the person you end up marrying."

"I wish I had your optimism, sweetheart." She laughs a bitter laugh. "Now, tell me where you're going looking like this?"

I look down at my shoes.

"Please don't lie to me. I can't stand more lies."

"I have a date, actually."

She smiles, and there's a tremble in her voice when she says, "Tell me about her."

I run my hand through my hair. "That would be weird."

"Take my mind off this, Aiden. Please."

"She's—" I can't seem to find the words. Nothing is good enough to describe Faith.

"Really? That amazing. Well, it's a good thing that I had to go."

"I'm sorry," I say.

She swipes her hand in the air. "Don't worry. I actually came here to break things off. My husband's assistant is breathing down my neck and if she got wind of you—even if we haven't done anything—I don't want anything bad to happen to you."

For the first time in the last handful of days I breathe easily. It's a weight that's been hanging over me.

"I'll move my things out," I tell her. "I understand."

"Don't," she says. "Room's paid for the week in cash. So I don't want to hear a peep about it. I'll wire you the money right now."

I push her phone down. "Don't, really. You didn't even see me. Honestly."

"Don't be stupid to turn down money, Aiden."

I shake my head. "It's not stupid."

"I'm sending it anyway. Donate it to a charity. Do whatever you want with it. But we had an agreement and I keep mine."

"All right." I look at my watch. Twenty minutes ago Faith texted.

Faith: *I'm on my way for real this time.*
And now she texts: *Here.*
"I have to go," I tell Ginny.
I hold her hand by her fingers. I kiss her knuckles. "Promise me you'll think about what I said."
"Promise me you'll treat her right."
"I will."
I turn around to leave. Fallon's still watching from the balcony, drinking my fucking beer. I give him a thumbs-up, which he returns with a less kind gesture.
"Angelique," I say, the minute I come through the doors. "Hey—"
That's the last word I get in before she slaps me across the face.

11

If You Only Knew

FAITH

There's no one in the store when I walk in. The only other time I've wandered into one is when one of my sorority sisters was getting married and they put me in charge of buying the most embarrassing toys.

I don't consider myself a prude, but all of the giant plastic penises in every color are arresting.

"Can I help you?" a slender white man asks. He's in a colorful tank top and he has the kind of facial expression that says he finds everything amusing.

"I'm going on a date and I want to make sure it's a night he'll never forget."

He tents his fingers and grins. "Direct. I like this. Backstory. First date? Third date?"

"Sort of third and maybe the last."

"A little mean, I like it. Are they adventurous? Reserved? Wildly explo—"

I cut him off. "I'd stay in the adventurous ballpark, but we haven't had sex yet. He's a bit more experienced than me."

"Well, you're lucky straight men are really easy to please."

I laugh. "I'm Faith."

Then he gasps.

Oh no.

"Faith Charles?" He takes my hand in his. "Don't worry. I won't sell your bedroom secrets to that terrible LePaige. Especially after she called my store lacking in vibrancy. Listen, bitch, the only thing that isn't vibrating is—"

"What was your name again?"

"Nando. How playful do you want to get? Because if left to my own devices, I'll change your life."

I adjust the thin purse strap around my shoulder. "Well, I don't really know what he likes."

Nando holds my arms out. "You're a vision. I'm not trying to shoot myself in the foot, but look at you. I'd start with some basics. Have you ever used edible underwear?"

"Once. It was messy. And those candy thongs are scary. What if he bites in the wrong place?"

Nando looks at me like I've grown a third eye. "They're for sucking."

Finally, I blush. "Oh."

I follow him down an aisle. It's like having a personal shopper for sex toys. There's an underutilized job position.

"This little gadget will have you seeing stars." He throws a vibrator ring into a basket. "Now for condoms, I'd go with these. They're better for your hoo-ha and seriously unbreakable. Like, I can fit my entire arm up to my elbow." He puts in a box. I add another. "Massage oil. This one isn't sticky and the smell isn't cloying enough to make you want to gag." He blinks. "Unless you're into that."

I burst out laughing. "I think this is a good start. I can't believe I'm doing this."

Nando rings me up and sighs. "I say that pretty much every Friday night."

I take my select trinkets in a discreet black paper bag that might be used at a boutique.

"Oh, shit," I say when I see my phone. "I'm late."

AIDEN

The sting of Angelique's hand is hard. Damn, she's strong.

"I know I probably deserve that," I say. I take a step back to give her room to seethe. "But can I know what it is I did?"

Angelique can't even form words. "I trusted you. I vouched for you. And you're with her?"

I suck in a breath. I glance over my shoulder to where Ginny is sipping her martini and looking out at the city. "It's not what you think."

"Then tell me, Aiden *Buenos Aires*. That's right. I looked up your name." She pulls out her phone. "I'm going to call Faith right now."

"Please," I beg her. "Please, just listen to me."

"Why?" Angie narrows her eyes at me. "Is that why you sat in front of me that night? Did the campaign pay you to fuck with Faith? Because that's beyond low, even for them."

"What? Why would her mom's campaign pay me?"

Angelique's brow is furrowed, but for the first time since she started yelling, she takes a breath. "Do you know who that woman is?"

"Ginny Thomas."

Angelique shakes her head. "You know what? I'm not going to be fooled by you again. You're probably a really good actor."

I reach out to touch her shoulder, but she slaps my hand. "Don't touch me."

I raise my hands and give her space. "Clearly we have a misunderstanding."

"This is what I know. I encouraged my best friend to have a one-night stand with you and it's backfiring on me because she's catching feelings for you and you're just using her."

I only hear one thing out of everything Angelique has said. "She has feelings for me, really?"

"Don't play stupid. You've been working with the enemy this whole time."

"Angie," I start.

"It's Angelique to you."

"Angelique. What enemy?"

"The Moreaux campaign hired you to seduce Faith and ruin her mother's reputation."

That name lights up something inside me. Mayor Moreaux. Faith giving that name to the reporter the night of the blackout. I stumble back and hit the wall.

I shake my head. "That's not what happened."

"Then tell me, Aiden. If that's your real name."

Ginny's husband's work. The things she said about him. They were always about *business* but she never specified. I try to find holes in her words. Something that should have alerted me sooner.

Faith is waiting for me downstairs.

My hair flops over again.

"Who are you?" Angelique asks.

"My name is Aiden Rios," I say and tug on the tie Fallon knotted for me until it comes undone. "I wasn't hired by the campaign. Ginny hired me. Just Ginny."

Angelique stares, confused. "What do you mean 'just Ginny'? Why would Virginia hire you if—oh."

Virginia. Not Ginger. My mind is spinning, each time trying to figure out some sort of clue I missed.

"I didn't know," I tell Angelique. "I swear. I know you don't have any reason to believe me. That night you met me it was a real low point for me. I thought I lost all my friends, my brothers because of a mistake I made. And Ginny hired me to keep her company for a week. Just company. We never—I never—She got called away that same day, though, and that's why I was alone. I didn't expect to meet Faith. I didn't expect to love her."

Angelique's eyes flash at me once again. "What did you say?"

The word hangs heavy in my throat. It strangles me. Because it has to be love, doesn't it? Even if I haven't felt it before? I know all the symptoms.

"I love her," I say. "I was going to end it tonight. I keep trying to tell her but I can't."

"You're a coward."

I nod. "I know."

"She said she's taking you to the ball."

I shake my head. "Undo my tie. I shouldn't go."

Angelique runs her tongue against her cheek and swears. "Look, don't tell her about Ginny. It'll wreck her so close to the election."

I make a strangled sound in the back of my throat. "I don't want to keep lying to her."

"Sometimes a lie is better than the truth. Leave town. Leave her alone."

And because it's the only thing I can think of, I nod in agreement.

"She's waiting for me."

"Then don't be late," Angelique says.

12

Nuestro Juramento

FAITH

When Aiden comes out of the hotel, my belly does that fluttering feeling. I squeeze my thighs because now that I know what's below the belt, I can't unknow it.

He gets in, but there's something off about him. His smile is tight. Not the usual happy smile he always carries. It's like he's trying despite himself.

"Everything okay?" I ask.

"Hmm?" he asks, distracted. He buckles his seat belt, hands nervous. Maybe he's just nervous. Then, he takes a moment to look at me. "You're stunning."

"You clean up nice yourself," I say. "So, I have a couple of things planned. Do you want to get dinner first?"

"Actually, is it okay if we walk around a bit? Wait, no, your shoes."

"I have flats in the car. They won't exactly match, but it's okay."

He leans into me and catches the bottom of my lip with his. "Thank you."

I park the car and lead him down the twisting streets. The weather is perfect this time, like the heavens are throwing a little luck my way after all.

He keeps my fingers threaded between his, a grip so tight it's like he's afraid to let me go.

"Okay, you have to tell me. Something feels really off."

"Do you remember the friends I told you about?" he says, and I nod as we weave through the Bourbon Street crowd. "They're in town this week and I haven't seen them in a while. I've been afraid of confronting them all day."

I lift my shoulder. "Well, sometimes the best thing to do is come clean."

"What about you? How was your morning?" he asks.

"My mom stopped by. Did you know your photo is in the *Gazette*? Not all of you, just, like, half of your body. But my mom asked me about you. I told her you're coming to the ball and she's fine with it."

"She is?"

"Yeah. Though, I apologize in advance for the interrogation you're going to receive from everyone in her campaign."

His fingers reach for his collar, like he was expecting to find a tie there, but instead, he fiddles with the first button. "I can handle it. So, where are we going to eat?"

"Have you ever had a po'boy?" I ask, and it's worth it just for the look on his face. We get to Pete's Po'boys and grab two seats in a dimly lit corner. "Sorry it's not a fancy place, but the food is amazing."

He takes my hand across the table, and my heart does that bubbly feeling again, like my insides are turning into champagne. "I love it. I can finally say I've been to a place where there's an alligator hanging from the ceiling."

I chuckle, but we both can't help looking up at the taxidermy of an alligator right smack in the middle of the ceiling, surrounded by light fixtures. There's a light bulb in its mouth, and the owner has arranged some dried grass to look like it's sprouting from the ceiling.

"That can't be real, can it?" Aiden asks.

"I mean, the owner is an avid hunter. When I was a little girl, I came in here and he told me a story about the time he made his first catch. He'd gotten himself lost in the swamp and thought he was fish food. But he followed this gator and it led him right back to where he needed to go."

"So he killed it?"

I brush the air with my fingers. "No! He caught the gator trying to kill his gator friend. It was very dramatic. The swamp critters never forgave him."

"You're fucking with me because I'm from New York."

"Is it working?" I lower my lashes and lean toward him.

His mouth hangs open as his eyes trace the whole line of my lips. It makes my skin heat up every time he does that. I knew I should have skipped the po'boys.

"Yes," he tells me.

The waitress comes over and takes our order. The place is bustling with people, abuzz with so many conversations that we don't stick out. Well, except for how overdressed we are. In the shadow of our little booth, we seem to fit in all right. The waitress brings over our drinks first. Two bourbon concoctions with ginger and lavender.

"What should we cheers to?" I ask.

"To the safety of all alligators," he says.

"You look like you have something on your mind," I say, after I take the first sip. The drink is refreshing in the heat of the evening.

"I've had you on my mind all day, Faith," he says.

I know, I know it sounds like a line. But the way he says it, without a trace of irony—I just don't know. I believe him. I let him take my hand in his. His thumbs trace across the tops of my hands. I can't think of the last time a man touched me like this. Like *holding my hands* was enough.

"I think I made a mistake," I say. I hardly trust my own voice.

His eyes are questioning. "What is it?"

"I should have taken you straight home."

We're leaning so far across the table that the little candlelight between us is warm against my chin.

"I mean, whatever happens tonight, we'll need some energy."

He's going to kiss me. I know he's going to kiss me by the way his whiskey-brown eyes search my face. He shuts his eyes and I would do the same. Except for the very inconvenient wait-ress who brings out our food.

Two po'boys. Shrimp and meatball marinara. I'm glad I have an entire pack of mints in my purse.

"Okay, you have to tell me your honest opinion," I say.

Aiden takes a bite of the shrimp. He shuts his eyes and bites so long that I think he's having some sort of attack. "It's not my tía Ceci's arroz con menestra y carne asada, pero, like, this is amazing."

I only understood half of that sentence, but it's enough.

When I first met Aiden, I knew he was the type of guy who enjoyed things. Food. Drink. Sex. Watching him enjoy the food of my city makes me want him even more.

We decline a second drink and can barely finish our orders. We take the rest to go. We fight over the bill, but I let him pay this one.

"Do you want to walk the food off a little?" I ask as we leave the restaurant. As much as I want to take him back to my place, or go back to his place, something is stopping me. I don't know if it's the vibes he was giving off before, or if I'm having second thoughts about being with him.

My mind likes to throw wrenches like that every so often. Angie says that that's why I'm single. But I know it has to be more than that. It would have been one thing if we'd had a fan-tastic one-night stand. But it was messy and awkward and it left me wanting more. Because I do want more of him. Holding his hand down the street even feels like being too far away. I shouldn't have these feelings for a guy I've only known for a handful of days, but I've spent more time with him than the ran-dom string of half-hour dates I've had the last two months.

It's time that's being compacted, used well. It's time I wouldn't trade for anything in the world.

He lingers in front of a Tarot shop. Voodoo Emporium.

"Have you ever had a card reading?" I ask.

He smiles that smile I love. "Actually, my friend Fallon's girl was at one of these places earlier today."

"They're in town?"

"Yeah, maybe you can meet them."

I bite my bottom lip because I want that very much. "Want to go in?"

"A nice Catholic boy like me?" he asks, but he's already tugging my hand in the direction of the shop. "When in Rome. If Rome had drinks this good."

The Tarot shop looks kitschy at first, but when we get to the second room, the altar they have dedicated to Yemaya is no joke. A man with heavy eyeliner, a sagging middle, and a long black ponytail comes out of the back. He dusts his hands of the scent of Chinese food that lingers in the air.

"What have we here?" he asks.

"Just some tourists in the Quarter," I say.

The man points a finger at me. "You, my dear, are no tourist."

I wink at him. I've never met the man before, but I like him already. He has a good *vibe*. Calm but strong at the same time.

"How much are readings?" I ask.

"Thirty each," he says.

I look at Aiden. "After you."

"I'm Harry," he tells us. "Do you want to both be in the room at the same time?"

Aiden and I look at each other and say, "Yes."

Harry smirks his thin, pink lips to reveal a soft dimple. He shuffles a set of cards with lush paintings of goddesses and knights and pages. Moons and stars are dotted in bright gold.

"Ladies first," Aiden says.

"Now, honey, do you have a specific question or are we thinking more of a general one?"

"What do people usually ask?"

Aiden sits beside me. The circular table is covered in a purple velvet cloth, and tiny white quartz crystals are dotted throughout, looking like tiny blinking eyes.

Harry sets the deck in front of me. "You're not usual people, honey. What do you want to know about? Job security? Family?" His deep-brown eyes flick to Aiden. "Love."

I do everything I possibly can to avoid looking at Aiden's eyes in this moment. The only thing I can't stop is the tickle right under my ribcage. Though that could also be heartburn.

"Just a general future reading is fine," I say.

Harry winks, not at me, but at Aiden. "Let the cards reveal themselves to you. Shuffle them. Break them into threes. Oh, I see it's not your first time around a set of cards."

"You would have done very well in Vegas," Aiden says, though a playful glare from Harry silences him.

I break the cards, favoring the middle. The last time I got my cards read was during a street fair last year. One of my college friends was doing it as a summer job and she had a deck her grandmama gave her. Though her grandmama was the real deal, Jolie not so much. She told me I was going to marry an actor and have four kids. I might as well have played a game of MASH.

Harry flips each card with a certain panache. There's a flair to his wrist, and each turn is accompanied by a very surprised little gasp. "Oh my, my, my. Very interesting indeed."

"What's very interesting?" I ask, though I'm trying not to laugh at his drama.

"Your cards are incomplete."

"What do you mean, 'incomplete'?"

"Well, you see this here is you. The Queen of Pentacles. And this here is the Seven of Wands. It crosses you. It means that your journey hasn't been easy. It's a classic line from work to the payoff. Here is the Queen of Swords. She's a strong character. It could be a mother figure, a boss, or someone with a feminine energy. It could be you as well."

"So I'm in the way of myself."

Harry purses his lips, but his humor is now focused. "That is a possibility. My mother always told me that the only way to move past an obstacle was to climb over it. But you can't climb over something when you're weighed down, bogged down. Whatever is holding you back, you have to: Let. It. Go."

I chuckle. "So then, what's incomplete?"

"See right here. This is the Ten of Pentacles. This is the bliss card. Utmost and total happiness. But it isn't in your ending, it's in your possibility."

"Okay, so I have to let my baggage with a mother figure go," I say, a little too dryly.

Harry places his hand over mine. "It sounds easy, but believe me, I know it isn't. And that's not to say that it guarantees you that happily ever after everyone raves about." He widens his eyes, almost comically. "Love is in these cards. I see four children."

I nearly choke on my own spit. "Excuse you."

Harry flips his thin black hair over his shoulder. "You dealt the cards, honey, I'm just the messenger.

"See this right here? With the exception of one wands and swords you have all pentacles. I see a man. A very fine, sexy, sculpted man." Harry is clearly looking at Aiden, who is visibly shrinking back to the edge of his seat. "Oh, here is the Knight of Pentacles. Very sexy, very dangerous. Be careful who you trust that little heart of yours with. Make sure they are deserving of that love. So many threes. That's a good number for you."

Harry is lost staring at the cards. I look up to see if Aiden finds this as hilarious as I do, but he's just as enraptured with the cards in front of me.

"The moon begins waning this Friday. It's going to be a time to shed all kinds of masks. Here, Justice symbolizes removing all the charlatans from your life. After that, once you LET. IT. GO you have a shot at this very fertile future."

I let go of a long sigh. "Whoo. Wow. Thank you."

"Do you have any questions for the cards?"

I look at them. I can't help but look at that final one. A couple under a rainbow and the knight. The thought that it could be Aiden makes that tickle in my ribcage grow. Maybe coming here was a mistake, even if it's supposed to be just for fun.

"I'm good, thank you, Harry."

I swap seats with Aiden, and he repeats the same movements as I did. Though his shuffling skills are not as good as mine.

"When's your birthday, hon?" Harry asks Aiden.

"October 26."

"I love Scorpios." Harry winks at me. "I love it. Now what do we have here? What do we have . . . here."

The last card he flips is the Death card.

"Now, don't be alarmed," Harry says. "It doesn't mean literal death. Out of all the cards, this one is my favorite."

Aiden has an elbow on his thigh, his hand toying with his perfect chin. "Why's that?"

"Because it means that all of this mess right here doesn't define you. I see a great loss from an early age. Recklessness. You haven't really had the opportunity to let go of the things holding you back. There's a great deal of wealth."

"That's not so bad," Aiden says, though his body is still tense from the first thing that Harry said to him.

"Maybe not, but there isn't any joy. But, ah, look at what we have here. The Ten of Pentacles. Everything in your life is leading up to this moment."

My heart gives a little tug. It's a feeling that I still reject. I want to reject it. Is it really that simple? Do I meet a gorgeous man at a bar and then, boom, the Ten of Pentacles? We get our happy ending. That's the thing about these places. They're designed to make you see what you want to see.

"What about family?" Aiden asks.

Harry nods seriously. "There's a break here. Something so deep that you carry it with you. You heard what I said about the waning moon? I want you to take a long, long salt bath. Do you like bath bombs? Don't knock it until you try it. Soak in a salt bath on Friday and then when you wake up the next day get ready to LET. IT. GO."

"All right," Aiden says, clapping his hands together. "Thanks, man."

"The answer to your other question is yes," Harry says.

Aiden's clear brown eyes flick up. "What other question?"

He points to the four cards that each have three symbols. "The cards show four kids in your future. Now, cash or credit?"

13

La Tortura

AIDEN

We come out of the Tarot shop a little dazed, but I still hold her hand in mine, even if we avoid each other's eyes.

"That was," I say, searching for the right word, but settling on, "interesting. Four kids. Damn. I didn't even think I'd get one."

"This is the second time I got the same reading," Faith admits, looking down at the floor. There's something cute and shy about the way she pushes her hair away from her face. "I guess no matter how hard I try I'm going to do what my mother always wanted."

"I thought you didn't believe in silly things like fate and Tarot cards," I remind her.

"You're right," she says, smiling. "I don't. So I won't worry and will go about my days."

But that's the thing. I do believe in silly things like the Universe and Tarot cards, and above all, fate. I'm superstitious. Can't help it. Grew up that way. But the thing the psychic said about my mother—if that's who he was talking about, it's going to keep getting to me if I don't stop my thoughts from cycling.

I don't want to think about those things with Faith.

I don't want to think about that reading anymore. *Let it go.*

He was talking about so many things. What do I begin to let go of? The memory of an anger so deep I haven't called my old man in years? The weight of my feelings for Faith? Faith herself. I have to let her go.

In turn, she has to let me go before she can have her happy ending.

But I'm weak. I'm selfish, and I can't let her slip away. I can't tell her the truth.

Not just yet.

Instead, I say, "I have to find a souvenir for my tía Ceci. Everywhere I go I get her a shot glass. I think at this point she has enough to have everyone at Christmas do a shot at the same time."

Faith blesses me with a smile. "Come, I think I know just the place."

She leads me down Dumaine Street, makes a right on Chartres, and then we're in Jackson Square, wading against the late-night traffic searching for bars or dark corners to make out. Inside a small shop with all kinds of trinkets and postcards. I can't decide between the glittery, gaudy tiny glasses, so I buy three. When we come out of the shop, Faith walks ahead of me. I reach for her hand to pull her back to me. Whatever our futures hold, I can't help but feel that in this moment, our hands should be entwined. She glances back, her eyes alight with something that tugs on a part of me I thought I'd hidden.

Then, there's a flash.

"A memory for the lovers?" an older woman asks us. She's got an old model Polaroid. It hasn't developed yet, but I can't imagine walking away without it.

I pay an exorbitant amount for the Polaroid, and we sit on a bench to watch the melee of people around us. A band of four people who look so different from each other but sound like they've played together their whole lives, dozens of small fortune-tellers with glittering tablecloths and tiny tea lights set over cards and around crystal balls. Artists painting on blank canvas, as if waiting for the moonlight for inspiration. Tour groups, mule-drawn carriages, and even a guy swirling batons on fire.

"This isn't a very good business model," I say, flapping the Polaroid in my hand.

"Don't do that," she says, and takes the white square from my hand. She puts it in a pocket of her purse. "The ink will run and make it blurry. And yes, usually they wait for you to say yes or no. But sometimes they just want to take a chance."

I stretch my arm around her shoulder, and she rests against me. She smells floral from her perfume and sweet with sweat. Some of the Tarot shop's incense clings to her clothes.

"I'm glad she did," I tell Faith. The square is better lit than other parts of the Quarter this late at night, and the soft yellow light makes her skin glow.

"So this is what you do. Travel the world with your boys and buy trinkets for your aunt."

"Well, you've got one part down," I say. I don't know if it's because I've been holding other stuff back, but I say, "I haven't spoken to my boys in a few weeks."

"Because of the mess you mentioned?"

I shouldn't be surprised that she remembers.

"So talk," she says.

I laugh. "It sounds so easy."

"It can be. I feel like we complicate things by keeping quiet and holding back. Have you apologized?"

"Don't you want to hear what I did first before you suggest I apologize?"

"Unless it's murder," she says. "And even then. If they're your brothers, your boys, you should at least try. Promise me you'll try."

And when she looks at me like that, I can't deny her anything. She could ask me for my still-beating heart and I'd find a way to rip it out of my chest. "I promise."

She sighs, glances around the square, and says, "It's getting late."

I nod automatically and take her hand. She takes a few steps, but I freeze.

Being in her presence fills me with so much of *everything*. It's like fucking sunshine and rainbows and all of that bubbly love crap that Fallon warned me about. I know I should say more. The thing that I was supposed to end the night with. But here we are, at the end of the night, and I can't bring myself to do the right thing, to be a good man.

"Faith," I say.

She whirls around. "Aiden."

Her smile makes my knees want to buckle, makes me want to fall at her feet for a chance to taste the sweet, hot wetness between her legs. She answers my inability to form words with a kiss. The pressure of her mouth against mine makes something in my heart explode, and my dick expands instantly. This woman is so fucking hot, she makes me forget with a single kiss, a touch, the barest fucking glance. It's like she sees right through me—not just a body, not just a good time.

I want to say more, but the wires in my brain are fried. "Can I walk you home?"

"I drove, remember?" she says. She takes a step closer to me. She knows exactly what her body does to mine. "Unless you want a nightcap."

Yes. A thousand times yes. I'm about to say as much, when there's a scream in the middle of the square. One of the fortune-telling tables has gone up in flames. At the center is a single flaming baton.

"Aiden, stop!" Faith calls me back.

But everyone has gathered, and the woman is in so much shock at seeing her cards scorched by fire that she isn't moving. It's going to catch on her clothes. I pull her back. Take off my jacket and use it to smother the flames. But whatever is in that fire only leaps up. I raise my arms to cover my face, but I feel the heat try to grab at me. I stomp on the jacket and table.

"Let it go, child," the older woman tells me. "Leave it."

My heart is drilling into the back of my ribs, when someone runs out of the restaurant across the street with a bag of salt. He covers the flames with it, and then there is only smoke. He slaps my back, asks if I'm fine.

But only Faith's relieved face matters. She takes my hand and pulls me out of the throng of people before we're trapped there.

"Bad luck is just following me," I say.

"Not luck," she tells me, reaching for my face with her gentle touch. "But you could have been hurt. Let me take a look at that."

I wince, but we stop on a dark street of closed shops. "Don't worry, I've had worse."

"You've had worse burns?" she asks, her thumb the only balm I need right now.

"I broke my wrist playing soccer once. My mom didn't even want me on the team because I hadn't hit my growth spurt yet. *Ow,* that hurt."

Her laugh soothes the sting of the small burn. She gets on her toes to kiss the spot just below it. "Better?"

"I've been told I'm too pretty for my own good so this might be a good way to make me look rough."

Her dark eyes bore into mine. "You don't need to be rough, Aiden. You're already—"

"Perfect?"

"I was going to say *wonderful.* But, yeah." Her voice lowers, like we're whispering secrets that we don't want anyone else to hear. That magnetic feeling returns when we're this close. Drawing closer and closer together until we're pressed against each other. She tilts her head up to me, her mouth seeking mine.

My heart races when she presses a kiss to that spot on my neck that makes me hard as diamonds. I touch her chin to guide her lips to mine. Her plush mouth is soft, so soft that we glide against each other. I meet her wanting tongue. Press my palms against her back and trace down that luscious spine of hers. Her ass was made to be worshiped, and I round out my hands along her thighs. I walk her backward, into a grate that rattles when I hit it. Voices and sirens ring out in the distance, music that doesn't seem to stop, and then there's the rapid, manic beat of my heart as she lifts her knee up and rests it against my hip. When I rake my fingers along her inner thigh, she sighs. When I drag my finger up to discover that she's wet for me, she gasps against my mouth, exposing her neck to me.

I kiss the tender spot. Sucking my way down to her collarbone.

"Do you see how much I want you, Aiden?" she whispers.

I want her, too. I want her more than I can admit. But this is supposed to be my great moment of honesty. My chance to tell her who I am. That I was Ginny Thomas's—Virginia Moreaux's—sugar baby.

All of those things are there on the tip of my tongue.

Just tell her.

But when she pulls away, her eyes full of adoration and passion, I'm too weak to tell her. Too weak to tell the truth, because I'm not strong. I'm not a good man.

There's a salacious whistle as a group of kids strolls past us. When I'm with her, I forget that we're not alone. That we're out in public.

"Was that my nightcap?" I ask.

"The night's not over, Aiden." Her smile is devilish as she leads me a couple of blocks farther to her car.

We drive with the windows down. The sleepy Southern streets cast a golden glow around us. I take her hand and kiss her fingers, the inside of her wrist where her pulse is frantic.

"That tickles," she says.

"I want to discover every part of you that makes you tickle."

I nearly jolt out of my seat when she hits the gas, and then we're zooming up the street. I think we run a light just before we get to her house. Faith looks at me, eyes full of secret whispers and kisses stolen in the dark.

And she says the words I want to hear her say over and over. "Come inside, Aiden."

14

Despacito

FAITH

In my house, in my bedroom, in the dark, I kiss Aiden.

I kiss him around the burn on his cheek. He thankfully let me put a salve on it. We didn't make it to the whiskey on my bar cart. We didn't make it past the front door without touching each other. His hands are everywhere at once, holding on to me with a fervor that almost scares me. Because I've never been held like this. Like I might disappear right before his eyes. Like he wants to make sure I'm real. Like he only wants me.

I push him onto my bed, a wicked smile widens on his face as he looks me up and down. I climb on top of him, straddling him on the edge of my bed. I can feel the outline of something in his pocket.

"What's this?" I ask.

He pulls it out and bites his lips as he draws out a condom. "Me making a wish."

I unbutton his shirt, surprised that my fingers are trembling with anticipation. That familiar tightness coils in the pit of my stomach as he lets me undress him. I lower myself to kiss the broad muscles of his shoulders. His chest rises against mine, his hands moving up from my calves and settling on my thighs.

"Faith." When he says my name, it feels like he's praying. He gathers my dress around my hips. We keep getting to this moment, and it's like something is trying to stop us. He believes in this all-powerful universe, but whatever that was, there's nothing to stop us now. I've waited for this moment for days.

I move farther up on his lap. A deep groan escapes his throat, because I know he can feel how soaking wet I am through my underwear. He wraps his hands around my waist and catches my lower lip, nips gently with his teeth. I return the bite on his ear.

"I want you," I whisper.

"I want you more," he says, kissing fast and hungrily across my neck.

I've never met a guy who likes to kiss as much as Aiden does. His full, warm lips dot kisses, like he's leaving breadcrumbs to find his way back. His clever fingers unhook the back of my dress, and when he tugs the zipper down, I wriggle against him. His cock twitches against my center, and I love the sound he makes when he reacts to me.

"Oh God, you're so fucking sexy," he moans, dragging his tongue across the tops of my breasts. He pulls down the lace fabric of my bra to release my nipples. They harden beneath the tickle of his tongue. I hiss when he bites gently.

"I want you inside me, *now*."

I feel his teeth against my skin when he smiles. "This time, I'm going to take my time with you."

"Tease," I say and gasp because suddenly, it's like we're dancing all over again, my spine arched back with one of his hands to support me. He kisses the space between my breasts, the place between my ribs that comes undone as he slides my dress down around my waist.

A deep, primitive growl escapes him as he lifts me into the air and flips me onto my back. He pulls my dress down my hips and over my knees. I help him kick it off. There's fire in his eyes when he stares at me.

"Why are you smirking like that?" I ask him.

"You're matching this time," he says, his eyebrow ticking up.

I finger the hem of my lace underwear. "Do you like it?"

"I would like them better in my mouth."

But he doesn't move. I reach for him because he's too far away and the absence of his weight on me is like losing something vital.

"Come back, Aiden," I whisper, tracing the same spot beneath my bra where his tongue just was.

"Tell me, Faith." He undoes his belt buckle, his voice gruff. "Where do you need me?"

I move my hands along the soft flesh of my abdomen. Rub down between my legs. "Right here."

"Show me," he says, and the hardness in his voice sends a thrill right through my core. "Show me exactly where you need me."

He pulls his belt in one swift movement and tosses it aside. Then he goes for his button.

When he unclasps it, I drop one of my knees to the side and let my fingers roam the top of my heat. I'm soaked right through. I push the fabric aside, unraveling myself in front of him. I thread my finger between my lips and find my clit. I gasp, surprised at how hard and sensitive I am.

"Aiden." I say his name. I rub circles around my clit with one hand and around my nipple with the other. My voice climbs an octave. "I need you."

He climbs out of his pants. There is absolutely nothing underneath except his glorious cock. He takes his dick in his own hand and strokes.

"Keep doing it," he tells me. Commands me.

"Not fair," I say, realize I'm pouting. I never pout. I've never done a lot of things like care about my matching underwear or touch myself like this, because girls like me should have restraint, control. Girls like me don't fall for guys like him. But when a shock of pleasure buzzes through me with my next stroke, I don't care what I should or shouldn't do. There is just Aiden and me and this feeling that I can't ignore.

He flashes a smile made for sin. "I want you to feel good, Faith. That's all I want."

"I'd feel better with you inside me." I press myself into the mattress. I lift my finger, watch him watch me as I bring it to my lips and taste myself.

He makes a sound that I can feel deep in my ribs because I've lured him back to me, his knees making the mattress sink on either side of me. He takes my wet, slippery finger into his mouth and sucks it clean. Kisses the inside of my wrist.

He nudges my thighs open with his knees. I can feel the heavy weight of his cock between my legs. I reach for him, but he takes my wrists and pins them on either side of me.

"So eager," he says playfully.

I wriggle beneath him to show him just how eager I am. The head of his cock slides between my wetness. I want to know what Aiden feels like inside me. And I know that this is dangerous territory I've never let myself explore.

"Fuck. Fuck me, you're so wet." He shudders against me, our bodies slick with sweat and desire. He keeps my wrists pinned down. His face is buried in my neck. "Everything about you sets me on fire, Faith."

"Fuck me, Aiden. Please, fuck me."

"Yes, baby," he says, letting go of my wrists, and finds the condom on the bed. He rips it open and slides it up the thick length of his cock. My heart skips a beat when he presses the head against my opening. I dig my nails into his back, and when Aiden slips inside, I could burst at the seams.

AIDEN

I wanted to take my time. To not have a repeat of the first time she put her delectable, unbelievable hands around my dick. I wanted to make her feel like she's never felt before. But I'm selfish. I couldn't wait. Hearing her beg my name, call out my name.

"Fuck me, Aiden. Please, fuck me."

How am I supposed to deny her? Wriggling her wet pussy against me. I grab her around her thighs and sink into her wet spot. I shut my eyes and bury my face in the crook of her neck. I feel the breath escape her when I inch inside. I can hardly breathe myself. She's so tight, her walls close around me. They nearly push me back out. She lets out a tiny squeal, and I'm desperate to hear it again. But I freeze, I don't move. I can't until I know she's okay.

"Am I hurting you?" I ask.

She shakes her head. I pull out. I need to hear her say it. "Faith? Look at me."

Her eyes are open. Her tits bursting through the sweet pink lace of her bra.

"No," she pants, and slaps my ass hard. "Come back inside. Please."

This time, I get in a little bit farther. I can feel the ripple of her walls around my shaft. If I close my eyes, I know this is the best dream I never want to wake from. I could bury myself inside her and never come out.

She slaps my ass again, and the shock of it makes me jerk deeper inside of her. She does it again and again, digging her nails in so hard that I think I'll bruise. And then I'm so deep inside that if I move, I'm going to fucking break apart, crumble into a thousand tiny pieces because I want to come all over her. Inside of her.

She wriggles against me, fucking me back. Her tits bounce up and down, and I press myself against her. Take one of her wrists and pin it back down.

When she cries out a moan, I catch it with my mouth. I pump my cock harder and deeper until she can't speak another word except my name, and the walls inside of her sweet cunt collapse around me, drawing the life out of me as she comes and screams my name.

It's the most beautiful thing I've ever felt.

It triggers something deep inside of me when she moans, "Come inside me."

In this moment I've never been as close to someone in my life as I am to Faith. I've fucked and banged and made love to women hundreds of times. So many times that sometimes I know I'm going through the motions, even when it feels good. But this—I don't think I've found the words for it. I am the spark of midnight on New Year's. Fire spinning, stars clashing, hearts racing. I am unraveling as the twisting, delicious feeling travels in my dick until it bursts, and I'm coming inside of her harder than I ever thought possible. I've been emptied out. My entire body wants to sink into her. A jolt of terror runs through me.

Because even after all of that, I want more.

FAITH

I haven't felt this relaxed in a long time. When was the last time I had a man in my bed? Share the same space? Fill me the way Aiden did. I don't have to think long on it before I realize that, yeah, the last man I dated on the real was two years ago.

But the last time I had someone in my home? That was longer. I don't let men spend the night. I'm no prude, but my sex life has always been perfunctory. Like I was trying to fill a quota of what I should be doing instead of my heart.

You can't think about your heart, I remind myself.

Not when it comes to Aiden.

This is what it is. Mutual itch scratching. Mutual needs being met.

Then again, if that were so, why is he tracing my thighs like I'm made out of the finest glass, like I might shatter if he holds me with too much force? Why do I have my arm and leg across his body? *Too* possessive. *Too* bare and intimate and all of the things that we are not supposed to be.

I let my fingers explore his fantastic abs. I don't usually like men that are so muscular. I love my men tall and beefy and thick. Aiden has definitely got the thick part covered where it counts. But he's got that dancer's build. Long, tight muscles I bet would chip my teeth if I took too hard a bite.

The thought makes me giggle. He traces the length of my jaw, guiding my face up to him. I don't think I'd ever get tired of the pools of honey that are his eyes. I get caught in them.

"It does a lot for my confidence that you're laughing at my naked body," he tells me.

My index finger makes a long line along the happy trail that points home. His dick jolts to attention when I do that.

"Not at you," I say.

"With me?"

"No. Just thinking about what it would be like if I bit you." I look back down at his abdomen. I feel something like satisfaction as his cock hardens with a single touch.

"It depends on which part of me you're biting," he says, his voice husky. "My body is yours for the taking."

That has my attention. Slowly I crawl back up on top of him. His erection is perched right between my ass cheeks. I can feel myself get wet, hot against him. I bet if I writhed against his abs, he'd make me come just with his muscles.

"Faith," he says, looking up at me in a way that makes a knot form in my throat. Why does he look at me so intensely?

"Aiden?" I shut my eyes and enjoy the slippery wetness of moving against him, and him sliding between my cheeks.

"I'd hate to be anything but a gentleman. But that was the only condom I brought."

"Oh," I gasp.

"Really?" he asks.

"Oh, no, not that." Well, almost that. I lower myself onto his chest, my breasts against his. His warm breath is sweet in front of me. "I bought some. They're in the car."

"Say no more." He gently pulls me off.

He slips his pants back on and grabs the silk kimono, all covered in pink flowers and leaves, that is hanging off my dressing chair. His thick head of dark hair is still, somehow, perfectly arranged as if by witchcraft. "You're going to scare Mrs. Friedman next door."

"With this face?" He touches his cheeks and chin. "I don't think so."

And then he's gone, and the absence of him is stark.

"This is ridiculous," I say out loud. I have to speak it out loud. What would my mother say if she visited me right now? The chances are slim, since it's past midnight, but still. I know what's on the line. I know what this means to my mother. But I can't stop wanting him. It's primordial, feral even. If I'm honest with myself, it's downright lust. Maybe the reason we're magnets is because we're both hurting in different ways.

And then a seed of doubt strikes me. What if we're not colliding because we're magnets? What if we're more like runaway trains and the inevitable crash that the psychic warned about. The Death card. The Seven of Wands.

"You don't believe in that stuff," I remind myself.

I go to my bathroom. I finish taking off my underwear and wash up quickly. I rub my favorite lotion on my arms and elbows. There's a dew on my cheekbones that no highlighter can replicate, and my mouth is plump from the way he bit me.

I squeeze my thighs at the memory of him. Because I can't stop myself. Because this train is on its course.

When I hear my front door open again, I flick the lights off except one and lean against the bathroom doorway.

"You're right. I did scare someone. But I don't think he minded—" He stops abruptly, short of dropping the little black bag in his hands. "Not that I don't miss the lace, but damn. You're so fucking sexy."

"How sexy am I?" I love the way he looks at me. It drives that sensation deeper into my core.

He throws the bag on the bed. Pushes my kimono off his beautiful muscles and onto the ground. "So sexy I feel overdressed. Look at what you do to me, Faith."

He steps closer, and even though he's only across my room, it's like wading through a raging river to get to him.

"What I do?" I let my finger slide from my collarbone, down my breast, and around my waist.

"You. Just looking at you. Being near you. The first day I looked at you my dick was so hard I couldn't even stand." He undoes his pants, his heavy erection bared for me. He keeps walking toward me like I've sunk a hook into him and I'm reeling him in. I shouldn't like this power. But who says I shouldn't? "Today, walking to your car was the longest minute of my day."

I feel myself pout. "Just your day?"

"My week. My whole fucking month. When I'm away from you? I can't think straight. I see your face when I go to sleep and when I wake up. When I fuck my own fucking hand because I couldn't be inside you."

I take his hand in mine and guide it to my aching apex. He lets go of a hard sigh when he sinks a finger in. He lowers his forehead against mine. A sharp hiss is on his tongue when I grab his thick cock. I stroke him just as he's stroking me, until we find a rhythm, until my legs are tumbling and I have to brace myself against him.

"Not yet," he whispers in my ear. When he withdraws his hand, I get that empty feeling again. Like I'm missing a part of myself.

He retrieves the bag I bought and makes himself at home in my bed. I love the way he looks there, like the king of the castle. My castle. My king. Like he's always belonged here.

"What do we have here?" he chuckles in a dark, devious way. How is he so good at being the perfect amount of playful and sexy? Most guys try too hard to be only sexy, but Aiden—he's effortless. "Oh, I like this."

"It was an impulse purchase," I say, climbing in front of him and resting on my knees. It's like fucking Christmas and I'm waiting to see if he likes the present.

"I've never used this," he says, holding the vibrating ring between his delicious fingers. "Or this."

"It's supposed to make you feel tingly. Down there."

"Mi reina," he says, squeezing my inner thigh with one hand. I love when he calls me that. "I don't need a gel for that. I told you. Everything about you makes me feel like that."

"Not everything," I say, skeptical. We've all heard that line.

He lies on his side, propped up on one elbow, and I mirror him. "Everything. The way your nose wrinkles when you're thinking hard about something. Your compassion. How you care about things others don't. Your mind. Your opinions."

"I have a lot of them."

"And you speak them. You aren't afraid to speak them. And every word you say is just made sexier by your absolutely fuckable mouth."

"You want to fuck my mouth?"

"I want to fuck every part of you." He brushes a thumb across my top lip. My eyes fall on the long stretch of his dick, the heavy head wet with precum. I take his thumb into my mouth and roll my tongue around it.

"I want to be crushed by your tongue," he says, a dark growl at the back of his throat.

I inch closer. Magnets. Trains. Whatever we are. I need to be closer.

It's strange being naked like this. Not trying to cover up the lines of stretch marks on my thighs I've had since my first growth spurt, or the way my breasts bounce when I edge closer to him. Though by the look of where his eyes fall, I know he doesn't mind.

"Your tits. God, your tits. I could suck on them for hours. For days."

"Be careful of the promises you make."

"Let me show you." He loops his arm around me and closes the space between us, burying his face between my breasts. I lean back and sink into the sensation of his thumb massaging one nipple while he nips at the other with his perfect teeth, tongue lapping at my skin like I'm water and he's endured a drought.

I hook a leg over his thigh and dig my heel into his ass cheek, and then we're tangled again. I never want to unravel from the feeling around us.

Aiden groans against my tit when his erection and my wet heat are lined up. And then he comes up for air. Only a moment, and then his eager mouth is on mine. I get a little too excited in the way I wriggle against him, so slippery that in the next movement I can feel the thick head of his dick press against my opening. The pressure of it sends an alarm through both of us, and I gasp.

"I'm sorry," he says, and pulls back. "I wasn't trying to—"

"I know, I know." I take his face into my hands and kiss his unblemished cheek. "I think we both got carried away."

That's a terrifying thought. Because I've never let someone inside of me without protection. I've never wanted to. But with Aiden, I want to feel every part of him, his skin, his muscle.

"Look," he says. "I just want you to know that I always wear a condom. Always."

His eyes are a bit terrified, and I wonder if it's for the same reasons that I'm afraid. That it felt too good. That I kind of want to know what he feels like raw and bursting inside of me. I've never known a man that way, and that heart-pounding fear takes root within me alongside the lust. I wonder if that's why I'm so drawn to him.

"It's a good thing I'm prepared," I say, and reach for the condoms on the bed, which he rips open in a frenzy.

And I'm glad I bought a whole box.

15

Sin Contrato

AIDEN

I make it back to my hotel in a hazy dream.

I take a Lyft blasting ska music, and I'm pretty sure it runs on old cigarette butts and Abercrombie & Fitch spray. But it doesn't matter because I spent the night buried deep inside of Faith Charles.

Her mouth, her sweet perfect pussy, her grabby hands.

You know, it's nice to be appreciated. But the best part of being with her is the face she made just before she came. Every. Single. Time. Like the sensation appeared out of nowhere, like she's never really ready for it, but when it hit her, it was a surprise, a wish granted—damn. I could die a happy man if the last thing I saw was her O face and I was the one who made her feel that good. It's starting to get me hard again, so I breathe in the cigarettes and high school football-player cologne and my wood goes away.

I walk into the Hotel Sucré wearing the same clothes I left with yesterday, minus a beautiful blazer, and the doorman gives me a knowing fist bump.

"What's up, paisa?" I ask.

"Life's good, can't complain," he says, and I feel that in my bones.

I go to my room to shower and change real quick before doing something that I promised Faith I'd do.

Although, I did break my promise to suck her tits for hours. I was distracted by the rest of her, soft and plush and mind-bendingly sexy.

But this is not a sex kind of promise.

This is something that I've been dreading for weeks. I hit up Fallon, and he gives me the information that I want.

I head two floors down and find room 413.

When he opens the door, I'm not sure if he's expecting me or if I never truly noticed how calm Rick Rocket is in demeanor. He's wearing what his version of casual clothes is, trading his brightly tailored suit jacket for a button-down and a pair of artfully distressed jeans. His dark blond hair is freshly cut and swept back. A few months shy of forty, Ricky is a man who pulled himself up by the bootstraps to create an empire of naked men and pleasure. And I'm among the most recent line of fuck-ups who let him down.

The silence that stretches between us goes on for too long, and then I'm like a fucking little kid toeing the carpet with my Adidas flip-flops and not saying a word. I never had an older brother to look up to, or a father who would reprimand me in the ways I might have needed. But I think that if I had, and I'm not talking about my dad, this is the feeling I might have had. Like he's not mad but "disappointed." For so long, I felt like I wasn't missing out on anything. Then being with Mayhem City and Ricky became the family I'd never truly had.

"Are you going to stand there all fucking day?" Ricky asks. Even after fifteen years in the States, he has a remnant of his Aussie accent just like I have mine. "Or are you going to hug me like a man?"

And maybe it's the emotional residue of last night's fuckfest (which I haven't 100 percent processed completely) or it's because I've missed him and all of my brothers. Whatever the reason, I wrap my arms around Ricky and squeeze tight. He's shorter than me but super built in that Hugh Jackman-in-peak-Logan kind of way. He gives me a solid pat on the back.

"Hey," I say, because I'm weak when it comes to more than just Faith. ,

"Took you long enough to write, didn't it?" he says. "Come in."

I walk into his balcony suite and make myself at home in the living room. From here there's a view of Dauphine Street, and it comes with all of the noise. It's ten in the morning, but it's New Orleans, and also, it's us, so he takes two beers out of the fridge and pops them open. We cheers, and for a moment, I'm about to ask, "What should we cheers to?" But that's my thing with Faith.

"Salud, my friend," he tells me, then drinks.

"I'm sorry, Ricky," I say, and launch into everything I've wanted to say to him since I quit. "I got wrapped up in all of the things I never had, all of the things that I wanted."

"I could have helped you get that. I thought that's what we were all doing."

I shake my head, drink my Abita beer, and keep talking. "It's just when this woman approached me about starting her own group, her own show, I thought it would be an amazing idea. I didn't know she was trying to screw you. I didn't think she'd leave me high and dry when all was said and done. It's what I deserved."

We do that thing guys usually do, stare down the bottle necks of our beers instead of look at each other in the eyes. Why do we do that shit?

"You were primed," Ricky says, leaning back into his arm-chair. I feel like I'm begging my mob boss to spare me a round with a gun, Al Pacino–style. "I was ready to hand everything over to you, Aiden. But do you know what my mistake was?"

I couldn't bear it if he said the mistake was trusting me. My whole life that's the one thing that I longed for. Someone who believed in me. Someone who put their faith in me.

And just like that, I'm thinking of her again. Faith's incredible smile, her asking me to promise that I'd do this. Even if it hurts, I'm glad I'm in this moment.

Something catches in my throat, and I take a swig of the cold brew to wash it down. I say, "I'm too immature?"

"That's the thing!" Ricky scoots forward. "You're not immature. My mistake was thinking you were ready. Don't get me wrong.

You've got years on where I was when I was twenty-five. At your age I showed up to this country with two hundred bucks in my pocket and a pair of croc-skin boots . . ."

"Which you still have," I finish for him.

"You're damn right I still have them," he says proudly. "It took me years to get to a place where I could build something. I thought you were ready, Aiden."

"I know."

"Then why did you fuck me over?" Ricky shouts. In a way, I've been wanting this shouting. It's cleansing. What did Harry say? Waning moon and all that. Before I think of letting this go, I have to face it. "Why did you leave the very week you were scheduled to take the show over for yourself? You didn't even tell me. You just *left*. What happened?"

I look down at my toes. I look into my beer. I think back to that day. "Margaret was waiting for me in the location she'd found. She'd been paying me a lot of money to keep her company at the blackjack table. I didn't have to do anything, just blow on her dice before she rolled. My usual deal. She was an heiress of whatever."

"Of almond milk," Ricky says, and I could fucking punch Fallon in the throat for running his mouth.

"Anyway, when I think back on it now, I see myself. A life-size toy there for her amusement. Because that's what she was doing. Fucking amusing herself at no cost to anyone. Except it cost me everything.

"One night she said she wanted to start her own show. She had a hotel, a slot, she just needed a guy to run it. I thought that if I turned her down, it would just slip through my fingers. I thought about everything I didn't have and I got greedy. I got so greedy and I don't think I'll ever be able to take that back. When I realized she'd been fucking with me the whole time, I panicked. I'd already no-showed on you for three days."

"We thought you were dead."

"I'm so sorry, Ricky."

He shakes his head. Those blue eyes of his stare past me to

the bright rays that break through the curtains. "Yeah, well. Can't change what's happened, can we?"

"No. But I want you to know that if I could, I'd do it."

I know Ricky's stance on people who screw him over. I've never seen it myself, but I've heard the stories.

"Well, you're doing all right for yourself these days. Fallon let me into your penthouse last night. We drank the whole minibar."

I let my face fall for a moment. When I was a kid, I'd always wanted brothers, and the time I spent with the guys of Mayhem City was as close as I was going to get. And I fucked it up. "He told you everything, didn't he?"

Ricky rests hands behind his head. He kicks his pedicured feet on the ottoman in front of him. "Oh, yeah. Says you've got yourself a girl here. But you met her while you were, *mm*, on call."

I can't escape the look he gives me. "It's weird. I've never—I mean, I don't—I mean, I have—Only, not with her—It's just . . ."

Ricky throws his head back and cracks up. I really do have the best kinds of friends in the world. "My boy, you are in trouble."

I swallow that familiar knot in my throat that forms every time I want to talk about Faith but I can't. "I know it. Believe me, I know it. I was supposed to tell her the truth yesterday. About what I do. Who I am."

"Who you are and what you do aren't always the same thing. Sometimes one is a means to an end."

"I don't think everyone sees it that way. Fallon didn't think so when he was with Robyn."

"Yeah, well, Fallon can be wrong, too. He's still an entertainer. Even if he's not a stripper. Why do you think he's here this weekend?"

I didn't think of that. "He said he was spending time with Robyn."

"I'm sure that's part of it. But I want to expand. That's why I'm here. That's why Fallon's here. That's why I'm interviewing local choreographers."

"You're going to go on the road *and* keep the Vegas slot?"

"That's the dream." Ricky finishes his beer and opens another one. Keeping up with him is almost a game in itself, but I do it. Because I want his forgiveness. Because I want my brother back. "I could have a spot for you here if that's what you wanted."

My heart starts buzzing. Here. New Orleans. Ginny and I are done. The only thing that was stopping me from telling Faith how I feel about her is that I didn't think I'd stay here. I didn't think I could. But if that's what Ricky's suggesting, then this could change things. Possibility fills my chest, and the first person I think about telling is Faith. But she's with her mother, handling campaign things. And I realize, maybe I shouldn't. Because a mayoral candidate doesn't need a male stripper as a son-in-law.

Son-in-law. What the fuck is wrong with me? Aiden Rios might believe in a lot of things, but marriage is not one of them.

"There is a whole lot of shit happening in your head right now," Ricky says. "And I want to help you deal with it, I do. But you have to tell me, Aiden. What do you want?"

I want him to forgive me. I want to run and find Faith and kiss her, find every secret part of her that makes her sigh those delicious noises she made last night. I want her to choose me. I want her to choose me despite what I have to tell her.

I want to dance. I want to dance with her in my arms. Fuck. I thought I'd let it go, but a part of me craves the center stage.

"I don't want to tell you one thing and then change my mind," I tell Ricky. "But I've missed you guys. I've missed the show."

"But do you want to be back?" he asks, always a straight shooter. "Do you want back in?"

"Can I think about it?"

Ricky nods a few times, tugging on his short beard as he gives me the once-over. "Fallon says you've got a masquerade thing next week. Do you have a tux?"

"I'm living out of a suitcase," I say, but I'm sure Rick Rocket travels with a tux no matter what. "No. I was going to rent."

He makes like he's going to smack me, but smooths the side of his hair. "Have I taught you nothing? Finish your beer. I'm taking you to my suit guy."

"You have a suit guy in New Orleans?"

Ricky smirks that devil-may-care smirk. "I have a suit guy just about everywhere."

16

Lovefool

FAITH

"You look mighty happy," Sunny, my nail tech, says, a telling look in her bright green eyes. Her braids are piled high on her head, giving her the look of wearing an artful crown.

"I'm always happy," I say, and follow her to one of the rows of pristine tables.

"You're always pleasant." She takes the seat across from me. "There's a difference."

"You're too much," I say, not wanting to spill about Aiden. But something in my heart bubbles like the tang of champagne after a good shake. When she sits and takes a look at my situation, she purses her lips in a way that lets me know I'm not off the hook. "This new place is great. Even if it's a little farther from me."

Sunny's the only person I let near my nails. Once, I went to a place where I got an infection from a nail clipper. I almost lost a finger. When I was growing up, my mother and aunts always insisted that we had to look our best. Put your best foot forward to the world. Someone is always going to have an opinion about what you wear or what color you paint your nails—or ask if your hair is natural. I never believed them until I went to school and started internships in conservation agencies. When I came back home, finding Sunny was the best thing that could have happened to me after nearly losing a finger to some foul nail clipper. When she moved to a luxury spa, I was just glad it was in the Garden District by me.

"Well, thank you for bearing the traffic to come see me," Sunny says, getting to work with my usual blush-pink color. She sets up the UV machine, brings the emery boards and all.

"Actually," I say. "I want something different. Let me see your reds and pinks."

"Finally. Can you let me give you some extensions, too? Maybe then you'll stop biting your nails."

I pull my hand out of her intense inspection. "I do not bite my nails." Then add "Anymore."

Because for a long time, I was bloodying my thumbs raw from anxiety. It's gotten better, and treating myself to this every two weeks *definitely* helps. It's not a long-term solution, I know. I go through the red and pink palettes. There's one shade, a bright red that looks the way Aiden makes me feel. A red that is bright and full of life. The red of azaleas and the sway of his hips against mine. The red of kisses stolen on dark streets.

"Faith Charles, is that you?" A cheerful woman's voice snaps me out of my Aiden reverie.

It's probably a good thing, because I have to cross my legs to calm the pulse between my thighs. The downside is the person sitting at the station beside me. The place is packed with clients, and it's just my luck that Virginia Moreaux sits next to me.

"How are you, Mrs. Moreaux?" I ask, and stick my hands into the warm water Sunny has put out for me. There's no reason why this woman's presence should make my heart rate spike. I'm glad I can keep my fingers busy with the smooth marbles at the base of the water bowl.

"Please, call me Ginny. It's been a long election season for all of us. I hope you don't mind if I sit here. My usual girl's out."

"Of course not," I say.

Virginia Moreaux, the first lady of New Orleans for two election cycles, has always been immaculately dressed. Her family comes from old Massachusetts money. It was her grandfather who lost it all, then her grandmother left the old man, took his two kids, and moved down south to start over. She found success in leather goods and started a small empire. Virginia More-aux might be married to a caricature of the Monopoly man, but I respect the women in her family. She even has a scholarship program under her maiden name for high school girls in Louisiana. That doesn't mean it isn't awkward to see her after her husband's campaign has tried to slander my mother.

"What've you got going on this weekend?" Sunny asks me, trying to save me from having to talk to Virginia.

I hold my hands out for Sunny to dry them. Then she gets to filing them almond shaped. "Just quiet nights in, you know."

"I heard there's a new club going to open soon," Sunny says. "Lots of business coming in this next year."

Lots of business that may or may not hurt the city in the long run. Virginia's husband created policies that would allow for other companies to get bigger tax breaks than the local ones. It's not blatant, but written in small ways. We look at each other at the same time, and I wonder if she's thinking the same thing that I am.

I smile, and she smiles, and it's on the edge of awkward.

"Faith, you're so young," she says. "I know I'm just being a big old buttinsky, but live your life! You're only twenty-five!"

"Twenty-nine, actually," I say and laugh. "Next month. I've always been okay with staying in."

"I wish my Lena were more like you," she says. "Don't get me wrong. She's got the Campbell spirit—starting protests with her friends and boycotting nearly everything in sight. I blame my own mother."

"You're a Campbell, too," I remind her, amused that this is what Virginia Moreaux worries about.

The woman sighs, her hand out for the nail tech to file into short squares. "A mother's worst fear is that she won't do right by her kids. I just want her to succeed. I want her to have all the things that I didn't. Travel the world. Fall madly in love."

"Didn't you do that?" I ask, trying my best to not be judgmental. "I remember seeing pictures of you from when you were younger. You and Mr. Moreaux in Italy and Hungary."

Virginia takes a deep breath and smiles. But I've lived my life so long with my mother being in the media and in front of audiences and cameras and constituents. I know what a fake smile looks like. The kind that masks a deep hurt.

"Oh, of course." Her voice is airy. "What about you, dear?"

"Well, after my mother wins," I say light enough that we both chuckle amicably and everyone around us eavesdropping chuckles as well, "I'd like to return to conservation. There's so much of this city that we can't lose to developers."

Virginia's smile becomes genuine. "The apple never falls far from the tree. But what about love? Anyone special in your life?"

I shake my head. "Not really."

That's when Sunny snorts. And I could kill her. The last thing I need to be doing is talking to Virginia Moreaux like she's my love therapist.

"Now, why don't I believe that?" Virginia says. "You're positively gorgeous. You're educated and you're your own woman. I can see why some of the local men would be intimidated."

"You flatter me," I say, trying to match her tone. "There's someone. He's sweet. Kind. I took him to the conservation center."

Virginia's big green eyes go wide. "My, you really put that boy to work. Wherever did you find him?"

I can't tell my mother's opponent's wife that I picked up a man at a bar. Besides, why am I telling her all of this anyway? All I know is that there is a fluttering sensation in my chest when I think of Aiden. It's a great big butterfly that turns into a thousand little butterflies, and those go on and on. I feel sick.

"A mutual friend set us up," I say, which isn't not true. "He's from New York. Which is weird."

"A city boy," Virginia says. "Even better. Make sure you take him for a dinner at Sylvain. I'm sure you have your own connections, but if you can't get a table, drop my name."

I do, as a matter of fact, have my own connections. "Thank you, I appreciate it."

Sunny starts painting the azalea red on my nails, and she makes a face that tells me she also thinks Virginia is too much.

"A New York boy," Virginia continues. "I do hope his football team isn't set. That might present a conflict with your father."

I laugh. "It's not serious, don't worry. Plus, I don't think he's into football. He was born in Colombia but grew up in New York."

"Does he call you 'mi reina'?" Sunny asks, and the memory of that phrase makes me see that shade of red behind my closed eyelids. My brother-in-law does that."

I answer with a restrained chuckle. Beside me Virginia has gone rigid. I shoot Sunny a wink because maybe that's all it took to make the first lady of New Orleans blush.

We go through our manicures in pleasant chitchat, commenting on the new menu at Galatoire's and how we hope it doesn't rain on the day of the masquerade ball. She no longer pries into my personal life, and other than parties, we don't talk about the campaign that has linked us this way.

"What a pretty color," she tells me as I examine the bright shade, so strange after my usual muted pinks and beige. "Very exotic."

I cringe inwardly at the word, but smile all the same. "See you next Friday."

There's something strange about the worry frown on her brow. "Will you be bringing your not-so-serious gentleman?"

Aiden in a tux? "That's the plan."

"Good for you. Good, good." She takes a deep breath, pulling her purse open to fish for her lipstick and compact. When I was little, I always admired how she was so put together, like a Barbie. That was before I realized how trapped Virginia Moreaux always seems, a deer skittering around a forest she doesn't know. She draws on her blush-pink lipstick. My mother doesn't get to bother with lipsticks because the campaign managers tell her that it's distracting. And I wonder, why do women always get relegated to two very different types of people? "Take care of yourself, darlin'. It's important to find someone that makes you radiant from the inside out. Someone who sees you for who you are and not who the world wants you to be. That's how you make love last, I think."

Sunny and I trade confused glances. "Time for your facial, Faith."

I don't have a facial scheduled, but I can tell she's giving me an out.

"Thank you, Mrs. Moreaux."

And I'm left wondering why a woman like her would say such a strange thing to me.

17

Deuces Are Wild

FAITH

"She said what?" Angie says. She's in my backyard in front of the fire, holding a glass of pale pink rosé in her slender hand.

I told her about my meeting with Virginia Moreaux. She stares into her glass so long I think she's trying to figure out if something in there is pollen or a bug. I walk round the patio chairs and settle in with my own glass.

"It was really strange," I say, scratching my scalp right behind my ear. "But you know, she's always been weird. Last year during a fund-raiser, she spent half the time in her room drinking and crying. I only noticed because we passed each other in the hallway. It's so weird."

Angie breathes in long and hard, the way she does when she's about to drop a truth bomb, or tell me she's bored with my subject. Really, it's a terrible thing she does, but I wonder if she does it to keep me on my toes.

"Faith."

"Angie?" I giggle.

"Why are you giggling?"

"I mean, I thought you would have been all over me after yesterday."

She frowns like she truly doesn't know what I'm talking about.

"Aiden," I say. I almost feel stupid saying his name. Aiden. Ayyy. Den. "He spent the night last night."

"He did, did he?" She licks the underside of her lip. "I thought you two were done."

I shrug and grab the bottle of wine from the chiller. "I don't know. It was supposed to be a one-and-done thing. He was so embarrassed about the first night. I was embarrassed, too."

"You got yours, though," she says.

And we cheers to that.

I take a sip, and the dry, cold wine coats my tongue. The sun shines through the trees gently blowing in the autumn breeze. "I know it doesn't make sense. But you're the one who told me that I don't take risks. I always do what's expected of me."

"I like the nail color choice," she says.

"It's more than that. When I'm with Aiden, I feel like a different person. Like I'm willing to be myself in ways I wasn't before. I'm still me, it's just like I'm waking up after being asleep. You tell me all the time that I'm hiding in my mom's life instead of living my own."

"Faith," she says. "It's just dick. You can find some anywhere."

I grab the pillow and throw it at her. "Why do you have to be so crass?"

"Have you met me?" She gets up, her coiled curls bouncing as she goes to the deck to grab two bottles of water.

"Do you not like Aiden or something?"

"I'm the one who pushed you at him." I recognize the guilt in her voice.

"You didn't push anything I didn't want. I wanted him from the moment he stood in front of me."

"I just want you to be careful. You haven't had a relationship in two years."

"It's not a relationship," I say, tracing my finger around the rim of my glass. "I'm not dreaming. I mean, I kind of am. But I know that he's not staying for a long time. I know that it's not permanent. I just want to enjoy the time that we have together, you know?"

"Good," Angie says.

The sound of a bell rings out from the front. I slap her knee. "Get that. It's him. I have to change my clothes."

She huffs and puffs, and I give her a kiss on the cheek as I duck into my bathroom to change out of my pajamas.

AIDEN

My entire body is buzzing being back here. I get out of the Lyft and smooth down the front of my shirt. I squeeze the bouquet of flowers and look at my reflection in the glass of her front door. Jeans, button-down, and a deep-red blazer. She didn't want to tell me where we were going, and I figured this combo will make me look equal parts casual and professional.

I don't expect that she's going to take me to some function where her parents are going to be. That's not where we are. I want to think she'd give me a heads-up, but you never know.

My thoughts flash to the first school dance I ever had. I was eleven and money was tight, so my mom didn't have enough money to buy me new clothes. So she tailored one of my dad's shirts. My ma was fucking magical with her sewing machine. She made me a tie out of the bottom of navy-blue curtains. The shoes were borrowed from one of the older kids in the neighborhood.

"You look great, papito. No matter what you wear," she said. Then she made the sign of the cross over my body and kissed my forehead.

Truth is, I don't know if I looked terrible or not. I remember that there was a boy in my school who made fun of my "Dollar Store Outfit." And the girl that I liked who laughed at me. And the guy's friend who saw a thread on my shoulder and pulled at it, so the whole shoulder came undone.

I can't fucking think about that shit. That was the past. This is the present. The future, if I'm even a little bit lucky. I slap my cheek and hold the flowers behind my back and ring the door.

"What do you think you're doing?" she asks me.

"Hey, Angie," I say, my body deflating a little at the sight of her. But then panic surges again. Did she tell Faith about Ginny? Did she blow up my spot?

"You can relax," she says, letting me inside. There's a glass of wine in her hand, and by the way she rolls her eyes at me, I know that I'm in the clear. "Faith's getting ready."

"Listen, Angie," I say.

"Angelique."

"Listen, Angelique," I say again. "I know I told you that I was going to tell her the truth but I couldn't."

"So you took her to bed instead."

I blank. "Wow, you're really straightforward, aren't you?"

"Are you not used to forward women?"

I shrug and take the seat across from her at the kitchen is-land. "You should meet my tía Ceci. I have a feeling you'd get along famously. Anyway, I'm going to tell her."

She shakes her head. "Don't."

I frown. Run my hand along the side of my hair. "I'm really getting whiplash here. I don't know what to do. Everyone in my life is telling me the opposite thing to do. Fallon is like one thing and Ricky is another. You're a whole other category."

"Listen to me," she says, and her sweet accent dances with the wine on her tongue. "None of us matter. I've never seen Faith as happy as she is these last days with you. She's no fool. She knows you're leaving."

Only, with the opportunity that Ricky's presented me with, I'm not sure if I am. Would I really stay if Faith asked me to? I never planned on being here, on staying. Then again, I never planned on meeting her. On tasting her. On finding myself deep inside her beautiful, sweet pussy.

I clear my throat. "I appreciate the advice."

"Don't appreciate it," Angelique says. "If you hurt her, I'll cut off your favorite part of your body."

"My hair?" I ask, and wink, and even Angelique throws her head back and laughs at that.

It's the perfect moment, really, because that's when Faith walks into the kitchen. In dark jeans and a blue top, she looks casual and sweet. Her hair is in soft waves over her shoulders, and I want to lick that sticky gloss off her mouth, feel the back of her throat.

"Well, I'm glad you two are getting along," she says.

Faith takes me to a small diner called Millie's.

We stand out, but I think I stand out about most places when I'm here. There are some girls at a table coloring the thin place-mats covered in alligators and fish, their hair segmented in rows of braids with colorful bows. A row of old men in fedoras and dress clothes line the diner's countertop.

When they all see Faith, they have a smile reserved for her, and I know that she's brought me somewhere that means a lot to her.

"It's nothing fancy," Faith says. "But my mom worked here when she was putting herself through college."

She sits in the booth across from me. I take her hands in mine, loving the way she receives my touch with a tender smile and the flutter of her lashes. I feel her cross her legs, and I wonder if the flutter applies to the spot between her legs.

"Hey, stranger," a young woman says. The waitress has dark skin and a yellow dress that places her in a different time period. "What do we have here?"

"Aiden," I say and hold my hand out.

"Jade," she says, giving me her fingers, like I'm meeting royalty. It seems to be in good humor, and Faith is giggling behind her menu.

I follow Jade's lead and kiss the top of her hand. "Good to meet you, Jade."

"Jade, oh my god," Faith says, and hides behind the menu as if I can't see her. "We'll have some pecan pie and coffee. Where are the folks?"

Jade exhales like she's been holding a great burden. "They left me all by myself. Went down to Pensacola for their anniversary. Don't worry, they'll be back for the primaries."

"There was no doubt in my mind," Faith says.

"Milk and sugar?" Jade asks us both.

"Yes," I say, and she runs back behind the counter.

Jazz music pumps from the speakers in the corners of the diner. There's a lot of wear on the ceiling, but the countertops are clean and shiny, like they've recently been replaced. I take Faith's hands in mine again. In the soft afternoon light, with her hair down and her cheeks glowing like she's been thoroughly fucked for hours, I feel like the proudest man alive. Because I put that glow there. At least, I hope I did.

"I like your nails," I tell her, holding up her hands. The lacquer is smooth under my thumbs.

"You noticed," she says, genuinely surprised.

"I notice everything about you, Faith."

"It's not something men usually do," she says.

"That's crap," I say. "If a guy doesn't notice it's because he's too busy to care or he actually doesn't. When I was a kid, I watched as my dad ignored the way my mom got her hair done and tried her best to look nice for him. To make him happy. I told myself that I would never be that way."

"So you pay attention to show affection."

"And because I love looking at you. I could look at you every second of every day and never be tired of it."

She narrows her eyes at me, like she's trying to figure out if she can call bullshit on my words. She doesn't.

"Well, what I noticed when I saw you was that this is a jacket I haven't seen before." She leans forward. Her fingers trace the front of my blazer. Even through the layers of fabric, her touch ignites a primal want within me.

"I took your advice and met my friend Ricky," I say, holding her hands up to my lips. I kiss every knuckle. "He took me shopping."

That makes her laugh. "I'm sad I missed it. Was there a montage of you trying on different outfits? Because I'd pay to see that."

"I'd pay to see that, too," Jade says, appearing with the tray of our food.

"I wouldn't," one of the men at the counter mutters into his coffee.

"Go on, get," Faith says, and shoos the grinning girl away.

"I hope you're ready for the best slice of pie you've ever had," Faith tells me.

I grab a fork. "I have to tell you, I've never had pecan pie."

Her eyes widen. "I'm about to change your life."

I lean forward, lower my voice so only she can hear me. "You already did that last night, Faith."

When she closes her eyes, I can see her long lashes touch her cheeks, and that motion is so sweet, so sexy, so telling of what she's thinking about that I'm hard. I'm so fucking hard at Millie's diner holding a forkful of pie. All because of her eyelashes.

"Talk to me after you've had your first bite," she says.

It really is the most delicious thing I've had in a long time. Well, second, when it comes to her.

"This party next week," I say, leaning back in the booth. "Should I do anything to prepare for it?"

"Like what?"

"Like meet your parents? I don't know, I feel like I might be crashing something important. I just don't want them to be surprised when they see me."

She takes another bite of her pie. "My mom has already run a background check on you."

I nearly choke on my food, and drink the scalding-hot coffee to wash it down. "She has?"

"Yeah, I'm sorry. It's a security thing. But you don't even have a parking ticket."

I grin. "It's a good thing, since I've never had a license."

"How do people from New York even function?"

"It's a secret called the subway. It takes you almost anywhere you want to go and it's almost even on time."

"You seem nervous."

"I've never met a girl's parents before," I say.

"Not even in high school?"

I grin. "I stopped going to school dances after junior high. And I never had dates. I told you, I was a late bloomer."

When she looks at me like that, with her chin resting on her hands, I find it so easy to talk.

"My mom's intimidating, but she's even worse once you get to know her. My dad's a teddy bear. Just don't tell him you've seen me naked and we're clear."

I burn my tongue on another sip of coffee. "Good to know. I doubt he'll want his daughter dating an unemployed dancer who's going to be crashing with his best friend and his fiancée soon."

"Uh, your fellow unemployed friend prefers the term *in between* jobs," she says. "I had a small trust from my grandmother and I put it all in my house. Now I just have to figure out the rest of my life. And why are you going to be crashing with your best friend? What happened to your room?"

I clear my throat. "It was only booked for a week and they won't extend it because the place is full. Something about American football."

She glances around. "Down here it's *just* football. And just for the next two weeks, you might want to be a Jets fan and not a Giants fan."

"There's hockey in the South?"

Faith stares at me blankly for a long time. Even Jade, who is folding napkins while listening in, nearly drops a fork.

"I'm kidding," I say, holding up my hands in defense.

"*Anyway,*" Faith says, tapping her finger on the top of my hand like she's sending some Morse code up to my chest. "Hm. I don't know if this is weird or what, but you can stay with me."

"Really?"

"You're staying through the ball. The least I could do is save you the trouble of shacking up with your friend."

"Stay with you." Something about repeating those words fucks me up inside. Not in a bad way, like I'm going to run out of here. It makes me want to break apart in this seat, like something that has to be inspected before being put back together to make sure it works. It's like my entire body is being rebooted and I don't know what my primary function is.

This tells me that I have to stop watching science fiction

movies when I can't sleep. And also that I shouldn't move in with Faith. Even if it's for a week. I've known her for a week and I'm coming apart at the seams.

So I say, "I can't wait."

She holds her coffee cup in the air. "To slumber parties."

"I'll cheers to that." We both drink, and I feel my phone buzz. It's Fallon, a selfie of him and the others at a bar. It's a stupid thing. It doesn't make any sense. What I'm about to ask Faith is too soon. But this timeline is already wrong. "Hey, do you want to meet my friends?"

She tilts her head to the side, that youthful little scrunch on her nose.

"Aiden, I would love to."

FAITH

When we walk into the lounge, I'm not sure if Aiden is clinging to me or if I'm clinging to him. The Daisy is so new to the Quarter that the couches still have the new-leather smell. The walls are dark red, with white sconces of light, and aluminum roofs that remind me of 1920s speakeasies. Old-school reggae floods the room, and I find myself moving my shoulders as we get to the small group tucked away in a quiet corner.

It's still early in the night, so the music isn't so loud we can't hear each other. There are so many guys I can't exactly remember who Gary and Vinny are, but I'd pick Ricky out of the group without having met him. He's the best dressed out of them, and the most charming. Even more charming than Aiden, if that's possible. His blue eyes wink at me, and his close-cropped blond beard brushes the back of my hand.

"My lady," he says.

Aiden wraps a hand around my waist and shoos Ricky away. They all laugh, and someone offers me a drink. I order a scotch on the rocks with a twist, and they laugh when Aiden orders a hurricane.

"What?" he asks. "They're mad good! Robyn, help me out."

A young Latina with ropes of black hair over her shoulder

smiles. She's sitting perched on a guy Aiden introduced as Fallon. They're the only ones in a couple, with the exception of two of the guys whose names escape me.

Robyn holds up her drink. "I'm with you. They're delicious."

"So, Faith," Fallon says. "What are your intentions with our Aiden?"

"Okay, we're leaving," Aiden says, smiling as he takes my hand. One of the bearded guys pulls him back so we're on separate sides of the wraparound couch.

"Come, Faith," Robyn says, and Fallon gives up his seat so the two of us can sit together. "It's just us girls. And a bunch of bros. You're lucky because usually they're running around naked."

I catch Aiden's eye to let him know that I'm fine. That I can tell how much they feel like family. It's something that I'm used to. A light hazing whenever someone new comes along. I've never done it for something that wasn't permanent, but it's still part of the fun.

"Don't worry," I say, "I got a preview."

They make *ohhhhh* noises, and on Aiden's side he's pulled into conversation with three of the guys and Ricky. I want to ask how Angie's audition went, but I also don't know if that's a line I shouldn't cross in case it didn't go well.

"Have you been to NOLA before?" I ask Robyn and Fallon.

But just then the waitress rolls around with a tray of drinks, and I take my scotch and Aiden takes his hurricane. It is almost a foot tall and has fruit that don't even belong there.

"That's extra," I say. "Even for a tourist drink."

"A toast," Ricky says. He stands, tugs on the bottom of his black velvet blazer. He taps his finger right at the center of his torso. "To always remembering where our family is."

We cheers, and when I catch Aiden's eye, he moves his lips. I can't be certain, but I think he says, *To us.*

"What was that?" Robyn asks me, catching the exchange between us. She playfully nudges my arm, her brown shoulders have recent bikini tan lines.

"Oh, it's just this thing Aiden and I've been doing," I say.

Fallon chuckles, like he knows something Robyn and I don't. "What's so funny?" Robyn asks Fallon.

"I just like being right." His green-blue eyes are like sparkling gems, and when they fall on Robyn, all of her, they light up even more. "So, Faith, give us some recommendations. We might actually be staying here a little bit longer."

"How come?" I swallow a sip of my drink.

"Well, Ricky's looking to expand. It's not definite. But just in case we find ourselves here for a little while."

At the thought of Aiden here, my heart gives a hard squeeze. I do my best to not look at him, but it doesn't last for long. He's all smiles, that flop of his hair falling over his eyes. I want to reach across the couch to move it. Then I realize, Aiden being here for longer could complicate things. Good, bad—I'm not sure. All I know is I hate the idea of *thinking* about our inevitable good-bye. I'm the one who pushed him to talk to his friends again. Maybe there's something to this fate universe woo-woo stuff. Maybe . . .

I drink my scotch, but even that makes me think of him, because it's like imbibing the color of his eyes. My mind goes through all of my favorite places in town.

Fallon lowers his whiskey and ginger and points from me to Aiden. "Tell Robyn about the swamp."

Robyn takes my hands in hers. "Oh my god, I want to go. Aiden said you took him into the wilderness."

"I did not." I look over to him and stick my tongue out. "We have very different definitions of what *the wild* means."

"She almost turned me into gator food," Aiden shouts over the music.

"Those chicken legs?" A tall blond man, almost blinding to look at, says. He slaps his beefy hand over Aiden's thigh. "You skipping leg day, bro?"

"He really hasn't," I say, just because I love Aiden's body so much I can't bear to think of someone disparaging its glory.

They fall into a bevy of howls and laughter. We get another round, and the blond guy, Patrick Halloran, begins an ab contest.

"Don't mind Pat," Fallon says. "He's the middle child of three brothers and didn't get enough attention."

Robyn shakes her head, leaning into Fallon. They're so comfortable together that their happiness radiates.

As if he's reading my mind, Aiden's at my side.

"Do you need a judge for this ab contest?" I ask him, taking the hand he offers me. Maybe it's the whiskey, maybe it's the red walls, the dimly lit room, but I let my fingers wander up his shirt and along the happy trail over muscle.

I look over my shoulder. Robyn and Fallon are kissing so sensually, I can't believe they haven't set fire to their corner of the couch. Ricky is consumed by something on his phone, and the other guys have abandoned their contest for the pool table in the corner.

"Come here," he says, pulling me against him.

My body goes willingly. Pressing myself against him is like arriving to a destination I didn't know I was trying to reach. We stumble down a dark corridor. It's a series of VIP rooms that are marked *reserved,* ready for tonight's festivities. There's one that's completely empty. The furniture hasn't been set up, except for plush gray walls.

"Wait," I say, and he stops kissing and lets go. I point into the empty room and step inside.

"Faith, what are you doing?" Aiden asks, but he knows what we're doing because he follows, his whiskey-colored eyes bright with mischief.

I shut the door and twist the lock.

His eyebrow raises as he presses his fists on either side of my head. "Someone could try to get in here."

I kiss his jaw.

"The furniture isn't set up, Faith," he says, nuzzling into my neck.

I slide my fingers into the front of his jeans. "Then fuck me standing up, Aiden."

He makes a grunting noise as he presses himself so hard against the wall, I think we might melt into it.

I knew I should have worn a skirt the moment he parts my

knees with his and rubs his fingers between my legs. I shut my eyes against the feel of his thumb searching for my center and finding it right away, like a road he's committed to memory.

"I've thought about fucking you all day," he says. "Even while we were sleeping."

"I know," I say. "I could feel you when you woke up this morning."

He grabs my hips and flips me around. The movement is so fast that I squeal. He lines his rock-hard dick between my ass cheeks.

"Is this what you felt?" he asks against my ear.

I lean into him, my hands pressed against the wall in front of me. I can't find my breath for a moment, my heart is racing so fast. "Yes."

"Tell me what you want, Faith."

All I can answer with is a moan. "Touch me."

He moves a hand around me, finds the front of my jeans, and snaps the button open.

I feel his forehead press between my shoulder blades, his legs tremble as his fingers slip inside me.

"Your pussy is so fucking hot and wet."

"For you," I say. "Only for you."

"This is my pussy." He slips in a second finger, and something inside of me jolts in response to the way he drums them back and forth and I rock myself against his hand.

"You're going to make me come," I say, moving my hips against him.

"That's all I want, baby. To make you come with my fingers, my dick, my mouth."

He pulls out his fingers and brings them to his mouth. "You taste so sweet."

Then, Aiden grabs the sides of my jeans and slides them down to my ankles. I reach behind me without turning around. I pull the zipper strained by the bulge within. He lets go of a hard sigh when he's free. There's the metallic rip of a condom.

"Aiden." I say his name, full of anticipation.

He places a hand on the back of my neck. Drags his nose from there to my ear. "Say my fucking name again."

"Aiden," I say, harder.

He holds his cock by the base, toys the top of it between my legs, at my opening. I push myself back, but he teases me. Grips the back of my neck. It's rough and delicious and I want more of it. More of him. I can't stand it, so I turn around. I place my hand on his hard, beautiful ass and pull him against me.

"I need you to fuck me right now," I say.

He scoops up my weight in his hands, keeps us upright by sinking us into the wall. All of the breath leaves my chest when he slips inside of me. Traps my mouth with his as he slides his swollen, hard dick in inch by inch.

He kisses me like he hasn't done it before, devours me like I'm the last slice of pie. I wrap my arms around his neck, and he bounces me up to keep me from sliding.

"Deeper," I whisper into his ear. He rolls his pelvis against me, pushing farther in until my voice is strangled. I've swallowed him whole. I want to keep him inside of me. He moves fast and hard. The wall is thankfully sturdy, the bass of the music thumping to the rhythm of us, until my belly's ignited with the spark of his essence. I need something to hold onto, and I want to grab hold of every part of him.

"I'm going to come," I manage to say.

"Oh, God, Faith," he says, grabbing hold of one of my knees. I can feel the walls inside me constrict, tighten around his hardness, and when he buries himself within me so hard, shockwaves pulse from my core.

And then he follows, his breath heavy and hard and spent.

AIDEN

When we exit the empty room and return to the others, it's clear exactly what we were doing. Partly because we were gone for so long and neither of us smoke, but mostly because the smell of Faith's sex clings to me.

We say good-bye, and I'm fucking proud of the flush on her perfect cheeks.

"Thank you for coming with me," I say.

She glances up, a smart smirk as my reward. "That was a first for me."

"Meeting someone's friends?"

"No, silly. Finishing at the same time."

"Me too."

"I want to try again," she says in that way she has of making my heart race.

The closest thing is my hotel room. It's going to be empty tomorrow, and the room *is* the penthouse suite. It expects more sex than it's had.

We kiss all the way up in the elevator, and I know if she only had on a skirt, I'd be so deep inside of her I'd graze her cervix with my dick.

I let us inside, and for a moment, the fear of everything I am, everything I've been doing, hits me. What if Ginny surprised me here? No, she wouldn't because she's the one who called the whole week off.

"Do you want anything to eat?" she asks. "I just realized the biggest thing I ate today was pie."

"Of course," I say. "Order me a burger, medium rare."

I walk through the room and look for anything that might be out of place. I know that at this point I'm paranoid. No, not paranoid, guilty. Because I know that even if I've never had sex with Ginny, it matters that she paid for this room and that she's the whole reason I'm here.

Maybe that was what the Tarot reading was talking about. Letting go and all that. Because everything is going to be fine with me and Ricky and it gives me something to consider. A prospect. A job. A life. A woman.

A woman who makes me come alive in a way I didn't think possible. In a way I thought was missing from me. This whole time I thought that maybe I was built wrong. That the reason I could have random hookups, the reason I could get paid for my time, was because I didn't care.

Only, now I care. I care because I want every part of me to be Faith's. For her pleasure and hers alone.

I hear the click of the phone in the bedroom. Then the rustle of clothes. The familiar snap of elastic that makes my dick salute like it's the first day of basic training.

I walk toward my room, and I feel like I'm wading through the best dream I've ever had. Because Faith Charles is spread across my bed on her belly, propped up on her elbows, ankles crossed behind her.

"I'm starting to think you like having sex when you might get caught," I say.

"Who's going to walk in?" she asks.

"Room service?"

She rubs the mattress in front of her. "Then you'd better get to work."

I unbutton my shirt in such a frenzy, a button goes flying off somewhere. My pants and underwear land in a heap on the floor.

"Leave the socks on," Faith says, harkening back to that first day.

I climb on the bed, and part of me wonders how I can joke around while I'm naked with her. Some women try too hard to act sexy, like it's a game, but with Faith, I want to smile and laugh and act like we've done this a million times. I want to get to that million, and I want to be able to say that it still makes her feel good.

"I never noticed this," I say, and trace the delicate arrow tattoo on her ankle. It's pointed toward her toes, like she is only ever meant to go forward. I love being so naked with her that there are still things for me to discover.

"Freshman year rebellion," she answers and rubs my dick. As if she even needs to do that to get my attention.

I rip open the condom, and this time she helps me get it on. I love the way my dick looks in her hands. The way she cups the base and runs a wet finger across my balls.

Faith climbs on top of me, her luscious tits pressed against my chest. She's got a face that was etched by the hand of God, and when she sits up and sits on my cock, I'm blinded by her beauty.

I arch my back to push into her tight cunt, and she pushes right back. I lick my finger and bring it to the cluster of nerves at her center. She moans harder when I rub her little clit, and she sinks so completely against my dick that I tremble at being all the way inside her. She reaches for my hands, shuts her eyes, and holds on. She rocks against my dick, her breasts bouncing so much that I do a full fucking sit-up just to take one into my mouth and suckle on it.

She screams with the shift of my dick, like I've found a part of her that makes her wilder, wetter. She holds me tight, and I'm afraid I've hurt her.

"Don't stop," she begs, her voice climbing half a dozen octaves. "So good, don't stop."

I've had a lot of sex and I know what gets me off. But never, in all my life, has a single sharp cry made me want to come so fucking hard. I grab her by her shoulders, her legs are draped around me, and I press her down on me. I choke on my own pleasure as she tightens, writhes like a snake, the ripple of a wave reaching out to snatch me, and then I'm coming hard and long inside of her and she's crashing and tightening around my dick so hard that it's like she's drawing the life out of me with her pussy.

We collapse onto each other for a moment. Just in time for the door to knock with our food.

Food that goes cold because she unwraps another condom and I'm so ready to lose myself in this woman that I don't care if I starve.

18

Heartbreaker

FAITH

Sleeping tangled in Aiden's bed is terrifying because of how normal this feels. He sleeps on his side, his lips slightly parted, his hair flopped over the side of his face. I'm not sure why I can't sleep. I should be tired, and I am, but part of me is wired with *feeling*. All feelings all the time. I don't think I like feeling like this. His hand is pressed on the soft skin of my belly, and for the briefest moment I think of what it might look like in a different time. A time when my belly is expanding with life, his and mine.

That's why I can't sleep. Because I can't deal with thoughts like that. I'm not sure where my career is taking me, but fantasizing about having a baby with a guy I just met isn't in the cards. Even if that guy is as sweet and kind and giving as Aiden. I suppose it also helps that he has a big dick. It rests against my thigh, and I reach out to trace the tender pink head. My pulse thumps at the base of my throat. My thighs ache and I feel rubbed raw in the best way.

I giggle at the thought of waking him up with kisses. I love the way he reacts to my touch. At the movement of my ribs, he mutters something, and then turns around in his sleep. He takes his arms with him, and I know I shouldn't miss someone who is three inches away from me.

But I do.

I miss Aiden filling my best parts with his. The way my heart plummets through my stomach when I'm near him, when I think of him. He's going to stay with me for a week and then what?

Are we just these moments to be remembered some time later? Are we helpless to what's prewritten in the universe, some cards stacked and shuffled and drawn at random?

The idea that we don't end up together makes my chest ache in a terrible way. That's why I can't sleep.

So I sneak out. I write a note and brush a kiss on his cheek. Then I dress and head out of the hotel at seven in the morning. There are still people partying, and for the second time in my life, I'm one of those stumbling home after a long night in the Quarter.

Angie would be proud, I think. My mother would give me a quiet stare and tell me to think of our image. My daddy—well—he doesn't seem like the murdering kind, but I don't believe he'd approve of the way I act when I'm with Aiden. Reckless. Wild. Impulsive. He brings out a part of me that I never let myself explore. I wonder, am I confusing this adventure with—love?

I shake the thought as I get into my car and drive home. I pick up a giant iced coffee at the Dunkin' Donuts drive-through and scarf down a Sausage Egg & Cheese. This is a series of firsts. The first time I'm driving home after a long night of sex. It's actually not even safe for me to drive right now because I might close my eyes, close my legs at the thought of Aiden. Aiden Peñaflor, who can move his hips better than any man I've ever met. It's the first time I've wanted to rip a condom off someone, to feel them bare and unobstructed inside me. The first time I've had six orgasms in one night.

The first time I've left before the other person woke up.

The first time I wanted to say *Screw it all*—the election, the pressure, the expectations—and just get back into bed with Aiden, where everything is safe and good.

The first time I nearly shouted "I love you" while I was in the middle of coming.

I pull into my driveway and do a double take. The front porch definitely has the furniture I bought over the summer, and the lawn ornaments are being eaten alive by my front grass, so I know it's my house.

But there's someone waiting for me on the porch chair where I like to read my paper and drink my coffee on most mornings. Mornings that are not today. I grab my half-eaten breakfast sandwich and my coffee, the warm day melting the ice already.

The woman sitting there looks familiar, but I can't place her. Not at first.

She doesn't belong in this memory I'm trying to create. One of cozy postcoitus whispers and the man of my dreams.

"Something I can help you with?" I ask Betty LePaige. She's not in her usual body-hugging colorful suits, clutching that irreverent notepad between fingernails sharpened to look like claws. You have to have claws in an industry where you can't always trust your sources, I suppose. That's why I always preferred animals, water, earth. For their constancy.

Betty stands when I get to the top of the porch. In modern gym clothes, and with her hair still wrapped up in a scarf, I can tell she must have rushed out of her house. A visit at seven thirty in the morning isn't casual or even friendly. Nervousness floods my gut like a sputtering volcano. There's an envelope in her hand. The flat kind that people usually slip under doors or pull out of trench coats in the middle of parks, depending on what movie you're watching.

"Is this about my mother?" This is the first time I've raised my voice at a stranger.

She stares at me, a small but imposing woman. "In a way. I have something that concerns you."

"Me?" I glance around the street. Some of my neighbors are walking their dogs, taking themselves out for a jog before the day gets too hot. "Come inside."

"I won't stay long," she says, but still follows me in when I open the door. My eyes rarely leave the envelope in her hand.

This is the first time I'm afraid of what an envelope may hold.

Not even when I got into my undergrad and grad programs was I afraid, because I knew I had the grades and I had the recommendations. I was good on paper.

"What is this about?"

"I want to be honest here and start off by saying that I've been hired by the Moreauxs to find a story on you." She crosses her hands in front of her, the envelope still clutched in one.

I try to think of what I could have done. Aiden. Taken Aiden to the refuge, to the nightclub. I press my hand on my chest to steady my heart. It couldn't be pictures from that night at the blackout, because they would have surfaced sooner. Me with my mouth on a man's crotch in public, albeit pitch black. Me getting fucked against a wall in a brand-new room where the furniture hadn't even been put together. Me going into a hotel room and leaving so early in the morning.

"Why would they ask you that?"

"Because your mother is clean. Your father has nothing in his past worth mentioning. And they're getting desperate. Your mother is polling higher than he is by thirty percent. They want something. Anything."

"And that right there is what will upset them?"

"It's about that boyfriend of yours."

I scoff, put on my best imitation of my mother. "The people of New Orleans won't care about a former male entertainer."

Betty raises her eyebrow but doesn't smile. "Perhaps not. But I believe they would be interested in this. Something that the Moreauxs are not prepared for."

She's holding that envelope right in front of my face, and so I snatch it. I press it against my belly. Aiden's hand was just there.

"So what? You're going to try to sell this to both sides? I suppose you have multiple copies."

"Contrary to what you might think of me, Miss Charles, your mother is a great inspiration to me. I took her humanities course when I finally decided to go back to school. No one has this photo. It's the only copy. I deleted the file, but I have others. Like I said, the Moreauxs won't want that getting out, even if they've already paid me for my labor."

"What do you mean?" I'm trying to wade through the sludge of her words. What wouldn't the Moreauxs want to see?

"I'm sure I'll see you soon," she says, and leaves me standing here.

I don't lock my door. I don't do anything at all except hold this thing in my hands. I know that I have to look at it. I know that I will look at it eventually.

So why can't I?

I shut my door and take my breakfast to my bed. I don't bother to wash my face or get out of my clothes. I take long, even breaths because it's like being asked to look at the way you might die, to stare into something that might hurt you, and I'm not ready for that.

My phone buzzes, and I know that it's Maribelle reminding me that I have to be at the offices today. Has it been only a week? Or, it's Aiden noticing that I'm gone and reading my note.

My whole mouth is dry as I slide my finger under the sealed tape. I get a paper cut and suck it until it no longer stings.

Inside there's a single photograph. It's dark; the outline of the camera's flash gives them the look of being caught in headlights. But they're not looking at Betty's camera, only each other. Virginia Moreaux and Aiden sitting together. She's facing the camera. Aiden has his back to it, but I know it's him even with the sliver of the profile. So close I know it's not an accident. So close that I can see his hand on her knee. The hands that were all over me last night and that night. Because I realize that he's wearing the charcoal-gray suit he wore on our date when we were both running behind schedule. When he seemed off and strange and I made excuses because I wanted to kiss him, to have his eyes only on me. I wanted to be his in a way that was primal and urgent. I wanted a man who has been lying to me, who was going to hurt me to the point of no return.

I've made a mistake.

I drop the photo and climb into bed.

This is the first time my heart breaks so deeply that my body shuts down and I fall into a heavy sleep.

19

Si Una Vez

AIDEN

Faith is gone when I wake up. I search for her in the blankets of the king-size bed, but all I find is a piece of paper. For a moment I think that she's come to her senses and decided that she doesn't want me to stay in her house or meet her family. I'm always waiting for the other shoe to drop like that. But instead, her neat, slanted handwriting says:

Have to run errands for my mom.
Meet me at my place for dinner.

♥

Faith

I trace the outline of that heart. Is this what Fallon feels all the time when he's with Robyn? Because it's kind of nice even if it's ridiculous smiling to myself when no one's looking.

The clock on the bedside table blinks 8:00 a.m. in red letters. When I get to the living room, there's a tray of food on the dining table. I lift the covers and help myself to a couple of bites of the burger. I pick the tomatoes off the salad, load them with salt, and call that a very unhealthy breakfast. Faith's grilled chicken looks sad in its little salad.

My phone is buzzing somewhere in the room, and it takes me a little while to find it.

Fallon: *Get your ass down here to the gym.*

Me: *Good morning to you, too sunshine.*

But I pull on my gym clothes. I make a pile of suits that I'll drop off at the hotel's dry cleaners. I suppose I can do the rest of my laundry when I get to Faith's later tonight. I splash some water on my face and look at myself in the mirror. There's a mark on my chest where Faith got a little too excited. I don't usually like things like that, especially in my line of work. You can't show up to a woman's house covered in someone else's love bites.

I don't want to show up at anyone's house other than Faith's. It's the scariest thought I've ever had. When would a guy like me think he could be with someone like her? We come from different worlds. I know I could never keep up with the politics and the kinds of conversations well-to-do folks have. But I've been around enough bored housewives and heiresses that I've learned how to fake it well enough. I don't have to lie about myself. If anything, people love an immigrant story that has a happy ending. It's the other kinds that no one wants to hear about.

Is that what I am? A happy story?

My mind flashes to my mother's last moments. It's been nearly a decade, and everything from that day swells within me. How she was dying and my father was out there getting drunk. How my tía Ceci told me where he was and that was the moment I snapped. Skinny as fuck and weak. I still went into that black-tinted-windowed bar on Hillside Avenue where my father was sitting. He was laughing into this woman's neck. I can still smell her rank perfume, her flesh spilling out of her spandex dress. My father's cigarette on the ashtray.

So I hit him. I hit him and it didn't even do anything. It was like a fly running into a glass window. He only brushed me off with his fist, and I wasn't strong enough to get back up or defend my mother. He always liked to tell us that we ruined his life, but I don't think he understood that all my mother did, all we ever did was try to love him until we finally decided to stop.

After that I walked back to the hospital with a bloody nose and a fat lip, and I never saw him again. Tía Ceci heard from some friend of a friend that he went back to Colombia, and I wonder, how different would our lives have been if only he'd left earlier? But it was like my mother held on. I promised myself that being in love with someone like that—it was something I couldn't do. So I didn't let anyone get close. I made these rules. I told myself that no one gets hurt if there are rules in place.

But where did that get me? Celebrating my birthday, getting drunk alone in a foreign city.

Faith walking in was my saving grace. If I stay, if I want to truly be with her, I know I have to come clean about everything. Otherwise she'll always be with a stranger, no matter how close we get. No matter how much I love her.

My phone buzzes again. Fallon sends a couple of gym related emojis.

Me: *Be right down, DAD.*

Fallon: **middle finger emoji**

I shoot Faith a text as I grab my key card and head down.

Me: *Mi reina. I got your note. See you tonight <3*

The gym is empty except for some of the guys. I've always been amazed at the dedication they put in even after a night out drinking. Fallon, Patrick, Vin, and Gary are spread out around the weight machines.

"Eyyyy," Vin shouts. He shakes my hand and we hug, slapping each other on the back. "Sorry I missed you last night. I was at this strip club. They don't wear panties here, man. Have you been?"

I laugh and grab a towel, shake my head as I get to a weight rack. "Nah, man. I've been busy. How's your brother?"

Vin's twin brother also dances with Mayhem City. The only way I can tell them apart is when they're shirtless, because Vin's got tattoos all across his ribcage.

"He's good. Keeping busy in Vegas. We miss you, man."

"I'm sorry, guys," I say, and I feel a different kind of peace knowing that they forgive me. Ricky asked me back. Faith and I are getting dinner tonight and then moving in, for a week. Everything's coming up for Aiden Rios.

"Though with you gone I got center stage," Pat says, twirling on his toes and making a dirty hand from his dick to me.

Gary makes a hissing sound with his teeth. "You don't need no center stage. Dude's face is in every airport in the country."

Pat stands in front of the mirror with a set of fifty-pound dumbbells. "And Canada."

"Wait," I say, starting by stretching my legs. "I've been gone a little while. Why is your ugly Viking mug in every North American airport?"

"Didn't you get the newsletter?" Fallon says, sarcasm clinging to his every word. "Patrick Halloran is no longer just headlining a male revue, but he's a cover model."

"Got signed by the biggest agency in LA, too," Pat says.

"This Thor mothafucka," Vin says. "You almost didn't do that photo shoot."

I grab a bar and load it up with plates. I can't actually remember the last time I went to the gym so I don't go too heavy.

Pat stares at his face in the mirror. He's got the kind of face that always looks freshly shaved. He was in Mayhem City a season before I was, but never made it to New York—out in Los Angeles chasing a modeling gig that went nowhere. He met up with us in Vegas, and the rest is history.

"This woman came to the show," Pat says, looking at me through the mirror with those green eyes. "Got a VIP pass and all. We got to talking and she asked me to be her cover model. I thought, sure why not?"

"Anything for a fan," Gary says, raising his voice to mimic Pat.

But Pat only grins his perfectly straight teeth. "Anyway, practically overnight her book is number one on the *New York Times* bestseller list. That's how they rank sales."

Fallon throws his towel at Pat's head. "We know that, asshole."

"Anyway, they printed like thousands of copies and had this

huge billboard in Times Square for a week. Then it sells even more copies. I'm surprised you haven't seen it."

Fallon rolls his eyes, but I know he's happy for Pat. Sure, he's a bit shallow, but so are the rest of us on some level. Everyone loves something, might as well be ourselves.

"I promise the next time I'm at the airport I'll pick it up. What's it called?"

Pat pulls out his phone and Gary snaps his fingers. "That's the longest he's gone without showing someone a picture. You all owe me a drink."

The other guys and I gather around to look at the phone. In the cover, Pat stands shirtless with one hand behind his head to extend his already long torso.

"Your nipples look mad pink," Vin says, and a hand comes out of nowhere to slap his head.

"*The Sky's Not the Only Big Thing in Montana,*" I read the title out loud.

"A little on the nose," Gary says. "I prefer those historical ones where they're like 'oh, no, you've ruined my reputation.'"

Pat's all grins as he says, "It's pretty good, too. The author's from Montana, and grew up near my hometown."

"I'm happy for you, brother," I say and slap him on the back. "And you guys don't listen to me when I talk about fate."

That's when they groan and roll their eyes at me. After an hour of weights, we move on to cardio. I tell them about Faith, but save all of last night's stuff, which is weird because I'm definitely the kind of guy to kiss and tell. Or I was. But everything to do with Faith—I want it for myself. Even the memory of her. Though I have to stop thinking of her when we're all in the steam room.

I spend the better part of the day with them. Each and every one tries to convince me to stay and help make the New Orleans season happen. It's temporary, but I'd get to be with my brothers. I'd get to be with her.

I realize Faith hasn't responded to my text even though she read it almost a minute after I sent it.

She must be busy with her mom's campaign.

My nerves twist in my gut, though. Like I might have done something wrong. Scared her somehow. I know I wasn't the only one who felt the spark between us last night. Like we could set the building on fire.

Around five o'clock, when I say good-bye to the guys and head back to my room, I still haven't heard from her. I decide to call, but when I get out of the elevator, Ginny is standing right in front of me and my entire body flashes hot.

"Ginny!" I say.

She looks from side to side like she's scared someone will come in. "Hey, sweetheart. I threw away my keycard after I last saw you. I didn't want to risk texting you. But I left my earrings in the safe. They were my mom's and I haven't worn them to the last couple of dinners."

"They're in the safe?"

I pull out my key card and let us in. My hand is shaking because the first thing I think is that Faith is expecting me for dinner.

But Ginny is only picking something up, and I'm leaving this room forever in a few hours, and I'm not doing anything wrong. Then why are the hackles on my back standing on end?

Ginny's hands are trembling, too. That's when I realize she's been crying. Even with her sunglasses on, the redness spreads down her cheeks.

"What happened?" I ask.

She's turning the safe lock in the closet. It clicks and she opens it. She brings out two pink diamond earrings the size of dimes. "Reggie knows."

I suck in a breath but do my best to stand still. I manage to say, "How?"

"His perky little intern *casually* mentioned that she'd seen me here. Then he got this photo from a some sniveling reporter he hired to dig up a scandal on the Charles family. Irony's a bitch, isn't it?"

"Should you be here now?"

"My husband doesn't actually care. He's with a sweet little

intern half his age now and I'm picking up my earrings and—"
Her hands shake so much that she drops one of them.

I bend down to pick it up and hand it to her. "Ginny, sit
down. I'll pour you some wine."

She nods and settles into the large couch. I bring her a glass
of wine, the one she left for me but I never opened. I spill some
of it on the counter, and I'm so nervous I decide to pour some
for myself. Every single one of my movements is punctuated
with the thought of Faith waiting for me at her house. But Ginny's
so hurt, and I can't just throw her out the door. She's still a person who needs a friend.

"Does he know who I am?" I ask her.

"Don't worry," she says, taking the glass. Her red lips leave a
mark on the rim. She pulls her legs up. I've never seen her *this*
scared and sad. Not even when we were on the phone. I'm so
used to this confident, radiant woman who possesses everything
she touches. "You can't make out your face in the photo. He
won't recognize you at the masquerade ball."

I never mentioned the ball to her.

"I know, sweetheart." She drinks again and takes off her sunglasses. Her eyes are red and puffy. The green of her irises dull,
like someone snuffed out her happiness. "I was at the salon and
Faith was so radiant, so in love, and mentioned her New York
beau. Why didn't you tell me you were Colombian? This whole
time I kept calling you—"

"Ginny," I say, sitting across from her in the armchair. I place
my hand on hers. "It's all right. I've been called much worse
than Argentinian. Right now, I'm worried about you. I watched
my mother die with regrets of being with a man who cheated on
her, who didn't treat her like the treasure she should have been
to him."

She looks at me and shuts her eyes. "It's not that simple. What
would people say? His campaign would attack me for days. My
Lena's in college—"

"You have your own money and your daughter would understand as long as you're happy. Also, who cares what people would
say? Your happiness is the one that matters."

"You're so innocent, Aiden," she says. "And kind. I'm sorry I tried to take advantage of you."

I shake my head. "You didn't."

"I'll get through this," she says, taking a deep breath. For a moment, the woman who picked me up in that hotel lobby is back. She brushes her blond hair out of her eyes. "Faith's a good girl, Aiden. Be good to each other."

"I know. I will. I'm supposed to go to her now, actually. Just waiting for my dry cleaning."

"Say no more." She finishes her drink and leaves it on the table. Her ears wink as she checks herself in the mirror. She pulls me into a hug and kisses my cheek lightly, wipes off any residue she might have let. "Don't be offended if I don't look at you at the ball. You'll agree it's for the best."

There's a knock on the door, and I go to get it. I laugh as I walk. "Don't worry, it won't be the first time."

There's a twenty in my hand for the laundry service, but when I turn to the door, the face that looks back at me is tear stained. Angry. Hurt.

"Faith," I say, my voice strangled.

"Who's in there with you, Aiden?" she asks.

I look down at my feet. That red-hot feeling coursing is through my veins. Every part of me is stunned into silence, so she repeats herself. Her dark eyes are narrow in their fury, her eyelashes wet. She must have been crying in the elevator. But how—?

That's not the question I should be asking myself. It isn't "how did she know?" It's "why did I do this?" It's "why did I fucking hurt her?"

She pushes past me, and I try to grab her arm.

"Don't you fucking touch me." She walks into the living room, and even though I can't see Ginny, I know what it looks like. Virginia Moreaux, her mother's opponent's wife in my penthouse with two empty wine glasses on the table.

"Oh, Faith," Ginny says, shaking her head sadly.

"How did you get up here?" It's the wrong thing to ask but I am not thinking straight.

"Not that it matters, but I have friends on shift."

She must mean Angie. I hate myself for trying to find an excuse. For the next words that sound hollow. "It's not what it looks like."

Faith lets go of a shuddering sigh. She closes her eyes, and the single tear that falls from her left eye is like a punch to my stomach. I did that. I made her cry. I hurt her.

I finally see that there's something in her hand. A manila envelope. It's a little worn. Like she crushed it and then tried to smooth it out.

"Tell me, Aiden," she says, her voice steady as a drawn knife. "What is it really like? Because from where I'm standing, you were hired by the Moreaux campaign to be with me. To get in my head."

"No," I say. To be honest, I'm not sure what story is worse.

Ginny gives me a tiny nod, like I have permission to tell the story of us. Because that's the thing. I wouldn't just be giving away my story, but her privacy as well, and of course that's one of my stupid fucking rules.

"Ginny," I say and immediately know it's the wrong thing because Faith repeats the name.

"Ginny," Faith says, hurt evident in her voice at this woman's nickname on my lips.

"I met her as Ginny Thomas," I say, holding my hands up. What am I defending, really? "When I was in Vegas, I took a bad deal with this woman. A client. That's how I ended up turning my back on Ricky and the others. Then Ginny hired me to spend a week with her. We were both in a bad place. The minute I arrived here, she had to go. That's the day you met me."

"Hired?" Faith says the word.

I've never been ashamed of myself or what I do. And yet, the hurt on Faith's lips makes me wish I could scrub everything in my past just to get rid of that.

"I'm an escort," I say.

"Faith," Ginny says, starting to make excuses for me.

"Don't," I say softly. No more excuses. No more lies. No more half-truths. "Faith, I never expected to meet you. To care about you so much that I wish I could be a different person. Someone better. I never expected to fall in love with you."

Her eyes snap up to mine, and the anger there deepens. She takes out the photo. I remember that night. Me and Ginny on the rooftop.

"You don't love me," she says, as if that picture proves it.

"That was the night we called things off. We never—It doesn't change the fact that I love you, Faith."

"Don't say that. You don't get to tell me you love me! Not when you've lied to me."

"I didn't—" I want to say that I didn't lie. Half-truths and withholding the truth are just as bad.

"Your real name isn't even Peñaflor."

I look down at my feet. "That's my father's last name. I stopped using it but when you met me you already saw my ID so I thought it would be easier. Faith."

"Don't say my name." She composes herself. She tosses the photo on the couch, where Ginny sat only moment earlier. It's my fate in life to be surrounded by women who are hurting and not be able to do anything about it. To be the cause of it. "Don't look at me. Don't text me. Don't call me. Pretend I don't exist."

It's completely the wrong moment, but Fallon's words spring to mind. *"I'm single for life,"* I said. And he shot back, *"Famous last words."*

And they were, because I feel like I'm been parted in half. I'm dying. My whole body is hot and I want to throw up. I want to fall at her feet and beg her. I want to tell her that I'll never hurt her again.

Maybe deep down inside I'm still that stupid kid with the torn handmade shirt, that weak little boy who couldn't compel his father to go to the hospital. That scumbag who chose his own pleasure to honesty.

I'm weak. I'm a fool. I don't deserve her.

And as she storms out that door, I know that psychic was right about one thing: I have to let her go.

20

I'll Never Break Your Heart

FAITH

After a while, Aiden's words start to blur together. I stop listening. There's those whiskey eyes, that mouth that made me feel like I was coming out of my body. It doesn't feel right being in this room.

Virginia is so still I almost forget that she's in here. She's the most dressed down I've ever seen her, like she's trying to blend in. But she'll never blend in, even if she wears jeans and a simple top. Her dazzling diamond earrings wink at me in a cruel way. Did she look this way when they met? Did they meet at a bar like I did? Was he working that night?

I know the answer in my heart. He couldn't have been, because I don't think even Aiden could have faked that kind of sadness.

It doesn't matter. Even if I could forget the fact that he's an escort, I can't ignore that he lied to me. That this picture is how I found out. Would he have told me eventually?

He says that they called things off, that moment captured in this overexposed photograph.

Of all people, why did it have to be her?

I can't listen to him tell me he loves me because it doesn't mean anything now. All of that love, that stupid head-in-the-clouds love I had this morning is gone. So I just start talking. I throw the photo on the table. Her wine glass is there with her lipstick on it.

"Don't look at me. Don't text me. Don't call me. Pretend I don't exist."

I walk out that door and he doesn't stop me.

But Virginia does.

God, he calls her *Ginny*.

I'm going to be sick. I hit the door close button, but she gets in anyway.

"I don't want to talk to you," I tell her, rage foaming at my mouth.

"Faith, please. You have to understand."

I press the ground floor button, but the elevator stops at the rooftop balcony level. I need to get out. These metal walls are too close, too tight. Everything about this enclosed space makes me want to scratch my skin raw. Her perfume is too cloying. Does he like to smell her? Her freshly manicured nails, the red blush on her cheeks, catch the hazy yellow light.

"You knew," I say, pushing through the confused hotel guests that get in. I step out and she follows me. "Yesterday at the nail salon. You knew it was Aiden. That look on your face."

Even with her splotchy, teary-eyed face, she manages to look regal. Women like her, they can have everything. Why did it have to be this one thing, too?

"I figured it out," she says. "You have to know—"

"I don't have to know anything. It's done. I'll see you with your *husband* at the masquerade ball." All I can think is that I need to run. But I can't stand here waiting for the next elevator. Angie's working tonight. She's at the rooftop bar. At least, I hope she is, because I know that one look from Angie and Virginia Moreaux will shrivel into her sensible Chanel loafers.

But she's relentless, and she's right beside me as I pull the glass door open and step into the pool area. Angie's at the bar, but there's a swarm of people trying to get drinks. The sun is setting, casting cotton candy light over the white furniture of the rooftop. The pool has a dozen tipsy bodies in the shallows and one on an ice-cream-shaped floaty in the deep end, so I stand there.

"My husband is cheating on me," she says.

She holds herself so elegantly, like she's used to standing beside someone who is angry and fuming at her. Like I am right now.

I glance around to see if anyone is paying attention to us, but almost everyone is drunk and in their own worlds. For her to say that out loud—she must really want me to listen to her.

"Does that make it okay that you did the same?" I ask her.

"We never slept together, if that means anything to you," she says.

"It doesn't."

"I was lonely and angry. I was tired of the same old song and dance. I felt trapped by everything I'm supposed to be. Aiden happened to be there and he just shines. From the inside out."

I want to say that I know that. I know that Aiden feels like sunshine on my skin. That I bask when I'm with him. But my lips tremble and my throat burns, so I don't chance speaking.

"The day Aiden and I called things off, I already knew he'd met someone. That was you. He shouldn't have kept things from you and I'm not saying to forget all of this, but to believe when he says he loves you."

I take a step closer to her so she can look into my eyes. "Love isn't enough."

She shakes her head. "Sometimes it can be."

I hate that this woman is here telling me all these things, as if she knows my life. But I spent all morning asleep. My body shut down at the sight of that photo, and all of a sudden, everything was too much to process. When I woke up, I crumbled the whole thing up. Then I grabbed it from the trash.

Everyone was trying to get in touch with me, but all I could do was scream and cry because I should have *known*. I should have been smarter.

When I glance over my shoulder, Angie's eyes are wide. She's making her way to me.

The worry in her eyes and the sadness in Virginia tugs at my anger. It deflates, and now all I'm left with is the hurt part. It's hard to talk to her because I don't want her pity. I don't want her life lesson.

"Today," I say, taking one last step so we're shoulder to shoulder, "today it's not enough."

I go.

I don't look back. She doesn't follow.

And neither does Angie.

21

Ten Minutes Ago

AIDEN

I can hear the guys talking in the small sitting area of my hotel room. I'm under the covers. This new room is a couple of floors down. It's almost exactly like my old room, only not a penthouse and with no Faith. Fallon and Robyn said I could stay with them, but I want to be alone.

"What should we do?" Pat asks.

"It's been three days," Vin says.

"I could get him a copy of my book."

"You didn't even write it," Gary says, and there's a slap.

"Should we take him to a strip club?" Vin says.

Another slap. Gary says, "How is that supposed to cheer him up?"

"Leave him be," Fallon says, thankfully the voice of reason. "Though, we should probably get him to take a shower because this place smells dank as fuck."

"I do not fucking smell!" I shout. I pull off my covers and walk out to the living room, where they're drinking my booze and eating my chips. "Get out."

"We can't leave now," Vin says. "We just ordered *Cancun Gone Wild #15*."

"Vinny," Fallon says, and Vinny slumps into the couch. "We're just worried about you, bro. We'll leave if you want."

Of course I don't want them to leave. I'm tired of being alone.

I don't do well *alone*. Maybe that's why I was so good at my job. Because I needed to be with person after person. No, don't go down that road.

"Don't leave," I say, sitting on the couch.

"Okay, but do you want to, like, put clothes on?" Vin asks.

I try to think of the last time I changed my clothes. After Faith left, after I let her walk out, I grabbed all of my things and checked out of the room. I couldn't stand being in there. Couldn't stand myself. I didn't see Ginny, but I suppose that was the last I'll see of her. Thing is, I still want her to be okay.

I lift my armpit and take a sniff. Wow, okay. They're not wrong about the smell. Vin tosses me one of the beer cans, and I pop it open. My body's going to hate me for this. But I drink it.

"You have to get over her," Vin says.

"It's only been a couple of days, lad," Gary says.

Pat gives me another beer. "I don't have relationships. Every woman I've ever tried to be with has a complete change in personality after the first month. You're better off going back to how you were before. You were happier then."

I was happy. I had my clients. I dated. I traveled. I danced. Then that stopped. My only client was Ginny, and there was no dance. I put on a good face because, let's face it, it's always a good face. I tried to be the same person I always was, but it didn't feel right.

Then there was Faith and Faith was—is—everything I didn't know I was missing.

"Tell me what to do?" I ask the room, but I'm looking at Fallon.

He rubs his face with his hands. If anyone knows what I'm going through, it's him. "Do you want her?"

"Yes."

"I walked away from Robyn and it was the dumbest thing I've ever done. Even when I look at her now, when she's in my arms or when she's sleeping, that feeling that I hurt her just kicks me in the gut. But Robyn came after me."

"So what are you saying? That I should just let Faith make the next move?"

The other guys tense, but don't agree or disagree with Fallon. "I'm saying that she told you not to contact her. Respect her space."

"Do nothing."

"Wait until she wants to hear from you," Fallon says.

Something twists hard in my gut. I want to punch him, so I settle for crushing the beer can in my fist. I regret it instantly because there's still liquid in it and it spurts all over my face. Anger surges through me, and I knock the can across the room.

This isn't me.

This can't be me.

And yet, I'm the one doing it. I know that if I looked at myself in the mirror, I'd be the person I hate the most.

Fallon's right. I have to respect what Faith asked of me. I don't deserve her and I never did.

Still, when my phone buzzes, I lunge for it on the table. My heart sputters like an old motor and my blood rushes to my neck. Please, please, please, let it be her.

It isn't.

It's Ricky.

We all have the same message.

Ricky: *Naked Avengers Assemble.*

"What the hell is he talking about?" I ask.

Vin slaps my knee. "You're coming home, brother."

And Pat says, "But you should probably shower first."

FAITH

I'm at the campaign headquarters with my mother, Maribelle, and Raquel, the campaign manager. There's a steady quiet between us, the kind that simmers like milk on low heat. At any moment it's going to boil over.

"You *left* the photo in that hotel room?" my mother asks, a hiss in her voice I haven't heard since the day I came home from my first year in college and she saw the tiny arrow I had tattooed on the inside of my ankle. She chased me out of the house, and I ran around back. I might have been nineteen, but she's still my mother. That was bad. But this is worse. It's everything she's worried about, and I was headstrong and foolish and blindsided by this feeling I couldn't control.

"I'm sure he destroyed it," I say.

"Because you know him so well?"

"Daria," Raquel St. Helen says, holding up her hand in a peaceful gesture. She's worked with some tough campaigns, getting a small town in Texas their first openly gay, Mexican American mayor elected. New Orleans's next woman and Black mayor should have been a breeze, especially when the Moreauxs are down in popularity. "Faith, how are you so sure that he wouldn't use the photo himself? Sell it from under Ms. LePaige's nose."

I should say that I have no idea. I should say that I can't trust him because I don't truly know him. Not the way I thought. But deep within me I know I'm right when I say, "He wouldn't."

"Do you love him?" my mom asks.

I frown. "That's not why we're here."

"It's exactly why we're here, Faith Abigail Charles. Don't you talk back to me when you've put everything I've worked toward in danger. For what? A good time? You couldn't wait a couple of weeks to take him to bed?"

I slam my hand on the table, trembling with hurt and rage and a sadness I fear will shake me apart. It's been four days.

"You're the reason I met Aiden in the first place!" I yell.

Maribelle zips past us and pulls down the office curtains. The doors are already closed, but when I shouted, dutiful volunteers and interns stopped their phone calls and started peering over.

"What are you talking about?"

"Aiden was there for me when all you could do was criticize every little thing I do. So no, I couldn't wait a few weeks to take him to *bed,* Mother. Because I needed him then. Everything I do is to try to please you and it isn't enough. This is no different. So just tell me what to do to fix it."

I can't meet my mother's eyes, because if I do, I'll break. I can't bear disappointing her yet again.

"If I might," Maribelle says. "Betty has done us a small favor. The Moreauxs wouldn't act on anything. Even if they tried to shame Faith, it would be even worse on Virginia."

I take a deep breath and hold it for as long as I can before releasing it. Even without the photo, I see it as clear as day. It's all I've been thinking about. How that day I was smirking like a fool buying condoms, Aiden was on a rooftop having a drink with Ginny.

We called it off.

We never slept together.

It isn't my business if they did. Aiden isn't mine.

I can't stop the little voice in my head from whispering, *He should be.*

"What about Betty LePaige?" my mother asks, her voice all strategy.

"You're her idol," I say. "She didn't have to come to me with what she knew. She could have left it alone. They did hire her to follow me. They knew I'd be your wild card."

"Faith," my mother says.

"If anything, Betty admires you." I look at Raquel. "What should I do?"

Her brown eyes are kind when she looks at me. She brushes her long blond bangs back. "At the moment there's nothing to control. This Aiden's face can't be identified, not unless he comes forward."

"He won't," I say, too hard. Why am I defending him?

Raquel presses her lips together, understanding. "I would refrain from having contact with him for the time being."

"We're not together," I say, and I swallow the strangle in my throat. "Anymore."

Raquel nods, with a concentrated look that tells me her wheels are spinning. "Good. Good. I believe this will blow over. I'll put some feelers out there to see how the other side is doing. In the meantime, this doesn't leave this room. The only way to truly know where we stand is at the ball on Friday."

I grab my things and start to leave.

"Faith."

I shake my head. "I'm sorry, Mom."

Then I leave, trying to keep my head up as I walk past a group of interns. Is this a fragment of what Virginia feels like every time she walks past the intern she knows is having an affair with her husband? Why is it that we can't understand what others are feeling until it happens to us?

I get in my car and go find Angie. I promised I'd be supportive of her new gig, and I will be.

I know she's still at her week trial with Mayhem City. I head down to the Quarter and park before I realize that Aiden might be there. And that my heart swells with the idea of seeing him again.

Pretend I don't exist. My last words to Aiden were said in the heat of the moment. I don't want him to pretend that I don't exist. I'm still so, so angry, but a part of me feels withered. Numb to anything that has to do with love or my own anger.

I haven't let myself sleep because my mind spins. It creates all the scenarios that I start confusing for reality. I imagine that instead of walking into Aiden's suite to find him and Virginia sharing a drink, I caught them in the throes of passion. I know that's not what happened, but sometimes you can convince yourself of your worst fears.

What is my worst fear?

It isn't a man cheating on me. Aiden didn't *cheat* on me. Not physically. When I was little, I was afraid of drowning. But then I learned to swim. I was afraid of sleeping outdoors, but if I wanted to be a part of conserving national parks, I had to learn to pitch a tent. I brought bug spray. I slept with a flashlight.

What was my answer to my fear of being hurt?

To take Aiden to bed.

To see him the next day.

To see him again after that.

To crave him. To feel—

A second line band comes rounding the corner, the loud brass snapping me out of a reverie that would get me nowhere except confused.

I get out of my car and walk into the warm afternoon. Blue-

and-white stickers with "Charles for Change" decorate some of the walls and businesses.

Inside, a fast hip-hop beat fills the former theater space. All of the lights are off except for the stage. The middle space is empty, expect for a few round tables.

I keep myself against the wall, though I'm sure my simple red dress stands out against the black. Angie is in blue workout leggings and a cropped matching top. Her hair is piled up high on her head, and she's walking across a stage of six shirtless men. I recognize Patrick and Vin but don't remember the others' names. Fallon is off to the side flipping through a bunch of papers with Ricky. Angie calls out motions, and they follow her every word. She stops Vin to correct his posture, to show him how she wants him to undulate his hips.

All of this is silly when you think about it. A bunch of grown men stripping down to their underpants for a horde of screaming women. I remember going to a show in college with my sorority sisters. But it was corny, not sexy. This is somehow different. It's a spectacle, but their movements are more about creating a connection. Angie is a great choreographer, and I know she's going to give this her all.

When Aiden waltzes out from somewhere backstage tugging off a white tank, my body betrays me. It starts with a straining blush along my neck and cheeks. It moves down across my chest, my ribcage. I shut my eyes, but the memory has already been pulled, a memory of Aiden gripping my waist. His nails raking down my hips as he shouldered between my legs to place his mouth on the aching knot of nerves there. My stomach floods with emotion at the boom of his laughter.

Even from here I can see him smile. It's so easy for him to smile, isn't it? That's what I loved so much about him.

He folds his arms over his chest to confer with Angie. Do his arms look bigger than I remember? I shake my head. I shouldn't be here. It feels like I'm forcing myself into his presence. I suppose I am, since our paths will cross because of Angie. If he's going to stay here, then I'm going to have to get used to the idea of him. In my life. Two trains going off the rails, ready to collide.

I make to move, but my heel gets caught on the carpet, and I sail forward onto a table. I catch myself, but my heel is stuck tight in there.

Aiden does a double take and stares at me. Everyone onstage looks at me, unsure of what to say or do. Angie waves at me, but Aiden looks away, swinging his arms and stretching.

I'm the one who told him to pretend that I don't exist, didn't I?

Truly feeling that makes me numb. The part of me that is hurting fights the part of me that longs to feel the brush of his fingers against my skin.

"Faith," he says.

He's getting off the stage, but the surge of adrenaline in my body makes me turn and walk out the door.

I get out onto the sidewalk, a strange feeling on my sole, and I realize I left my shoe.

"Faith," Aiden says. My sensible black leather pump is in his hand.

"Right," I say, and take the shoe from him. "Thank you."

Up close, I ache in the same way I did when I held that photo in my hand. I also ache in a different sense—a dangerous one, like he's the ocean and I want to throw myself against the expanse of his chest. Drown in him.

"I'm sorry," he says. He raises his hand to scratch his hair. He got a haircut, but a short beard cuts a rugged line along his jaw. I want to laugh because he thought the burn on his cheek would make him look rough, but it's already gone.

Although, his narrow nose is red, like he's been out in the sun too long. I want to rub lotion on it, tell him to take care of his skin like that day on the Jaguar. That feels so long ago.

"I'm sorry," he says again. A broken record. A needle scratching across my heart. "I know you didn't want me to contact you. I understand. I mean, I will understand. I just didn't want you getting an infection from walking out here."

The center of my body squeezes, like an accordion being smashed of air right in the middle. "Still cleaner than New York, I bet, though."

We laugh.

It hurts to laugh like this with him.

He licks his lips. Someone walks past us on the street and whistles at him. He's still shirtless, his sweatpants slung low on his hips.

Stop looking, I remind myself. I clear my throat and lift my foot to slip my pump back on. I wobble, and the first thing I grasp is Aiden.

He catches me like he was waiting for me to fall, like he was ready. I look down to avoid his whiskey-brown eyes. I trace my fingers back and forth on his shoulder before I push myself off.

"I'm sorry," I say.

"Faith." He says my name. Just my name. "Can we talk? Let me explain?"

The street is fairly empty for this time of day. My car is directly behind me. I can leave. I can walk away like I did before. But instead I say, "Okay."

"Really?"

I look at my watch. "I have five minutes."

He nods, that relentless chunk of hair falling over his face once again. "Before I met you I had a bunch of rules. I thought that they would help me keep things simple. Rule #1, don't play games. Rule #2, no lies. Rule #9, treat her with the respect she deserves. I could keep going."

He takes a step closer, and I'm anchored into place. He looks down at me, and I wonder what we look like. Me in my dress, and him so bare in nothing but sweatpants and sneakers. Why do I care what we look like? Why do I care what other people think?

"But I broke every rule with you, Faith. I'm not ashamed of how I made my living. The only thing I'm ashamed of is that I might have been a fraction of what my father was like. I'm ashamed that I hurt you, most of all."

"*Made* a living?" I ask, finally lifting my eyes to his. I was right. I should have kept my eyes averted. The anguish in his eyes mirrors mine. But is that enough? "You're not staying with Mayhem City?"

He nods once, licks his lips. Those lips that even now send a shiver down my spine at just their memory. "I am. But no more extra clientele. I don't want to be the cause of anyone else's hurt."

"What do you expect me to do with that information, Aiden?"

"Nothing. I wanted you to know in case it matters to you. I love you, Faith. You're in my heart, buried deep in my skin."

I swallow the emotion that gathers in my throat and wants to bubble over. I fish for my keys in my purse.

"Thank you, Aiden," I say. And in this moment I know I'm more like my mother than I ever thought possible. What I always saw as cold, hard emotion was only ever a shield against a world that wasn't built for her. "I wish you all the best."

AIDEN

So far, I've consumed thirty beignets.

Pat's going to have something to say to me tomorrow morning at the gym, but right now, even the waitress looks concerned for my health. It's nearly ten at night, and there's a lonely saxophone playing somewhere in the distance. Somehow New Orleans has answered exactly how I feel at the moment.

A woman appears in front of me. Pulls the empty chair and sits. She's in an elegant blue blouse that ties at the throat and storm-gray slacks. Almond-shaped nails and hands just like her daughter's.

I nearly choke on powdered sugar when I realize it's Daria Charles herself. "I'm so sorry."

She hands me a napkin. "So, Aiden Rios Peñaflor."

"It's just Rios now," I say.

"You took your momma's last name?"

I nod. "She raised me all on her own. Until the very end."

"I'm so very sorry you had to go through that. And so young."

I arch my eyebrow, settling into my chair more comfortably. "You've looked into me."

She nods. "I have friends in New York."

I smile and shake my head. The way she pushes her hair back, the way she stares at me, as if her actions are so obvious, remind me so much of Faith. "You must not be impressed."

She sets her hands on her lap and sighs. "You moved in with your aunt Cecilia Rios when you were sixteen after one month in a juvenile detention center for assault."

I clench my teeth. Close my fist because sometimes I can still feel my father's fists on my face. But I do what I do best. I brush it off. I smile. I shove my hurt down my throat like bitter medicine. "To be fair, my father had it coming."

"Your father?"

"My mom was in hospice. He'd stolen her mother's necklace and given it to someone else. I went to get it back."

Her brows knit together in that way older women have when they feel sorry for me. Only Daria Charles isn't a client. She's a woman who has been touched by my mistakes.

"You dropped out of high school the following year."

I nod. "We had to pay rent. Besides, I was getting tired of hearing I was good for nothing. I started dancing. Eventually I met Ricky, the owner of Mayhem City. Or rather, he found me. I was at this dive in Jackson Heights. I can't believe I made it out of there alive. Gave me a good job. Good hours. Taught me how to shop for a suit."

She nods along to my story. On paper, I'm not the kind of guy you bring home. To be fair, Faith never brought me home, and yet, here is her mother.

"And your side business," she says in the most politically correct way she can.

I chuckle, mostly blushing because this isn't some stranger. She's the mother of the woman I'm in love with. "People get lonely. I tried my best to make sure that what I did was legal. And that no one got hurt."

"You failed at the hurting people part this time," she says.

I nod, and look down at the six beignets left in front of me. Three dozen really was too ambitious. Suddenly, I'm nauseous.

"Why are you still in New Orleans, Aiden?"

I dust sugar from my fingertips. "I guess, when I got here I was hiding. I couldn't face my brothers but now that I have, I know that the right thing is to see this through."

"And where does my daughter fit in this?"

I stare into her deep-brown eyes, and I find that if I looked at her long enough, I'd tell her everything she wanted to know about me. "Faith asked me to stay away from her. If that's why you're here, then you don't have to worry. I shredded the photo she brought and then I set it on fire. Set off the fire alarm, too, and blamed it on my smoking. I—uh—don't smoke, I just said that."

She puts her hand up to save me from my rambling.

"Anyway, you don't have to worry. I'm going to respect what she wants."

"I'm not worried," she says, and when she says that, I believe it.

For a long time we sit like this. She asks about my life and I tell her. We talk about her favorite books and we discover that we both have a collection of Chernow biographies. I know she's fishing to see if I'm going to be trouble for her campaign. All I can do is show her who I am. An immigrant kid from the Caribbean coast of Colombia who dropped out of high school but still managed to make a life for himself. Even if it's not the road others would have chosen.

At the end of our conversation, she takes the last beignet. "It's a shame to waste these, son."

"Believe me," I say. "I haven't wasted any of it."

I stand when she does. She's shorter than me, but I lower my head. When she places her hand on my cheek, it just feels good to have a mother's touch, even if she isn't mine.

"Promise me," she says. "You'll go."

It hurts to say this, more than anything. But I say, "I promise." This is one I intend on keeping.

22

¿Dónde Estás, Corazón?

FAITH

I'm not keeping count, but it's been six days since I walked out of that hotel room. Two days since I left Aiden standing in the middle of the street, bare chested and vulnerable after telling me that he's sorry. That he loves me.

No, I'm not keeping count at all.

Instead, I'm bathing in mud.

"Why did I let you talk me into this?" I ask Angie. I've spent the last two days with her. We're dipped in mud baths up to our throats, facing the spa's window, which overlooks a huge garden lawn. Thankfully, we're in the tubs inside because we cannot handle the mosquitos out there. "The ball is in seven hours and I still have to pick up my dress from the dry cleaners and get my hair done."

Angie drinks her cucumber-lime water. Spa Palace is her favorite place. She usually drags me here when she's stressed out about work or her shoulder is particularly bothering her. This time, I'm the one spiraling. Reorganizing my closet to donate clothes I haven't worn in over a year. I bought a grill that has so many gadgets I don't even know what to do with. I rented a floor waxer, and it's still there in my mostly empty kitchen.

My mother and Raquel have both agreed that the best thing I could do for the campaign was keep a low profile. Every morning when I pick up my coffee, I grab a stack of newspapers and scour them for any hint of my name.

I did all the dutiful daughter things. Stood beside my mom during her speeches in the middle of Jackson Square. I smiled and nodded and agreed when people reminded me that my mother was strong and wonderful and would be the best thing for this city.

There has only been one incident where I had to see the Moreauxs. The hair on my arms bristled when I had to lean in and kiss Virginia's cheek. Then, of all things, my mother placed her hand on my shoulder and stood with me. We didn't talk about Aiden or what transpired. She was simply there for me, and I was there for her. It was something I wasn't prepared for and I remind myself that everything my mother does is because she loves me.

"We can pick up your clothes on the way to the hair salon," Angie says. "You're looking for things to freak out about, Faith."

"I am not."

"You are, too." She sets her drink on the wooden board between us. "Every time you're anxious or stressed you give yourself more things to do. Then you're like this little angry bee zipping back and forth, and anything around you gets stung."

"A bee can only sting you once," I say, and shoot her an unimpressed glare.

"Why don't you just admit that you miss Aiden?"

"Because," I say.

His name gives me a hot flash.

Just his name.

More than his name, actually.

I don't close my eyes. If I do that, I'll remember us. Instead, I stare at the glass wall and the trees out there, the women lounging around the pool with tiki torches lining the ground. Focusing on something else helps.

"Because admitting that I miss Aiden means that I'm not over him and I can't accept that."

"Faith, that boy is a wreck. He's a zombie stumbling across the stage. It's ruining my show."

I chuckle. "So, what? I take him back so that you have a good season?"

"No. You talk to him because right now you're punishing yourself."

"How am I punishing myself?" I take my ice water filled with crushed petals and sip the flowery sweetness. "That makes no damn sense."

"You've always done this. After you failed the bar, you bought a house that had no floors and a bathroom that was leaking."

I frown. "It was a great investment in that neighborhood and it's worth twice what I paid for it and the renovations."

"When you broke up with Stuart after he proposed to you two years ago, you took a clerkship with your dad's firm even though what you really wanted was to work at the refuge with Gladys."

"That clerkship looks great on my résumé." I drink ice water so quickly that it gives me brain freeze. "None of that changes the fact that Aiden lied to me. Even if I do want him still, even if I—it doesn't matter because I'll always wonder if he's going to do it again. I'll have that in my heart and my memory and I don't want to be one of those women who just turns the other cheek because she's in love. Love isn't enough."

"Faith," she says, voice full of guilt.

I set my water beside her and sink as far into the mud as I can without it touching the hair at my nape.

"Abbie," she says. "I knew about Aiden and Virginia."

Even though I don't expect her to say that, I breathe deep and long, and the mud around me resists against the expansion of my body. "Everyone knew except for me, it seems. You're right. I'm a terrible judge of character."

"That night," she says. "I saw them talking. I slapped him."

I chuckle. "Thank you."

"I told him to break it off or I'd tell you. I wanted to tell you, but then you were so happy. I haven't seen you open up like that in so long. Your love was plain as a cloudless day, darlin'."

I bite my lower lip. "Why are you telling me this?"

"Because you're being as stubborn as your momma, bless her. You don't want to see it but you're the same person. And yet, your daddy still looks at her like she's the sun to his moon. That's how Aiden looks at you. When he's not messing up a routine by forgetting a step."

I know I'm as stubborn as my mother. "Aiden said he was afraid of becoming his dad and yet, here we are."

"He recognizes that. You do, too. It's one thing if he looked in the mirror, said it, and then kept making the same mistakes."

"I don't know how to accept his love," I finally say. "I'm scared of it. When I'm scared of something, I can conquer it. But this? I can't conquer this. I can't fix it or beat it. That's not a feeling I'm comfortable with."

"Oh, Abbie. You're not supposed to conquer love. If you go in thinking it's a war, then you're never going to win. You embrace it, but only if you want it and it wants you back. Believe me, this time, it wants you back."

We stay in the mud bath for a bit longer, enjoying each other's presence. I'm still unraveling the strings in my heart, hoping none of the threads break.

As promised, Angie drives me to the laundry to get my dress, and then we get our hair done. She gets a wash and an updo that makes her look even taller than she already is. I keep it simple with soft waves parted at the center.

When we get to my house, she curses. "I left my shoes at home. I'll be right back."

"Why don't you just pick them up on the way?"

Angie gives me an incredulous side-eye. "I'm not driving tonight. If I'm going to be your date, your ass is ordering a car service so we can both partake in the fancy champagne."

With that, she's gone and I'm going up my porch, fishing for my keys.

There's a package on the porch chair. I look around the area, but other than Mrs. Friedman out for her evening power walk, the street is empty. My heart seizes at the thought of it being another mystery package from Betty LePaige.

The package is wrapped in brown butcher's paper, and my name is scrawled in sure, strong letters. FAITH.

My movements are robotic, hand turning the key, walking inside, kicking off my shoes, and sitting at my kitchen table—all from muscle memory because I know beyond anything that this package is from Aiden.

I carefully unwrap the package. Blink. Aiden pulling down the zipper of my dress.

I push the paper apart. Blink. Aiden parting my legs with his hands.

I open the pale wooden box. Blink. Aiden pushing deep inside me.

The box is light to the touch, like those shadow boxes you get at voodoo shops in the Quarter. Only instead of it being filled with straw and crystals and tiny painted porcelain skulls, there's a single piece of paper and a red velvet baggie.

The card is one sided, thick and soft to the touch. The initials RR are stamped in the corner, and immediately I know it's Ricky's stationery. Aiden wouldn't have stationery. But he would have a wooden box, and he'd have sloppy, almost indecipherable handwriting.

I brace myself as I read.

> *Dear Faith,*
> *This has weighed me down all my life. My mother told me to give it to the woman I loved. I can't imagine anyone else having it. No matter what. No strings attached. Adiós, mi reina. Mi vida.*
> *Aiden*

I press the card to my chest for a long time. Mi reina. My queen. I don't know what the other word is, but I set the card down for the baggie. I hold my hand out and drop its contents on my palm.

A glittering citrine set in a vintage gold pendant and delicate chain. I trace the jagged cut edges with my thumb. Something like this must have meant everything to Aiden.

And yet, I find myself putting it on. It sits delicately in the spot between my collarbones. I stare at myself in the mirror and try to see the woman who owned this. Aiden's mother, the only person he loved more than anything.

I pick up my phone and call him. It's like the gem is in my throat as it rings and rings and rings.

Just like that I'm angry that he's given this to me. Thrust this on my doorstep today. I pick up the card again. It's not dated.

I look at that word again. Adiós. Good-bye.

I grab my keys and speed all the way to the hotel. How can he just leave this here? It could have been stolen. What if I never noticed it? My fist lands on the horn to get through traffic almost until I'm in front of the hotel.

"I won't be long," I tell the valet, who recognizes me.

I march up to the reception desk. "Can I have the room number for Aiden Rios or Aiden Peñaflor? Please, it's urgent."

The girl looks around the room, as if she's afraid of being caught.

"Please," I say.

She types in the name. "I'm sorry, Miss Charles."

"Please." I don't even care if she knows who I am. If she'll tell others.

"It's not that. I can't tell you his room. Mr. Rios checked out yesterday morning. I called a car service for him myself."

"To where?"

"The airport, Miss Charles."

I whirl around because I don't want her to see the way tears sting my eyes.

"Are you all right, Miss Charles?"

Breathe. Count to ten. I do all the things I've learned to do to cope. I turn to look at her, and I find my words are failing me. So I nod and leave.

Angie is on my porch when I pull my car in the driveway behind hers.

"What the hell happened?" she asks. "I was about to call the cops. I was going to break your window with a rock."

I shake my head. "I forgot something."

"What did you forget?"

I forgot my heart. This bloody, messy, terrible thing in my chest. "Aiden."

Her anger leaves in an instant, and then she's holding me until I finally let myself cry. I tell her about the necklace and that when I got to the hotel he was already gone.

"I didn't know," Angie says. "There was no rehearsal yesterday. Maybe he's coming back. Maybe he just went to Vegas or New York."

I pull out of her hold and wipe the corners of my eyes. This is what I wanted, and now that I have it, I regret everything I did to push him away. I can still call him. I can still—

I shake my head. No. I asked him to stay away from me. I told him to pretend I don't exist. My words were drenched in hurt and anger. Now all that's left is a second heartbreak of my own making.

"No," I say. "No. Now I know. I have to let him go."

23

Here I Go Again

AIDEN

"Are you sure this is something you want to do?" Ricky asks me.

"I'm positive," I say, taking his hand in mine. In front of us is a set of signed contracts. "Thank you, Ricky. I mean it. I won't let you down."

He squeezes my hand. "I don't give second chances easily, my boy."

I tense as the force of his shake threatens to break my bones. I smile and slap his arm. "I know. Believe me. It's good to be back. I need this. But first . . ."

"You're going to go get your girl?"

"Actually, I have to go to New York."

Ricky smooths his beard with his index finger and thumb. "What for?"

"I haven't seen my mom in a while," I say. "Actually, in five years."

"We have a show in two weeks," Ricky says.

"I'll be there." I point to the contracts. "You already signed. No backsies. Don't worry. You won't even know I'm gone."

I grab my bags, head to the front desk, and check out.

New York feels different because I'm different. The wind is too cold. I should've worn a jacket. I should've shaved.

But my mother wouldn't have cared if I shaved.

"It's okay, papito," my tía Ceci says, holding my hand as we walk into St. Mary's cemetery in Queens.

She's exactly as I remember. Same shoulder-length hair she dyes blond every three weeks. Same bright top showing more cleavage than I was comfortable with as a teenage boy. Her heeled boots barely bring her to my shoulder, but somehow it feels like she's holding me up.

I get up to the headstone for Amada Helena Rios, querida madre y hermana. The grass is well taken care of and there's an old bunch of roses Tía Ceci must have brought last month. She always comes on the third of every month to visit her sister without fail.

I remember the day when I stopped coming. It was the first time I got punched in the face by somebody's husband. My head was full of my mother's face—disappointed, disheartened, disillusioned with me—and I just stopped visiting.

My chest hurts with the cold air, car exhaust thick even within these rows of dead. Cemeteries even feel different than they do down in New Orleans.

Tía Ceci stands back while I talk to her. My mother's English was never very good, so I speak in Spanish. I place my hand on the headstone and it takes me three tries before I can say, "Pues, Mamá. Ya pasó. La conocí."

Well, Mamá. It happened. I met her.

"That was a good thing you did, papito," Tía Ceci tells me as we get on the train and go back to her apartment in Forest Hills.

"I should have done it sooner," I say.

She purses her metallic pink lips and holds her hand up, like she's agreeing with me but not. "Ya pues, it would have saved me two hours standing in the cold."

I told my mother everything. About Ginny. About Faith. About meeting Daria Charles and how we talked all night. I told Daria everything I could remember of my mother, even that

I hadn't visited in five years. I promised Daria two things, and this is the one that was the most pressing.

"I can't wait to meet her," Tía Ceci says.

"I don't know, Tía. There's so much that I can't take back."

"Don't take it back. Keep moving forward. Your heart is too big, papito. You have to leave some room in there for yourself."

In her house, she unwraps all of her shot glasses. Some of her neighbors and her latest boyfriend are over to watch Real Madrid play Manchester United. She lines up ten of the glasses I've brought her. Three from New Orleans, a couple from Vegas, one each from Miami, Houston, Ireland, Jamaica, and Kansas City. Gaudy, shiny little pieces of the places I've been.

We take a couple of shots with the others, but the cold tequila does not go down as smoothly as before.

"You know," I say, biting into a slice of lime, "Faith drinks whiskey."

"She misses you." Tía Ceci holds her shot the way a fancy woman might hold her teacup, with her pinky up.

"You can't know that."

"Of course, I do. How can she not miss you?" She goes off into her room, and I can hear rummaging from her dresser.

Rodolfo, Tía Ceci's boyfriend and a former marine, shouts at the television, though I can't tell if he's happy or crying. Is that what I look like when my team is losing?

"Here," she says, setting a small red velvet pouch in front of me, the kind Colombian people use to keep trinkets and rings and even finger bones in (seriously).

I shake my head. "No."

"Your mother told you. She told you what to do."

I drop the necklace in my hand. The last time I held this, I was bloody, and I'd just snatched it off that woman's neck. My father called me a thief, but by some miracle, the woman told the police that it belonged to my dying mother. My dad never dropped the assault charge, and the judge felt pity for me, so all she gave me was a month.

The gem might be the size of a dime, but it has the weight of the world to me.

I drop it in the front pocket of my shirt. "Thank you, Tía."

"Make sure she knows, Aiden."

In the morning, I take the first flight to New Orleans to go get my Faith back.

24

So Close

FAITH

The Mayor's Masquerade Ball is held every year in the Elms mansion.

My parents are already there, along with my mother's team. Angie and I watch the house for a moment, the white pillars lit from the ground with a beautiful light.

"Hm," Angie says, and I believe we're thinking the same thing. "Do you think the Confederate soldier turned merchant who built this place ever thought a Black female mayoral candidate would be having a ball in it?"

I give her a strong glance. "I hope he's turning in his grave."

"I'll drink to that," she says, and we head right in.

I gather the black skirt of my dress. It's a simple, sleeveless Christian Siriano with heavy silk that tapers to my waist. At the door, there's a man all dressed up in nineteenth century French regalia. I grab a black-and-red mask while Angie chooses a hot-pink-and-blue one to match her pink tulle gown.

The lights are dim, the music is not even remotely French, but at least people are already dancing to the DJ's Top 40 selection. The two teams of candidates are placed at tables on either side of the grand ballroom. My mother's deep in conversation with Judge Benthu and his wife. By their smiles I get a good feeling about this. On the Moreaux side, Reginald's almond-shaped head is covered by the mask, but nothing can hide the scowl on his face or the tight smile on Virginia's fine features. She's chatting with the election commissioner's wife, both clutching Marie Antoinette glasses fizzing with champagne.

A hot blush starts to creep across my chest when Virginia's green stare finds mine across the room. Her smile becomes more natural, and Angie places a hand on my arm.

"Look! Drinks," Angie says, swiping two glasses from a waitress. She winks at Angie and my friend returns with "Keep 'em coming."

"What should we cheers to?" I ask, and the words send a spike of memory through me. I touch the pendant resting on my chest.

"To winning," Angie says.

"Don't," I say.

"Because—"

"No."

"All I do is *win win win*." And then she's twirling on the dance floor along with a crowd of others.

She leaves me to my own devices. I go over and kiss my parents, smile and nod and play the role of the dutiful daughter. Today I mean it. Today it isn't a role at all. It's just me.

"What about you, Faith?" Judge Benthu asks me. "What can we expect from you soon?"

I look at my parents and back at the old man, his white skin crinkled at the corners of his eyes and lips. This is a man who has smiled and laughed his way through life. "Well, I'm applying to take the bar. There's a lot of land here that needs protecting."

"That's a fine mission, my dear," he says genuinely.

"I'm proud of you, baby," my dad says, pressing a kiss on my forehead.

"So am I," my mom says, and she takes my hand and squeezes. "I love you, Faith."

I can't be sure if she's doing this because we're in front of people. It doesn't feel that way. My mother doesn't give praise easily, and she wouldn't fake it for a crowd. In this moment, I am at peace, even if there's something missing.

"Faith!" A familiar voice comes from my right. A short, stocky, older blonde weaves through the hordes of dancers and pulls me away. I excuse myself from my parents and the judge, and follow my friend.

"Gladys!" I lower myself to embrace her. She's in a black-and-red frock that's all lace and fringe. She's brought a tiny alligator covered in glitter and clipped it to her messy blond hair. "You look wonderful. I didn't realize you would actually come."

"Thought I'd liven this funeral up. Everyone's so serious."

"There's a lot on the line," I remind her.

"Well, there's no mystery as to who I'm voting for, hon." She pulls me toward her. "But I came to tell you in person that we've got funding to keep all the programs running. I can hire more interns. Thank you, darlin'. Thank you."

My mouth must be hanging open, because she closes it by pressing her thumb on my chin. "What? What did I do?"

"The donation was made in your name, Faith." She pulls me into another hug. "Don't you go start crying on me now! It's a celebration. That tall drink of water's been staring at you since you walked in."

"Who?" I ask, because I don't see anyone.

But Gladys is gone.

I adjust my mask a bit because it's starting to pinch behind my ears. The song slows down to a pretty number I've never heard, with plucking guitars. People start to leave the dance floor, and only sweethearts remain, swaying back and forth.

There's a man across the room. When the crowd shifts, I make out a fine black tux that tapers just so, white gloves and all. A simple white eye mask over his smooth face.

A face I'd recognize anywhere now that he's unobstructed.

It's like I'm in that dream, where you're moving in one direction but you're not actually getting any closer to where you mean to go. That's what it feels like while Aiden strides toward me, a tiny smile on his face because I'm wearing his mother's necklace.

I'm still a bunch of nerves, all wound up and ready to spark.

I want to slap him. I want to kiss him. I want to embrace him and never let go.

He bows in front of me and holds out his hand. "May I have this dance?"

People are looking. Of course they're looking. I'm my mother's daughter and he is the most beautiful man in the room.

I take his hand.

AIDEN

I see Faith the moment she steps out of the car with Angie, and my heart stops.

She is a vision, a princess arriving at the ball, and I'm anything but a prince, but I know she's mine. Her perfect breasts are visible in the sweet V-neck of the dress. The black silk ripples like water in the mansion's lights.

I grab a drink and down it, then head back inside. I grab a white mask from one of the butler guys and find a place to wait for her. Even if I'm here on the invitation of Daria Charles herself, I can't ambush the future mayor's daughter. Instead, I cling to the walls.

That's the great thing about spending so much time trying to be anonymous. I've learned how to blend in. One woman in a white ruffly dress that makes her look more like a ghost than anything is already so drunk she tries to give me her empty glass to refill.

"Don't work here," I tell her, and she keeps on floating by.

When I see Ginny and her husband, the vein in my neck gives a little throb because he's got his thumb pressed on the inside of her wrist. I wonder if he knows who I am. I wonder if my being here is hurting her.

Ginny, on the other hand, has caught sight of me. She presses her fingers to her earrings and tugs. She gives the smallest shake of her head, then continues talking to the housewives and the important people in suits.

Angie walks toward me and does a double take. "What are you doing here?"

"I was invited," I say. I tell Angie all about my meeting with Daria and my quick trip to New York.

"Why didn't you say anything?" she asks.

I sigh. "I wasn't sure if I should come."

"Don't fuck this up," Angie tells me, digging her pointed nail through the fabric of my tux.

"Can you do me a favor?"

"Maybe."

"Can you bribe the DJ for a slow song?"

"You're lucky you grew on me," she mutters.

"Like a flower?"

"Like fungus."

Then she's off, and I'm holding my breath for the song to change. For the crowd to clear. For Faith to stand alone.

I wade to her, mi reina. Mi vida.

"May I have this dance?" I ask, and I'm a little proud that my voice isn't trembling or breaking. Dances like this have never been my specialty. The music becomes a romantic waltz.

I spin her to the center of the dance floor, her skirt swishing around her legs. Bring her against me. There's so much that I want to say to her now that she's in my arms, but all I can do is lead her in this waltz around the room. All I want to do is bask in her eyes, admire the way that gem fits perfectly against her warm brown skin.

But there's a tug of sadness on her lips, and I want to take her mouth in mine and right it. I press my fingers on her side to let her know which way to turn.

"I didn't know you could waltz," she says.

"I'm glad there are a few things about me that will still surprise you."

She stares at her hand on my shoulder, avoids my eyes. Her voice is so small, so hurt, when she says, "I called you."

"I was getting dressed," I say. "I'm sorry."

"You keep saying that but you still do things that hurt me."

I lick my lips. "I only did what you asked me to, Faith."

Her big, beautiful brown eyes finally fall on mine. "I didn't realize how easy it was for you."

"One of my rules is to not play games, mi vida." I spin her and she moves willingly, anticipating my next moves.

"What changed your mind?" she says as she falls back into my arms. But for a moment, her finger traces the gem on her chest.

"Your mother, actually." I tell her everything, and she's more shocked than I ever imagined. "My tía Ceci was the one who gave me the necklace. I wanted you to have it. I meant every word. No strings attached, Faith. I love you, and the woman I love will wear my mother's necklace."

"If you meant every word, why did you write 'good-bye'?" she asks, resting her fingers on my shoulders, lowering them to the top of my chest just like she did when I caught her in the street, when she wobbled. I want to catch her whenever she starts to fall.

"I wasn't going to come. I wanted the decision to be yours."

"What changed your mind?"

I sigh. "My greatest fault is that when it comes to you, I'm weak. I wanted to see you. When I saw you were wearing the necklace—"

"Don't test me," she whispers. "That's a game in itself and you don't like playing games."

"Hm. You're right."

"What if I wasn't wearing it? What if I still feel the same? What if it didn't match?"

We both laugh at that, and it feels so good to hear her laugh that I could weep at her feet. The music starts to slow down.

"Are you staying in New Orleans?" she asks, resting her head on my shoulder.

I lower my face into her hair, breathe her in. "I am. I have a contract with Ricky to open the show here."

"And then?"

"And then, I can do whatever I want."

She looks up. "What does *mi vida* mean?"

I laugh, and I feel her vibrate against me. "My life, Faith. It means my life."

Her eyes widen just so, and I lead her into one last spin. This time she comes back to me on her own. For the first time I realize that the entire dance floor is empty except for us at the center, that Ginny and her husband, and Faith's parents, and half of New Orleans are watching.

I couldn't care less because Faith repeats my words. "Mi vida," she calls me, and punctuates her words, this song, with a kiss.

There's a solid hour of speeches. I meet Faith's father officially, and while he doesn't smile at me, he at least shakes my hand. People come up to us, and everyone mentions our "sweet little kiss" on the dance floor.

It took every bone in my body (except that one) to stay still as Faith pushed herself up on her toes to kiss me. My dick gave a little jerk, jealous of my stupid mouth because it got to taste her lips again.

While Reginald Moreaux gives his speech after Mrs. Charles, Faith gives my arm a little tug. I blink and nearly lose her through the crowd. She goes upstairs, and I recognize the tiny twitch of her gloved index finger as she motions for me to follow.

The second floor of this mansion is empty, but I still look over my shoulder, my blood rushing everywhere but my head as she walks into a room and locks it.

"You keep doing that," I say, turning to where she's pressed herself against the door. She takes her mask off, and it's like staring into the sun. My sun.

"You keep following." She reaches for my mask and takes it off, adds it to the mask on the floor.

"I would follow you wherever you wanted me to go, Faith." I get all up in her space, and she brushes her hair off to the side. "Can I kiss you?"

She grabs the front of my tux and gives me a hard tug. "You can devour me, Aiden."

I capture her mouth with mine. Grab her by her small waist and plop her on top of a table. The room has one of those plush daybeds, but for what I want to do to her, this tabletop will do just fine.

She moans against my mouth, her sly fingers going right for the gold, rubbing my straining erection.

"Fuck," I gasp.

"Already?" she asks with a tiny giggle.

"I didn't bring protection."

She sinks her fingers into my waistband. Untucks my shirt. "I've been on the pill since I was sixteen."

I arch my eyebrow. "I thought you didn't lose your virginity until eighteen."

She rolls her eyes. "The pill is for more than birth control. I'll write you a list later. After you fuck me in this room where some nineteenth-century bride probably did her stitching."

"I love when you say words."

"Any words?"

I tap her lips with mine. "Any words."

"Mi vida," she says, shy, sweet, like she's afraid of getting the words wrong.

I catch her pouting bottom lip with my own. Well aware that there are over a hundred people downstairs, including her father and my ex-client, my dick is still fucking throbbing with need.

Faith pulls her skirts up her thighs, spreading her miraculous legs for me. She's wearing a devilish lace thong that's about to be in my fucking mouth. She fingers her slit and shuts her eyes. "I want you inside me, Aiden. I've missed the feel of you."

She slides a finger in and brings it to her own mouth. I could come just watching her do that. But first I get on my knees and drape one of her legs over my shoulder. I rub my nose against her soaked lace thong. I pull the fabric aside, and then close my mouth around her aroused clit. Lick my way into her wetness. I press my hands on her knees to brace as she crosses her legs against my back. I would bury my face between her legs for eternity if she keeps moaning like that.

"Aiden," she says, yanking at my shirt with an urgency that drives me wild. Because she needs me just as much as I need her.

I undo my belt, my button, in seconds. Her hands are a frenzy pushing away my shirt, and when she grabs a hold of my cock, it jerks in her hand. I'm dripping with pleasure as she strokes upward, grinding me to her tight little cunt.

But I fuck her leg instead, my dick leaving a trail of precum on the inside of her thigh. She kisses my neck.

"What's wrong?"

I can hardly breathe from the strain of my dick. "I just want you to know. I want you to know that I haven't been with anyone else since—"

"Mi vida," she whispers in my ear, and I find myself making a deep growling sound as I line my hips up with her and press the head of my cock inside her.

We hold our breath, and I feel myself coming undone with the feel of her. Sliding deep into her sex unobstructed is like seeing stars, like sliding across some unexplored galaxy where only she and I exist. She grabs my ass and brings me closer. She shuts her eyes, and seeing her react this way to me makes me harder than ever. I bring her legs around my waist, and she locks them, driving me in up to the hilt.

"You feel," I start to say, but I lose myself in the rhythm of her hips grinding against me, the shake of this old fucking table, the way my heart beats to the same spitfire speed as hers. "You feel like love, Faith."

She pulls back, and for a moment I think I've messed this up. That the trip and the necklace and meeting her parents has been one long dream. But she smiles against my mouth. "I love you, mi reina."

Even though I'm fucking inside her, I laugh. It sends a different kind of pleasure through me. "*Mi rey,*" I correct her.

"Mi rey," she says, giggling.

"I fucking love you," I say and lift her, keeping her taut and wet pussy tight around my dick.

I fuck her standing up. I fuck her while walking across the room. I fuck her as I settle her on this dainty pastel fainting couch.

I pull out and she gets on her knees, looks over her shoulder. I climb up behind her, pushing her skirts back to around her waist. She holds the ends up and watches as I part her ass cheeks with my hands.

"Aiden," she whimpers, and I drag my tongue from her wet pussy and up. I run my dick through her swollen wet slit and sink in again. Every. Fucking. Time. Every fucking time it feels like the first time. I keep one hand on the small of her back and the other around her ass, each second harder and harder to keep quiet.

With her like this, something wild and primitive sparks within me, and I feel myself start to shudder. I feel her walls, too, rippling around my cock, like they're trying to draw my come out of me.

She gives a tiny squeal as she comes, and that sends me over the edge. I try to pull out, but she pushes herself, further fucking my dick, and then everything I have is spent inside her.

I kiss her shoulder. Stay this way for a moment longer.

"We have to go back downstairs," she says. "The speech will be over."

I look around the room for something to clean her so her pretty dress doesn't get soiled. There are some handkerchiefs in a drawer, and they'll have to do.

"Thank you for not touching my hair," she says, and plants a kiss on my cheek. She admires herself in the mirror. "You wouldn't be able to tell I just got my brains fucked."

I come up behind her. Press my fingers to her chest. "Only if someone felt how hot your skin was."

"I can blame it on the heat." She turns and brushes my hair back. "You, on the other hand. Close your tux. We ripped a button somewhere."

"Casualty of war," I say.

She fixes my tie, and I could get used to this. Faith taking care of me. Fixing details about me. Her eyes widen like she remembers something.

"Aiden, that was so much money. You gave it all to the refuge?"

"It didn't feel right keeping her money."

"That's how much you make?"

"Made," I say. "My attentions from here on out are yours and yours alone. If you'll have me."

She takes my hand. "I want you, Aiden. I've wanted you since the first time I saw you."

When we leave the room, the coast is clear. Until we hear some shouting coming from the room beside us.

It takes me a moment to recognize Ginny's voice. I look down at Faith, who is also realizing something terrible is happening. That I'm going to act. I know that this can break everything we've fixed. I know that if I close my eyes, I don't see Ginny at all, but my mother calling for help.

"Aiden!" Faith calls for me, but I'm slipping out of her hand. I rush into the room.

Reginald has her cornered. His hand is clamped down around her wrist and the other is in midair as Ginny hides behind her own arms.

"Threaten to divorce me one more time," he says, then stops when he realizes they're not alone.

"Don't you fucking touch her," I shout.

I see red. I relive feelings I thought were gone. But they're not gone. They're right beneath the surface. I grab him around his shoulders.

"Aiden, stop!"

I underestimated him as a weak old man. He breaks my hold and sucker punches my nose. Sweat pours from my face. But when Ginny covers her face and screams, I realize it's blood.

"Aiden," Ginny cries.

Reginald snaps his gaze between us and then to Faith. "You're him."

There's a flash. A blinding pain in my right eye. I start to lunge at him, but someone grabs me around my waist.

"Easy, brother," Ricky says.

What the—?

He and Fallon are here, as are Betty the reporter, Robyn, and Maribelle.

"Get out," Reginald shouts. "He attacked me first. I'm going to press charges. I have witnesses."

I'm breathing so hard that blood keeps on flowing, a river of madness down my face.

"What witnesses?" Robyn asks in a steely voice I've heard her mother use. "When I walked in you were hitting your wife, Mayor Moreaux."

The man's blue eyes are wild, enraged. When he takes a step toward Robyn, I fight against Ricky and Fallon's hold.

"You're not helping her," Fallon whispers, and his voice brings me out of my rage spell.

"Virginia," Reggie says.

The woman stands tall. Something passes between her and Faith that I could never understand.

"I was so scared," she says, but she's not talking to her husband. She's talking to the reporter. And that's when I realize, this is Virginia's out. It's a needle of a shot, but she's taking it. "I blacked out when Reggie was hurting me. This young man tried to stop him. The next thing I knew, he was bleeding."

"You," Reginald says in a thundering voice. "I will destroy all of you."

"Try it," Faith says. "We've got pictures."

"And I've got pictures of that trash you call a man."

"No, you don't," Betty LePaige says. She presses her finger to her camera, and it makes dozens of clicking noises. The mayor's veins strain in his neck as he realizes what's happening. "I deleted them. Everything."

"I'm going to sue you."

She shakes her head. "I never cashed your check, Mr. Mayor. Unlike you, I decided to keep my dignity."

"We'll see you at the polls," Maribelle says as the mayor storms out of the room.

As Maribelle and Faith gather around with Ginny and Betty, I know that I shouldn't be here.

With Ricky shouldering my weight, we leave the room, take a back exit through the kitchen where no one can see. They put me in the car, and we drive in silence to the hotel, then get terrified looks as onlookers watch three guys in suits arrive covered in blood. We take the elevator up to my room, and by then I can walk on my own.

"How did you guys end up there?" I ask, and the surprise of the sting is worse than the actual cut on my lip.

"Well, as I'm creating jobs here, Mrs. Charles extended the invitation."

"Some of the guys are still there," Fallon says. "What were you thinking?"

"I wasn't. I had just made up with Faith and then I heard Ginny cry. It reminded me of the way my mom cried when my dad yelled and tried to hit her. It's like everything I wasn't able to do back then just came rushing back. It's still there." I rub my hands on my face and wince. That motherfucker got me good. I'm almost mad that they stopped me from hitting him back, but then how would that have looked? I would have gone to jail for sure. And then I would have lost Faith. That is, if I haven't already.

"We'll leave you be," Ricky says. "Clean yourself up. Then we can see if you need stitches."

"I'll be fine," I assure them. "Hey, guys."

Fallon and Ricky turn around.

"Thanks for saving me. Not just tonight."

Ricky smirks in that knowing way of his. "That's what family's for."

Once they're gone, I realize I dropped my phone and Faith can't even get in touch with me. I want to go back to the mansion, but that wouldn't help anyone. Not the way I look now. Instead, I take a hot shower. All cleaned up, I take inventory of my face. There's a bruise on my right eye, starting to swell, and a cut on the arch of my lip that's red and looks like I got stung by a bee.

I get some ice down the hall and use the plastic bag in the bucket to make a pack for my eye. At some point, I manage to fall asleep, even with the anxiety gnawing in my chest at not knowing where Faith is. Is she okay? What did she have to explain to her mother?

I must have fallen asleep, because I know I'm dreaming. Warm hands wrap around my naked torso. Kisses up along my arm.

"Faith," I mutter.

She kisses around the bruises and cuts. "Thank you for what you did. I know it must be hard for you."

I reach out, and it's like she's here. My eye's so swollen I can hardly open it. "Mi vida," I sigh. "I need you."

And then my body shudders as her mouth closes over my dick. Her tongue is so real. Her teeth playing with the sensitive skin around my head. Her perfect little mouth makes a popping sound that makes me raise myself up on the mattress. Fuck her soft, full mouth. She uses her hand to stroke my length. Jerks me up and down, rolling sexy licks with her tongue until I can't take it anymore.

"I'm going to come," I sigh. I push my pelvis up. In my wildest dreams I never would imagine this. Faith under my covers. Faith licking the life out of me. I shake and gasp, rake my fingers on her shoulders. Not in my wildest dreams did I conjure the sight of her taking my load in her pouty mouth.

Because she's here, her mouth glossy with my come. She licks it off the top of her lip and then she kisses me.

"You're here," I say.

"I'm not going anywhere, Aiden."

Even though my muscles ache and I can only see out of one eye, I climb on top of her. Faith parts her legs for me, wet and waiting, and I sink into her soft, tight life force. Both of us search for something from the other. Love. Sex. Desire. And I give it all to her, surrender myself to this love that has changed me, broken me, put me back together into a man who will deserve her.

25

You Are My Home

FAITH

For an entire week Aiden and I live in our private little world. We hibernate in his hotel, nursing his bruises and cuts. He browns by the pool, and I read *The Sky's Not the Only Big Thing in Montana* by Scarlett West because Patrick has a whole box of them in his room. It's a strange thing to picture the lumberjack in the book as the same guy who gets mani-pedis with me in the hotel spa, but it's only a cover.

Aiden drinks hurricane after hurricane, and I take my whiskey on the rocks. I don't completely eliminate the outside world. Maribelle keeps me up to date with the campaign, and my mother and I have started texting multiple times a day. Sometimes she asks me how Aiden is doing, because he left so early. I'll say that having your own mother use peach and heart emojis is the single thing that makes you feel like you're in bizarro world.

She's leading in the polls by record numbers, and I have a different kind of anxiety in the pit of my stomach, because it's one thing to show predictions but it's another to get people to actually vote this week. The Moreauxs hang over me like a raincloud. I keep waiting for Reginald Moreaux to start another slander campaign against my mother with me at the center. Virginia has assured me that he won't make a move. Not when he has more to lose.

I don't want to pity her. I know she wouldn't want that of me. But what I do have is a wish that she'll find her way through this and come out stronger.

Strength isn't always easy to find. Every time Aiden tells me a story about his life, about growing up in Colombia and having the kind of father who turned his back on his family, I'm reminded that Aiden is one of the strongest people I know. Just like my mother. Just like Angie. The people around me are beacons of it.

I know that I'm lucky.

I'm loved.

He doesn't let me forget it. All of it comes in different ways. In the way he searches for me in a crowded restaurant and finds I'm already looking at him. When we're spread out on the couch and his fingers trace my skin absentmindedly. It's in the way he pulls me close to him after hours of sex, how he loves my smell on him, how he makes sure I come first.

But mostly, I know it when he puts me on the phone with his tía Ceci and she talks to me for so long that I suggest she take my number instead of his.

I see it in the pendant glittering on my chest, a pale whiskey brown just like his eyes. A remnant of the woman who shaped this man's heart.

When the week is up, I stand in the middle of the room wearing one of his soccer jerseys and my underwear.

"Hey, baby," I say.

"Mi reina?" he says, eyes lingering on my freshly lotioned legs.

"We have to get dressed. Polls open in an hour."

"You can't go dressed like that." He climbs his way across the sofa, moving his torso and pelvis like he's practicing one of Angie's new moves. "I'll help you take it off."

AIDEN

I've never seen a second line so big before, but there's more than enough reason to celebrate.

Mayor Daria Charles celebrates right along with the city on a warm, sunny afternoon. There's confetti and music and so much dancing that if I close my eyes, I can almost envision being home for carnaval. Even if the music is different, the *feel* of it is the same.

I hang back and let Faith be with her family. Angie and the boys join the revelry on the streets. We grab drinks in one of the Quarter's bars that's waving rainbow flags and serving up a cocktail called Daria Darling.

Never in my life have I seen a city celebrate like this. It's like being in the middle of history, and for the first time in so long, I am more at home than I've been anywhere.

When I look at Faith, grinning from ear to ear as she glides down the street, I know that she's the reason.

We go our separate ways for most of the day. Family time is family time, and I understand that. I stay with Angie, Robyn, and the boys eating our fill of hot wings and drinking beer at a bar with an outdoor garden. When the sky gets dark, the entire place comes to life with ropes of white lights. Music pumps from the massive speakers, and even though there isn't a dance floor, Angie and Vin are dancing with a couple of girls they were chatting up.

Faith walks into the garden in the simple white dress she was wearing this morning, and my entire body comes alive when her eyes meet mine.

The lights above us flicker when we kiss.

"We have to stop doing that," she says, taking a seat beside me.

The song changes, the beat sexy and slow, and instead of letting her sit, I pull her to dance with me.

"Congratulations," I tell her.

She wraps her arms around my neck. "I can't believe it."

"Believe it." I kiss her nose, and she kisses my upper lip. The cut there is only the faintest pink scar. My eye has only the slightest shade of green. She always kisses those parts, like she's healing me with her own life.

A waitress comes over and gives us two celebratory hurricanes on the house.

"Your favorite drink," I tease her.

She rolls her eyes playfully, but thanks the young girl regardless. "What should we cheers to?"

"To your mother."

"To our mothers," she says.

We clink our glasses and we slurp the sweet liquor. She sets the drink on the table and takes my hand in hers.

"Time to go home," she says. Her brown eyes are so full of light. I want to spend my entire life making sure they stay that way.

"Do you need to get your things from the hotel?" I kiss her bare shoulder.

She makes the sweetest sigh. "Actually, I'm being presumptuous but I was hoping that we could both get our things."

"Faith Abigail Charles," I say, so close our noses almost touch. "Are you sure? What if my bathroom habits change? What if you hate the way I start chewing or breathing in the middle of the night or the way I fold my pants?"

"Believe me, if you're going to live with me, your bathroom habits are going to be pristine."

"Tempting." I pull back and take a gulp of my drink. "You don't have a gym, do you?"

"Aiden," she says, a playful whine in her voice.

I wrap my arm around her small waist, and even though she wriggles against me for a moment, she eventually sinks into me. Kisses me so deeply someone (Pat probably) at the table clears their throat.

"Let's go get our things," I say. "But I do expect turndown service."

"You're not getting any kind of service with talk like that," she says, but she can't stop smiling.

Before she can leave the garden, I pull her against my chest, cup her face in my hands, and stare deep in her eyes.

"I'll go wherever you want, whenever you want, Faith. I'd live here in New Orleans or in some wild place saving the world. Say the word and I'm there alongside you for as long as you'll have me, and do you know why?"

She juts her chin out in that way that captivated me so. "Why?"

"Because you're my Faith. You're my home."

Acknowledgments

This book would not exist without Natalie Horbachevsky and Sarah Younger. All of my readers owe Faith's and Aiden's adventures across New Orleans to you.

My endless gratitude to Adrienne Rosado for all your hard work, and my editor, Norma Perez-Hernandez, for being a ray of sunshine. Thank you to everyone on the wonderful Kensington squad, especially Lauren Jernigan, James Akinaka, Jane Nutter, Alexandra Nicolajsen, Vida Engstrand, Paula Reedy, and the production team.

Writers need a sound track. The one for *Hired* was 90 percent Maluma and the remaining 10 percent belongs to Luis Fonsi, Daddy Yankee, and "Despacito."

Lastly, to all of the incredible romance booksellers, bloggers, librarians, and authors who understand the changes romance will see in the future. Alexis Daria, Sierra Simone, Sarah Maclean, Rebekah Weatherspoon, Bea and Leah Koch, and Silvana Reyes, just to name a *few*. I'm so lucky to be part of this community.

Turn the page for a preview
of Zoey Castile's first
Happy Endings Novel . . .

STRIPPED

Available now

From Kensington Publishing

1

The Thong th-thong thong thong

ROBYN

The thong is covered in red, white, and blue sequins reminiscent of the American flag. Though I know it can't be *exactly* the American flag. One, because it's a sign of disrespect to wear the flag as an article of clothing, let alone a shimmering strip of fabric that gets wedged all up in your private bits. Two, I just went over this in my class when Freddy Dominguez asked how many times the flag has changed since Betsy Ross's original design. One thing led to another, and I suddenly found myself explaining to a class full of ten-year-olds why they could not make a dress out of the flag for an extra-credit class project.

Here, now, at seven o'clock in the morning, I hold the thong up to the light, like an archaeologist might hold a particularly curious desert find. Upon further inspection of the G-string, I don't think it'd be possible to fit all fifty stars and stripes on the triangle attached by flimsy elastic fabric. It's a rather large piece of fabric, all things considered. Either the owner is packing a lot of junk or has a huge vagina.

I take a deep breath. What a way to start the morning. I slept through my alarm, and while my coffee was brewing, I ran down in my pajamas to pick up my laundry bag from the place next door. Since the first item I took out was a thong I don't remember buying, I'm going to go out on a limb and say I was given the wrong bag.

It's pouring outside, and the ink on the receipt attached to the bag is too smudged to read the name on it. In twenty minutes, I'll start the countdown for being late to work. It's probably frowned upon for an elementary teacher to be late to class for the third time this week. It's only Wednesday. Unlike in college classes, my students don't get to pick up and leave after fifteen minutes of me not showing up. Plus, since my lateness is, uh, *recurring* the last couple of weeks, my little devils have taken it upon themselves to booby-trap my desk with pranks. Lately, it's been whoopee cushion central in room 412. Yet another generation has discovered the hilarity of fart noises. #Bless.

Anyway, when I opened up my laundry bag, I knew it wasn't mine. This leaves me with a few problems. One: I don't have any clean underwear or clothes, other than the ones I'm wearing now. Two: I'll have to run back in the rain and swap them out, leaving me with a desperate need to shower again after sweating my face off and getting soaked in dirty New York water. Three: Wouldn't the sequins itch once it got all up in the owner's butt crack? Finally, on what occasion, other than the Fourth of July, would someone wear something like this?

My second alarm buzzes, but at least I'm awake now. Murphy's Law is kicking my ass. No clothes, no shoes, no service. Well, I do have shoes, I suppose. I could be an Internet sensation. In local news, fifth-grade teacher shows up in pajamas and rain boots. My mother always said I have a face for TV.

Also, what is that dripping noise?

I slide across the living room in my dirty socks (better than Swiffering!) and get to my kitchen. My toe hits the river of coffee snaking across the slanted floor.

"*Breathe,*" I tell myself, looking down at the sight. "Breathe."

There was once a time when I was a hopeful twenty-one-year-old ready to graduate college early with honors. I woke up before the sun, without the help of six alarms spaced out by ten-minute intervals. *That* Robyn wouldn't wait for all her clothes to be dirty before sending them out to the wash. Hell, she would've walked the extra ten blocks to the Laundromat and sat there while paying her bills early. That Robyn was never late. Didn't even use the word *late* in her vocabulary, not even when commenting that *other* people were late to meet her. That Robyn had her shit together. That Robyn didn't forget to put the coffeepot *in* the coffee machine before it started percolating.

That Robyn was a fuzzy memory, replaced by this Robyn: twenty-eight and with a severe case of "chicken without a head." It's a very technical term, and it's real, my students are sure of it.

"Dammit!" I shout at my apartment in Astoria, Queens. I repeat it until I work myself up into a cocoon of anxiety. I'm answered by a truck horn, dozens of children screaming in the street, and the general cacophony that is my block at any time of day.

New plan: Clean this up. Run downstairs in the rain and swap out bags. Beg Principal Platypus to not fire me. Teach students how to not be a disaster using self as an example. Perfect. Great plan.

I step over the puddle of coffee and shove the empty pot in place to salvage at least one cup of precious java. Then I go to grab a fistful of paper towels. Empty.

I open the drawer for a dishrag. Empty.

I remind myself that the dishrags are in my gray laundry bag, which this is not. It is, however, *someone's* clean laundry.

"I can't do that," I tell myself, hopping back over the stream of caffeine. I do always tell my students to think outside the box. Sometimes the solution is right in front of you, and my solution might just be this.

I pull open the drawstring and grab a fistful of items off the top. The star-spangled thong, a black tank top too small to fit a human person, and a pair of giant gray sweatpants. As I place the so-fresh-and-so-clean clothes on the river of coffee, I consider that this person must have an unusually disproportionate body.

But who am I to judge? I'm cleaning my floor in nothing but my panties and socks. All of my bras are dirty. If I hadn't spent my after-school time yesterday trying to salvage my friendships,

I would've gone to Target to buy new underwear and socks. Aside from a temporary solution to my wet floor, maybe the bag contains something that would fit me.

I wring out the clothes in my kitchen sink and let the water run a bit. I look back at the laundry bag open in my living room. Why stop at three items of clothing? There might be a clean top that fits me. It could be like the Sisterhood of the Traveling Laundry Bag. They'll never know. I'll come straight home, wash everything, and return it.

Then again, the day I show up to class in semi-stolen clothes will probably be the day I start on a downward spiral. What's to stop me from stealing someone's grocery bag or underwear?

"Maybe I should take an Adulting 101 class," I tell myself as my third alarm *and* a knock on the door interrupt me. "Or maybe get a cat so I'm not talking to myself."

I take off my wet socks and tap the phone alarm silent. The knock on the door is quick and cheerful. I like to think that you can tell a lot about people by the way they knock on doors. At seven fifteen in the morning, no one should be that damn peppy.

I throw on my silky robe that's hanging from the couch and make my way to the door. The person on the other side knocks again in the fifteen steps it takes me to get there. I'm pretty sure they're trying to tap out the tune of "Single Ladies," which is *always* a great song to have stuck in your head.

"Who is it?"

"Hi, it's your neighbor," a male voice answers. "I think I got your laundry bag by mistake."

My stomach does a weird flip-floppy thing, like I've been caught doing something wrong. That's probably because I *am* being caught doing something wrong.

"Just a second!" I shout to buy myself time. I look around the room, but there's nothing I can do except answer the door. I clear my throat and undo the bottom lock, then the middle, and leave the chain lock intact.

"Hi," I say in my best attempt to be nonchalant, as in, "*Hi, I didn't just use your clothes to clean my floor.*"

At first, he's just a tall and blurry blob that my brain can't process because this is a terrible, terrible morning. It takes me a second to notice him. *Really* notice him. The door creates a shadow that obstructs his features. Then, he steps slightly to the right so we face each other through the three inches of open door and the morning light behind me illuminates him.

His strong chin rests just above the chain lock. He's smiling, and I was right. He *is* too damn peppy for this early in the morning. He's also too damn fine to be standing at my door. I rub one eye, just to make sure I'm seeing right, and, yep, he's still there—the most beautiful man I don't remember ordering.

I almost forget why he's here when he holds up a pink laundry slip with my name on it.

The back of my mind is going, "*All the single ladies—*"

He smiles and my brain forgets the rest of the words to the song. I zone in on his face, though I'm pretty sure the rest of him doesn't disappoint. I love faces. How unique and different every single one is. I love *his* face. His smile crinkles at the corners of his lips. It pushes all the way up his face, like he's truly happy to see me, despite this ungodly hour of morning. It's a shameless smile because he knows, he *has* to know, the effect it has on people. On me.

"Uhm," I start to say, trying to wade through the fog of thoughts.

"Your apartment smells amazing," he tells me, looking past me and inside. "Is that a Colombian roast?"

I can feel my face scrunch up with confusion. Then, I'm completely aware of how quickly this stranger looks at my toes, the long stretch of my bare legs, and tries not to linger at the silky robe that clings to my breasts. I self-consciously pull the robe closer. The dull pulse of a caffeine-deprived headache starts to ebb its way into my brain

"So," he says, because I'm just staring at his face. I'm shamelessly staring. "Are you holding my clothes hostage? Is that what this chain is for?"

Playful. Charming. It's too early to be those things, but he's managing it. When he smiles again, my belly drops straight through my body and down the six floors of the apartment building.

Dammit. Not now, I scold my mind. At least I still have a slightly reasonable part of my brain that works.

"Right! Give me a minute." I shut the door in his face and run across the living room where his open bag of laundry is. I face a decision: Come clean (pun intended) and tell him that I used his clothes as a mop. Or, I shove the clothes back in there and let him find the caffeinated surprise later on. At least I know he likes the smell of my coffee.

He knocks on the door twice.

I realize I don't like either of those options. There's a third. I could take a page out of my students' proverbial books. This option would make me both deceptive and a thief, but that is what I'm going to go with. Besides, I'll return everything later on. He has plenty of sweatpants in there. I don't even need to know about the thong anymore. I just want to get dressed and go to work. That is if I still have a job to go back to. So, I kick the soaked clothes into a corner of my kitchen, and drag the bag toward the door.

I undo the chain and face him.

"Here you go," I say, my heart racing from sprinting back and forth. My heart could also be racing because looking at him now without the door obscuring my view is twice as startling as just the sliver of him. It could be that it's been eighteen months and counting since I've met a man who made my pulse throb. Or because he's equal parts rugged and charming, which is my favorite combination.

In his navy-blue sweats and white ribbed tank, he looks like he could've just left the gym. A duffel bag rests on the floor right behind him, next to my laundry bag, and I realize the tank top I "stole" from him can't be his. His chest is too broad, too solid. I catch myself staring at the curve of his shoulders, and mentally bite him, while trying to restrain myself. Who needs self-control when you're already in a tailspin, amirite?

Down, girl, I think. I realize that there is only a thin sheet of silk between us. And a door. And, well, our laundry bags. Whatever. We are really, really close to being basically naked together.

He lifts his Red Sox cap and runs his hand across his soft, light-brown hair. There's a question marring his features. He doesn't ask it out loud but I'm sure it's along the lines of "Are you crazy?"

Instead, he says, "Thanks, darlin'."

I hate pet names. But when my neighbor says it, I don't seem to mind at all. Hell, I'm even getting warm and tingly. He shakes his head, as if dispelling the thoughts in there. I wonder what he was thinking. He picks up my laundry bag and swaps it out with his.

The exchange has been made.

"You're a lifesaver," I tell him. "I'm officially out of clean clothes."

He laughs, and I decide it's the most wonderful sound I've ever heard.

"I don't know," he says. "That silk robe is a pretty good look."

I feel the burning blush creep up my neck and settle in my cheeks. It's not that I'm impressionable. I'm not. Well, I don't think I am. It's that he's caught me off guard. It's early and I'm late for work. If I'm going down that road, I'm late for my life in general, but that's a can of worms I'd rather not open.

"*All the single ladies,*" my mind singsongs.

Then, my fourth alarm goes off.

Panic replaces my attraction to my handsome neighbor. I start to shove him out of my doorway. He budges easily, taking a step back when I take a step forward, like we're doing some sort of morning tango.

"Thanks again, but I've got to go. I'm late for work and the new principal is probably going to fire me, so thanks but—" I start to close the door when he interrupts.

"Where do you work? I could give you a ride."

"Why?"

"Because you're late and the new principal—"

"Don't you have somewhere to be?" I cut him off.

He shakes his head once, and I wonder if I'm imagining the glimmer in his eyes. "Just got home. The only place I have to be is my bed."

I can't help it. The mental image of him on his bed overpowers my thoughts. It's probably a very, very big bed. He looks like he spreads out on it completely naked.

I clear my throat and point to the window. "I teach up here by Astoria Park."

"I can drop off my things while you get dressed. I just moved into 5A a couple of weeks ago."

"You're right under me," I say. Then wish I hadn't.

"I am." He smiles his crooked smile and he leans a little closer to the door, careful to not step back in the doorway.

I recognize the implication in his grin, and suddenly, the silk robe I'm wearing feels more like a fur coat in the middle of July. I wonder where he's from and what his favorite song is, and whether he's a model or an actor because he's not normal-person attractive. He's a little too big and muscular to be the thin, European models in the latest issue of my *Vogue*. But his face. Damn, *dat face*.

God. I have to stop eating lunch with my fifth graders.

"You should wear the red dress," he says and winks.

As he picks up his laundry bag and slings it over his shoulder, I find myself stuck between being indignant and flattered.

"You went through my clothes?"

"Did you go through mine?" He laughs good-naturedly.

I cross my arms over my chest. "No."

I realize I sound more like one of my students than the twenty-eight-year-old child I truly am. Deny until you believe your own lie, right?

He bares his teeth and I swear that he's letting me get away with it. That's when I realize that I really, truly can't get a ride from him. Not just because he went through my undies (Hey, Pot! Meet Kettle!), but because it would be harder to return the clothes that are bunched up in a corner of my kitchen floor. I don't want anything to do with him after the laundry exchange. I can already feel the warmth of his smile creeping along my skin and that just can't happen. There is no room for this feeling in my life right now. Plus, how do you look a man in the face and say, "*Btw,* here's your sparkly thong. I washed it."

Plus, plus! Stranger danger. How can I caution my students about getting into strangers' cars when I'm minutes away from doing the same?

"It's really nice of you to offer," I start. I want to close the door and get to work. I want to hit the restart button for the hundredth time this week. I want to stay and talk to him because I feel a bud of something wonderful flowering in my chest. And that can't happen. Not right now.

"But?"

"But, it's totally fine. I usually walk. I'm not very late anyway. Sorry about the laundry mix-up."

He nods once, a suspicious grin on his lips. It turns to a yawn, which he tries to stifle.

"Sorry, long night," he says. "Okay, 6A. Have a good day at work."

He walks away, and I start to close the door when he whirls around. I catch the doorknob just before it slams on the hand he reaches out to me.

"Would you want to get a drink Saturday night?"

I want to say yes.

For the past year, I've been complaining about how hard it is to date in New York City. All of the dating apps in the world weren't able to give me a One True Match. I've waded through a Sea of Douche Bags for so long that I haven't just lost interest in going on another bad first date—a part of me has lost all hope in finding any semblance of love.

Could it be this easy? I give him a quick glance from head to toe. Honestly, he deserves more than a glance. He deserves a thorough inspection.

"*All the single ladies,*" my mind hums.

Single ladies. That's when it hits me. "I'd love to but I have a work thing."

"On a Saturday night? Where's that New York hospitality you never hear about?"

My fifth alarm goes off.

My mind is frazzled, tugging between the mess in my apartment and the potential in the hallway.

"Say yes," my heart urges.

He has a sequin thong in his laundry bag. And a girl's shirt. *DO NOT ENTER,* my mind practically screams.

When there's a war between my heart and my mind, then my mind always wins.

"I really have to go," I say.

I'm too old to date guys like this, anyway. He just got home at seven in the morning after partying. Then, a ray of light hits the beautiful stranger standing in my hallway. It's downright angelic, is what it is. He doesn't even look tired. His eyes have a mischievous glint, like one night with him could turn my world upside down. His body is tan and the sweat that's dried on his skin fills my senses. His lips—they're full and slightly parted as he patiently waits for me to close the door. His foot taps ever so slightly, and it's the only sign that he's perhaps nervous. But then I see something else that adds to the decision that, no, I should not be seeing a guy like this. I did not imagine the glimmer in his eyes. The glimmer is, in fact, everywhere.

"Also, you have glitter on your neck," I say.

He looks confused for a moment, then gives me an understanding closed-lip smile. An understanding that the glitter had to come from somewhere, someone. He nods again and watches me close the door.

"You know where I live if you change your mind," he says quickly.

After I shut the door I wonder if I've made a mistake. I look through the peephole and my heart gives a little tug because he's still standing there. He looks like he might knock again, but he hesitates. Instead, he smiles and shakes his head. He picks up his laundry and shoulders the weight, grabbing his duffel bag with his free hand.

Then he's gone.

I don't have time to pine for him, even though a sick, twisted, sexually deprived part of me wants to.

But my phone goes off again. This time it's not my alarm. It's my best friend, Lily, calling. Lily teaches in the classroom next to mine. I told her if I wasn't in the teachers' lounge by seven thirty, to call me.

I let the phone go to voice mail, and hurriedly pour the salvaged coffee into my travel mug. I rummage through my laundry while scalding my tongue with coffee. It's okay. Taste buds are overrated. So are hot men with glitter on their necks and bedazzled thongs and women's clothes in their laundry.

I shoot Lily a text. *Traffic! Cover for me, please!*

Lily responds with a side-eye emoji. *Hurry up. Principal Platypus is patrolling the halls.*

That's when I see it, and an involuntary grin spreads across my face.

At the top of my laundry stack is my favorite red spring dress. I put it on.

FALLON

"She totally went through my clothes," I tell Yaz when I walk into my apartment.

Yaz, my five-month-old husky pup, barks in response. She runs around the laundry I drop at the foot of my bed. I take my clothes off on the way to the bathroom, leaving a bread-crumb trail for no one. Once upon a time, this Prince Charming wouldn't be coming home alone after a night of work. Wouldn't have gotten turned down for a "work thing."

" 'Also, you have glitter on your neck,' " I say, trying to mimic 6A's voice. It isn't high-pitched, the way her sweet, soft face gives the impression it would be. It's a perfect, rough alto. The kind of voice I can picture whispering dirty nothings in my ear.

Having spent the night surrounded by hundreds of women with high-pitched screams, the sound of her voice is a welcome reprieve.

I kick off my sweatpants and run the water. I've started a downside list of living in New York. My place in Boston was brand-new and three times as big for the same price. Astoria's got its charm, I suppose. Greek coffee and baklava at any time of the day is a pretty sweet deal.

Downside #1 is that it takes five minutes for the water to turn hot. I love hot showers, and I'm not just talking about the times I have someone in there with me. I'm talking scalding-hot water. Feel the steam in my pores. Feel my muscles unwind after a night of acrobatics.

It's the only way I feel clean after having bills shoved down my pants. Don't get me wrong. I love money. I love having it launched at me from willing MILF hands, fingers that have mapped every inch of my hard-earned muscles. I work for that paper. But I still need a shower.

Fucking glitter. Ruining my life one sparkle at a time.

I scrub my face and neck, knowing how hard it is to get rid of this stuff. Glitter is the herpes of the makeup world. On that note, I think of 6A in her pretty silk kimono instead.

Wrong. Not pretty. Not pretty at all.

Her in that robe was the hottest wet dream I've ever had come to life; it was a gift from the gods themselves. She kept pulling it tighter around her full breasts and tiny waist, like she thought I had X-ray vision. I wish I'd been able to say something clever.

Well, if I'm wishing for stuff, I'd wish that she'd said yes. I pause and marvel at that. *She* said *no* to *me*. I must be losing my edge.

After a night of "yeses" I finally have one no. And it sucks. I haven't had a girl turn me down since I shot up a foot and had my braces removed in the eleventh grade.

I push the bath curtain aside and pull the cabinet mirror toward me. I wipe away some of the steam and take a look at myself. I've got some serious dark circles under my eyes. I resigned myself a long time ago to a life of sleeping in the day and working at night. It's part of the glamorous life I live.

I wink at my own reflection. That wink has gotten me out of

speeding tickets, brought in thousands of dollars in tips, and earned me passing grades up until I dropped out of high school. There was a time when I didn't have to say a single word to get a date. A wink, a smile, and it was over.

Zac Fallon, lady-killer. Not literally, of course.

What has New York City done to me? I don't have the attention span. I work, I go home, I go to the gym, I go to work again. Lather, rinse, repeat.

My buddy Ricky likes to remind me that at thirty, I'm over the hill. Ricky himself is thirty-nine, but still thinks like a horny nineteen-year-old. Maybe I am old. Maybe I look tired. Maybe I'm overthinking it. Maybe I'm just *not* for her.

As if sensing my distress, Yaz barks from the living room.

I push the mirror back into place, leaving a soapy trail on the glass.

Once I've rinsed the glitter out of my pores, I replay my interaction with 6A. Incredulous. Judgey. She was *so* fucking judgey. You know what? I probably dodged a bullet with that one. There's no point in getting tangled up with someone when I don't know how long I'm going to stay in this shit city.

As the waterfall of metallic New York water washes the suds away, I truly convince myself that I was never interested in her. Not in her high cheekbones that turned perfectly pink when I winked at her. Not in the thick, long black hair that tumbled around her shoulders like waterfalls of ink. Not even in the round and perky tits she kept trying to cover with that flimsy robe.

I hope she'll wear the red dress.

I turn off the faucet and watch the tiny whirlpools of suds and glitter run down the drain.

"Fuck." I'm hard. I'm hard just thinking about her in that silk robe. In that red dress. I don't even know her name and I'm hard as fuck.

It's not that I don't enjoy a good hard-on. I spent six hours with hordes of women grabbing at my dick and nothing happened. There was a time ten years ago when the touch of a woman, any woman, during one of my sets would have me saluting my flag.

That went away right quick. Self-control and all that.

But here I am, like a maypole reaching toward the sky, and I blame her. Judgey, rude, messy, gorgeous, sexy—

She wasn't just the girl who stole my laundry. She was the girl who saw right through me. My dick is a fucking masochist.

I turn the water back on. Hotter this time so steam can rise. It's been a while. Not because I don't have opportunity. I always have the opportunity. But because, lately, I feel worn and torn most of the time.

I groan into the rising mist. I rub my hand up and down my shaft. I hold on tighter to myself and to the fleeting memory of a woman who doesn't want me. Think of the way her nipples pushed against silk. If that thin tie had come undone around her waist I would've been able to see everything that she was hiding.

"Oh shit," I grunt, and shiver despite the heat, releasing my load into the drain as 6A's full dick-sucking lips come to mind.

When my legs stop trembling, and the water rinses me clean (well, relatively clean), I dry off and jump into bed. Tomorrow is the beginning of June, and the New York chill refuses to let go. I stare at the ceiling and try not to think about the fact that the hottest girl I've seen in this city has been living one floor above me. Then, I think about work—there's so much that needs to get done. So much to decide. The show gets bigger every day. . . .

Yaz barks, then climbs up on my chest and passes out. At least Yaz wants me.

Rick and the club will have to wait until Monday. I haven't had more than three days off in a row, let alone a weekend, in about five years. I give myself permission to think of 6A once more.

That heart-stopping, breathtaking, world-changing face.

Okay, that's it. No more. Tomorrow I can forget about her.

Okay, once more. "She could be the girl," I say, touching the chilly part of my bed. She could keep my sheets warm. She could be a reason to be in this damned city. I could be charming and sweep her off her feet. I can't wait to see her again.

But another voice, a strange, sensible voice that's been quiet most of my life, whispers, "No. *It's just the past coming to haunt you. She's just the girl who took your laundry.*"